ROYALLY SCREWED

EMMA CHASE

everafter ROMANCE

EverAfter Romance
A Division of Diversion Publishing Corp.
443 Park Avenue South, Suite 1008
New York, New York 10016
www.EverAfterRomance.com

Cover Design: By Hang Le

For more information, email info@diversionbooks.com

First EverAfter Romance edition October 2016.
ISBN: 978-1-68230-775-5

To Billy & Molly – for every hilarious, sweet memory,
every awesomely awful story, for the laughter and love and for
being the best big brother and little sister in the whole world.

ACKNOWLEDGMENTS

It's not always easy coming up with a new story idea. Every author wants to write something epic—an entertaining, heartwarming book that will resonate with readers, with loveable, sexy, funny characters that will stay with them long after The End.

But sometimes, inspiration takes a holiday, leaving a writer to flounder with the question: What am I going to do next?

The idea for *Royally Screwed* and the Royally Series was a few months in the making. I'd had some thoughts about a few potential stories—even some outlines—but none of them grabbed me by the throat and said, "This…this is the story you have to write." A phone call with my amazing agent, Amy Tannenbaum, changed that.

I've often said that my first reading love was historical romance, but my favorite stories to write are contemporary romances. And I, like most of the public, am fascinated by the comings and goings of today's modern royals—it's such an elite, unique form of celebrity (and the babies are adorable!!). During my brainstorming session with Amy, those passions and interests created the perfect storm of inspiration . . . and *Royally Screwed* was born.

In the days that followed, I went on a writing bender. Frantically jotting down notes and outlines and little snippets of dialogue, not just for *Royally Screwed*—but for the books that will follow. That's not usually how I work. Typically, I'm consumed by one story—one couple's journey—and everything else fades to the background. But for this series, I fell completely in love with all the couples—every character—the entire world was a fantastic combination of realism and fictional. There was just *so much* to sink my writing teeth into.

First and foremost there was the romance—the exciting, entertaining, exhilarating journey of two people finding each other, falling in love and overcoming every obstacle that gets in their way. But there were other themes too—the intrusive public thirst to know every detail of a public figure's life, the idea of family obligation and the sacrifices we make for the people we love. The captivating idea of modern day royalty—these attractive, wealthy but also typical twenty-something's who are bound by rules and traditions that are literally centuries old.

I'm thrilled with how *Royally Screwed* turned out. I can't wait for you to meet Nicholas and Olivia, and the group of friends and family that surround them. I can't wait to finish writing *Royally Matched* and *Royally Endowed*, so I can continue to share with you the world and characters that I've fallen head over heels in love with.

Inspiration can be tricky—but if you're lucky, you have people around who'll help you cultivate and refine it. I'm very lucky.

And so, as always, I'm grateful to my agent, Amy Tannenbaum and everyone at the Jane Rotrosen Agency for your constant support and guidance and for working so hard to bring my books to fruition.

Thanks to my publicist, Danielle Sanchez and everyone at InkSlinger PR—it's been a joy working with you.

Thanks to my assistant Juliet Fowler who's always on the ball and is so good at everything she does.

Huge thanks to Gitte Doherty, of TotallyBooked, for always making me smile and for helping me make Nicholas a swoony, sexy, not-American sounding beast!

I'm sure I'm not alone in thanking Hang Le of By Hang Le designs for this absolutely gorgeous cover and for all her beautiful graphics. Much gratitude to Coreen Montagna for your always meticulous and terrific work.

All my thanks and hugs to Nina Bocci, Katy Evans and all my fabulous, awesome author friends!! It's always reassuring to know I'm not crazy—but the life of a writer often can be.

On that note, love and gratitude to my family—for your patience and understanding, encouragement and unending support. Thank you for putting up with me, I know it's not always easy.

And to my stupendous, wonderful readers—I love you guys!!! Your support and excitement is humbling and you make this writing business all the more joyful. Thank you for sticking with me from book to book, series to series.

Now . . . go dive in and get Royally Screwed! xoxo

PROLOGUE

My very first memory isn't all that different from anyone else's. I was three years old and it was my first day of preschool. For some reason, my mother ignored the fact that I was actually a boy and dressed me in God-awful overalls, a frilly cuffed shirt and patent-leather brogues. I planned to smear finger paint on the outfit the first chance I got.

But that's not what stands out most in my mind.

By then, spotting a camera lens pointed my way was as common as seeing a bird in the sky. I should've been used to it—and I think I was. But that day was different.

Because there were hundreds of cameras.

Lining every inch of the sidewalk and the streets, and clustered together at the entrance of my school like a sea of one-eyed monsters, waiting to pounce. I remember my mother's voice, soothing and constant as I clung to her hand, but I couldn't make out her words. They were drowned out by the roar of snapping shutters and the shouts of photographers calling my name.

"Nicholas! Nicholas, this way, smile now! Look up, lad! Nicholas, over here!"

It was the first inkling I'd had that I was—that *we* were—different. In the years after, I'd learn just how different my family is. Internationally renowned, instantly recognizable, our everyday activities headlines in the making.

Fame is a strange thing. A powerful thing. Usually it ebbs and flows like a tide. People get swept up in it, swamped by it, but eventually the notoriety recedes, and the former object of its affection is reduced to someone who *used to be* someone, but isn't anymore.

That will never happen to me. I was known before I was born and my name will be blazoned in history long after I'm dust in the ground. Infamy is temporary, celebrity is fleeting, but royalty . . . royalty is forever.

CHAPTER 1

Nicholas

One would think, as accustomed as I am to being watched, that I wouldn't be effected by the sensation of someone staring at me while I sleep.

One would be wrong.

My eyes spring open, to see Fergus's scraggly, crinkled countenance just inches from my face. "Bloody hell!"

It's not a pleasant view.

His one good eye glares disapprovingly, while the other—the wandering one—that my brother and I always suspected wasn't lazy at all, but a freakish ability to see everything at once, gazes towards the opposite side of the room.

Every stereotype starts somewhere, with some vague but lingering grain of truth. I've long suspected the stereotype of the condescending, cantankerous servant began with Fergus.

God knows the wrinkled bastard is old enough.

He straightens up at my bedside, as much as his hunched, ancient spine will let him. "Took you long enough to wake up. You think I don't have better things to do? Was just about to kick you."

He's exaggerating. About having better things to do—not the plan to kick me.

I love my bed. It was an eighteenth birthday gift from the King of Genovia. It's a four-column, gleaming piece of art, hand-carved in the sixteenth century from one massive piece of Brazilian mahogany. My mattress is stuffed with the softest Hungarian goose feathers, my Egyptian cotton sheets have a thread count so high it's illegal in some parts of the world, and all I want to do is to roll over and bury myself under them like a child determined not to get up for school.

But Fergus's raspy warning grates like sandpaper on my eardrums.

"You're supposed to be in the green drawing room in twenty-five minutes."

And ducking under the covers is no longer an option. They won't save you from machete-wielding psychopaths . . . or a packed schedule.

Sometimes I think I'm schizophrenic. Dissociative. Possibly a split personality. It wouldn't be unheard of. All sorts of disorders show up in ancient family trees—hemophiliacs, insomniacs, lunatics . . . gingers. Guess I should feel lucky not to be any of those.

My problem is voices. Not *those* kinds of voices—more like reactions in my head. Answers to questions that don't match what actually ends up coming out of my mouth.

I almost never say what I really think. Sometimes I'm so full of shit my eyes could turn brown. And, it might be for the best.

Because I happen to think most people are fucking idiots.

"And we're back, chatting with His Royal Highness, Prince Nicholas."

Speaking of idiots . . .

The light-haired, thin-boned, bespeckled man sitting across from me conducting this captivating televised interview? His name is Teddy Littlecock. No, really, that's his actual name—and from what I hear, it's not an oxymoron. Can you appreciate what it must've been like for him in school with a name like that? It's almost enough to make me feel bad for him. But not quite.

Because Littlecock is a journalist—and I have a special kind of disgust for them. The media's mission has always been to bend the mighty over a barrel and ram their transgressions up their aristocratic arses. Which, in a way, is fine—most aristocrats are first-class pricks; everybody knows that. What bothers me is when it's not deserved. When it's not even true. If there's no dirty laundry around, the media will drag a freshly starched shirt through the shit and create their own. Here's an oxymoron for you: journalistic integrity.

Old Teddy isn't just any reporter—he's Palace Approved. Which means unlike his bribing, blackmailing, lying brethren, Littlecock gets direct access—like this interview—in exchange for asking the stupidest bloody questions ever. It's mind-numbing.

Choosing between dull and dishonest is like being asked whether you want to be shot or stabbed.

"What do you do in your spare time? What are your hobbies?"

See what I mean? It's like those *Playboy* centerfold interviews—"*I like bubble baths, pillow fights, and long, naked walks on the beach.*" No she doesn't. But the point of the questions isn't to inform, it's to reinforce the fantasies of the blokes jerking off to her.

It's the same way for me.

I grin, flashing a hint of dimple—women fall all over themselves for dimples.

"Well, most nights I like to read."

I like to fuck.

Which is probably the answer my fans would rather hear. The Palace, however, would lose their ever-loving minds if I said that.

Anyway, where was I? That's right—the fucking. I like it long, hard, and frequent. With my hands on a firm, round arse—pulling some lovely little piece back against me, hearing her sweet moans bouncing off the walls as she comes around my cock. These century-old rooms have fantastic acoustics.

While some men choose women because of their talent at keeping their legs open, I prefer the ones who are good at keeping their mouths shut. Discretion and an ironclad NDA keep most of the real stories out of the papers.

"I enjoy horseback riding, polo, an afternoon of clay pigeon shooting with the Queen."

I enjoy rock climbing, driving as fast as I can without crashing, flying, good scotch, B-movies, and a scathingly passive-aggressive verbal exchange with the Queen.

It's that last one that keeps the Old Bird on her toes—my wit is her fountain of youth. Plus it's good practice for us both. Wessco is an active constitutional monarchy so unlike our ceremonial neighbors, the Queen is an equal ruling branch of government, along with Parliament. That essentially makes the royal family politicians. Top of the food chain, sure, but politicians all the same. And politics is a quick, dirty, brawling business. Every brawler knows that if you're going to bring a knife to a fistfight, that knife had better be sharp.

I cross my arms over my chest, displaying the tan, bare forearms beneath the sleeves of my rolled-up pale-blue oxford. I'm told they have a rabid Twitter following—along with a few other parts of my body. I then tell the story of my first shoot. It's a fandom favorite—I could recite it in my sleep—and it almost feels like I am. Teddy chuckles at the ending—when my brat of a little brother loaded the launcher with a cow patty instead of a pigeon.

Then he sobers, adjusting his glasses, signaling that the sad portion of our program will now begin.

"It will be thirteen years this May since the tragic plane crash that took the lives of the Prince and Princess of Pembrook."

Called it.

I nod silently.

"Do you think of them often?"

The carved teak bracelet weighs heavily on my wrist. "I have many happy memories of my parents. But what's most important to me is that they live on through the causes they championed, the charities they supported, the endowments that carry their name. That's their legacy. By building up the foundations they advocated for, I'll ensure they'll always be remembered."

Words, words, words, talk, talk, talk. I'm good at that. Saying a lot without really answering a thing.

I think of them every single day.

It's not our way to be overly emotional—stiff upper lip, onward and upward, the king is dead—long live the king. But while to the world they were a pair of HRHs, to me and Henry they were just plain old Mum and Dad. They were good and fun and real. They hugged us often, and smacked us about when we deserved it—which was pretty often too. They were wise and kind and loved us fiercely—and that's a rarity in my social circle.

I wonder what they'd have to say about everything and how different things would be if they'd lived.

Teddy's talking again. I'm not listening, but I don't have to—the last few words are all I need to hear. ". . . Lady Esmerelda last weekend?"

I've known Ezzy since our school days at Briar House. She's a good egg—loud and rowdy. "Lady Esmerelda and I are old friends."

"*Just* friends?"

She's also a committed lesbian. A fact her family wants to keep out of the press. I'm her favorite beard. Our mutually beneficial dates are organized through the Palace secretary.

I smile charmingly. "I make it a rule not to kiss and tell."

Teddy leans forward, catching a whiff of story. *The* story.

"So there is the possibility that something deeper could be developing between you? The country took so much joy in watching your parents' courtship. The people are on tenterhooks waiting for you, 'His Royal Hotness' as they call you on social media, to find your own ladylove and settle down."

I shrug. "Anything's possible."

Except for that. I won't be settling down anytime soon. He can bet his Littlecock on it.

As soon as the hot beam of front lighting is extinguished and the red recording signal on the camera blips off, I stand up from my chair, removing the microphone clipped to my collar.

Teddy stands as well. "Thank you for your time, Your Grace."

He bows slightly at the neck—the proper protocol.

I nod. "Always a pleasure, Littlecock."

That's not what she said. Ever.

Bridget, my personal secretary—a stout, middle-aged, well-ordered woman, appears at my side with a bottle of water.

"Thank you." I twist the cap. "Who's next?"

The Dark Suits thought it was a good time for a PR boost—which means days of interviews, tours, and photo shoots. My own personal fourth, fifth, and sixth circles of hell.

"He's the last for today."

"Hallelujah."

She falls in step beside me as I walk down the long, carpeted hallway that will eventually lead to Guthrie House—my private apartments at the Palace of Wessco.

"Lord Ellington is arriving shortly, and arrangements for dinner at Bon Repas are confirmed."

Being friends with me is harder than you'd think. I mean, I'm a great friend; my life, on the other hand, is a pain in the arse. I can't just drop by a pub last minute or hit up a new club on a random Friday night. These things have to preplanned, organized. Spontaneity is the only luxury I don't get to enjoy.

"Good."

With that, Bridget heads towards the palace offices and I enter my private quarters. Three floors, a full modernized kitchen, a morning room, a library, two guest rooms, servants' quarters, two master suites with balconies that open up to the most breathtaking views on the grounds. All fully restored and updated—the colors, tapestries, stonework, and moldings maintaining their historic integrity. Guthrie House is the official residence of the Prince or Princess of Pembrook—the heir apparent—whomever that may be. It was my father's before it was mine, my grandmother's before her coronation.

Royals are big on hand-me-downs.

I head up to the master bedroom, unbuttoning my shirt, looking forward to the hot, pounding feel of eight showerheads turned up to full blast. My shower is fucking fantastic.

But I don't make it that far.

Fergus meets me at the top of the stairs.

"She wants to see you," he croaks.

And *she* needs no further introduction.

I rub a hand down my face, scratching the dark five o'clock shadow on my chin. "When?"

"When do you think?" Fergus scoffs. "Yesterday, o'course."

Of course.

Back in the old days, the throne was the symbol of a monarch's power. In illustrations it was depicted with the rising sun behind it, the clouds and stars beneath it—the seat for a descendent of God himself. If the throne was the emblem of power, the throne room was the place where that sovereignty was wielded. Where decrees were issued, punishments were pronounced, and the command of "bring me his head" echoed off the cold stone walls.

That was then.

Now, the royal office is where the work gets done—the throne room is used for public tours. And yesterday's throne is today's executive desk. I'm sitting across from it right now. It's shining, solid mahogany and ridiculously huge.

If my grandmother were a man, I'd suspect she's compensating for something.

Christopher, the Queen's personal secretary, offers me tea but I decline with a wave of my hand. He's young, about twenty-three, as tall as I am and attractive, I guess—in an action-film star kind of way. He's not a terrible secretary, but he's not the sharpest tack in the box, either. I think the Queen keeps him around for kicks—because she likes looking at him, the dirty old girl. In my head, I call him Igor, because if my grandmother told him to eat nothing but flies for the rest of his life, he'd ask, "With the wings on or off?"

Finally, the adjoining door to the blue drawing room opens and Her Majesty Queen Lenora stands in the doorway.

There's a species of monkey indigenous to the Colombian rain forest that's one of the most adorable-looking animals you'll ever see—its cuteness puts fuzzy hamsters and small dogs on Pinterest to shame. Except for its hidden razor-sharp teeth and its appetite for human eyeballs. Those lured in by the beast's precious appearance are doomed to lose theirs.

My grandmother is a lot like those vicious little monkeys.

She looks like a granny—like anyone's granny. Short and petite, with soft poofy hair, small pretty hands, shiny pearls, thin lips that can laugh at a dirty joke, and a face lined with wisdom. But it's the eyes that give her away.

Gunmetal gray eyes.

The kind that back in the day would have sent opposing armies fleeing. Because they're the eyes of a conqueror . . . undefeatable.

"Nicholas."

I rise and bow. "Grandmother."

She breezes past Christopher without a look. "Leave us."

I sit after she does, resting my ankle on the opposite knee, my arm casually slung along the back of the chair.

"I saw your interview," she tells me. "You should smile more. You used to seem like such a happy boy."

"I'll try to remember to pretend to be happier."

She opens the center drawer of her desk, withdrawing a keyboard, then taps away on it with more skill than you'd expect from someone her age. "Have you seen the evening's headlines?"

"I haven't."

She turns the screen towards me. Then she clicks rapidly on one news website after another.

PRINCE PARTIES AT THE PLAYBOY MANSION

HENRY THE HEARTBREAKER

RANDY ROYAL

WILD, WEALTHY—AND WET

The last one is paired with the unmistakable picture of my brother diving into a swimming pool—naked as the day he was born.

I lean forward, squinting. "Henry will be horrified. The lighting is terrible in this one—you can barely make out his tattoo."

My grandmother's lips tighten. "You find this amusing?"

Mostly I find it annoying. Henry is immature, unmotivated—a slacker. He floats through life like a feather in the wind, coasting in whatever direction the breeze takes him.

I shrug. "He's twenty-four, he was just discharged from service . . ."

Mandatory military service. Every citizen of Wessco—male, female, or prince—is required to give two years.

"He was discharged *months ago*." She cuts me off. "And he's been around the world with eighty whores ever since."

"Have you tried calling his mobile?"

"Of course I have." She clucks. "He answers, makes that ridiculous static noise, and tells me he can't hear me. Then he says he loves me and hangs up."

My lips pull into a grin. The brat's entertaining—I'll give him that.

The Queen's eyes darken like an approaching storm. "He's in the States—Las Vegas—with plans to go to Manhattan soon. I want you to go there and bring him home, Nicholas. I don't care if you have to bash him over the head and shove him into a burlap sack, the boy needs to be brought to heel."

I've visited almost every major city in the world—and out of all of them, I hate New York the most.

"My schedule—"

"Has been rearranged. While there, you'll attend several functions in my stead. I'm needed here."

"I assume you'll be working on the House of Lords? Persuading the arseholes to finally do their job?"

"I'm glad you brought that up." My grandmother crosses her arms. "Do you know what happens to a monarchy without a stable line of heirs, my boy?"

My eyes narrow. "I studied history at university—of course I do."

"Enlighten me."

I lift my shoulders. "Without a clear succession of uncontested heirs, there could be a power grab. Discord. Possibly civil war between different houses that see an opportunity to take over."

The hairs on the back of my neck prickle. And my palms start to sweat. It's that feeling you get when you're almost to the top of that first hill on a roller coaster. *Tick, tick, tick . . .*

"Where are you going with this? We have heirs. If Henry and I are taken out by some catastrophe, there's always cousin Marcus."

"Cousin Marcus is an imbecile. He married an imbecile. His children are double-damned imbeciles. They will never rule this country." She straightens her pearls and lifts her nose. "There are murmurings in Parliament about changing us to a ceremonial sovereignty."

"There are always murmurings."

"Not like this," she says sharply. "This is different. They're holding up the trade legislation, unemployment is climbing, wages are down." She taps the screen. "These headlines aren't helping. People are worried about putting food on their tables, while their prince cavorts from one luxury hotel to another. We need to give the press something positive to report. We need to give the people something to celebrate. And we need to show Parliament we are firmly in control so they'd best play nicely or we'll run roughshod over them."

I'm nodding. Agreeing. Like a stupid moth flapping happily towards the flame.

"What about a day of pride? We could open the ballrooms to the public, have a parade?" I suggest. "People love that sort of thing."

She taps her chin. "I was thinking something . . . bigger. Something that will catch the world's attention. The event of the century." Her eyes glitter with anticipation—like an executioner right before he swings the axe.

And then the axe comes down.

"The *wedding* of the century."

CHAPTER 2

Nicholas

My whole body locks up. And I think my organs begin to shut down. My voice is rough with pointless, illogical hope.

"Is Great-Aunt Miriam marrying again?"

The Queen folds her hands on the desk. A terrible sign. That's her tell—it says her mind is made up and not even a gale-force wind could sway her off course.

"When you were a boy, I promised your mother that I would give you the space to choose a wife for yourself, as your father chose her. To fall in love. I've watched and waited, and now I've given up waiting. Your family needs you; your country needs you. Therefore, you will announce the name of your betrothed at a press conference . . . at the end of the summer."

Her declaration breaks me out of my shock and I jump to my feet. "That's five bloody months from now!"

She shrugs. "I wanted to give you thirty days. You can thank your grandfather for talking me out of it."

She means the portrait on the wall behind her. My grandfather's been dead for ten years.

"Maybe you should be less concerned with my personal life and more concerned with the press finding out about your habit of talking to paintings."

"It comforts me!" Now she's standing too—hands on her desk, leaning towards me. "And it's just the one painting—don't be obnoxious, Nicky."

"Can't help it." I look at her pointedly. "I learned from the best."

She ignores the dig and sits back down. "I've drawn up a list of suitable young ladies—some of them you've met, some will be new to you. This is our best course of action, unless you can give me a reason to think otherwise."

And I've got nothing. My wit deserts me so fast there's a dust trail in my brain. Because politically, public relations–wise, she's right—a royal wedding kills all the birds with one stone. But the birds don't give a damn about what's right—they just see a rock coming at their fucking heads.

"I don't want to get married."

She shrugs. "I don't blame you. I didn't want to wear your great-great grandmother, Queen Belvidere's tiara on my twenty-first birthday—it was a gaudy, heavy thing. But we all must do our duty. You know this. Now it's your turn, Prince Nicholas."

There's a reason *duty* is a homophone for *shit.*

And she's not asking me as my grandmother—she's telling me, as my queen. A lifetime of upbringing centered around responsibility, legacy, birthright, and honor make it impossible for me to refuse.

I need alcohol. Right fucking now.

"Is that all, Your Majesty?"

She stares at me for several beats, then nods. "It is. Travel safely; we'll speak again when you return."

I stand, dip my head, and turn to leave. Just as the door is closing behind me, I hear a sigh. "Oh Edward, where did we go wrong? Why must they be so difficult?"

An hour later, I'm back at Guthrie House, sitting in front of the fireplace in the morning room, handing my empty glass to Fergus for a refill. *Another* refill.

It's not that I haven't known what's expected of me—the whole world knows. I have one job: pass my tiger blood on to the next generation. Beget an heir who'll one day replace me, as I'll replace my grandmother. And run a country.

Still, it all seemed so theoretical. *Some day, one day.* The Queen is healthier than a whole stable of horses—she's not going anywhere anytime soon. But now . . . a wedding . . . shit just got real.

"There he is!"

I can count on one hand the number of people I trust—and Simon Barrister, 4th Earl of Ellington, is one of them. He greets me with a back-smacking hug and a glowing smile. And when I say glowing, I mean literally—his face is bright tomato red, and crispy around the edges.

"What the hell happened to your face?"

"Damn Caribbean sun hates me. No matter how much sunscreen I used, it found a way to fry me like a chip!" He elbows me. "Made for a creative honeymoon, if you know what I mean. Burn ointment can be quite sensual."

Simon married last month. I stood beside him at the altar—though I'd tried like hell to get him to make a run for it.

He's got a big heart and a brilliant brain, but he's never been good with women. The copper hair, milk-white skin, and pudge around the middle that no amount of tennis or biking will melt away didn't help. And then Frances Alcott came along. Franny doesn't like me and the feeling is entirely mutual. She's breathtaking—I'll give her that: dark hair and eyes, the face of an angel, skin like a porcelain doll's.

The kind whose head will spin around on its neck, right before it drags you under the bed to strangle you.

Fergus brings Simon a drink and we sit down.

"So, I hear the Old Bird finally brought the hammer down on the whole marriage thing."

The ice rattles in my glass as I gulp it down. "That was fast."

"You know how it is around here. The walls have ears and big mouths. What's your plan, Nick?"

I raise my glass. "A rapid descent into alcoholism." Then I shrug. "Beyond that, I don't have a plan."

I toss the papers at him. "She made me a list of potentials. Helpful of her."

Simon flips through the pages. "This could be fun. You could hold auditions—like *The X Factor*—'Show me your double-D talents.'"

I arch my neck, trying to dislodge the knot that's sprung up. "And on top of everything, we have to go to bloody fucking New York and chase Henry down."

"I don't know why you dislike New York so much—good shows, great food, leggy models."

My parents were coming back from New York when their plane went down. It's childish and stupid, I know—but what can I say, I hold a grudge.

Simon raises his palm. "Wait, what do you mean, '*We* have to go to bloody fucking New York'?"

"Misery loves company. That means road trip."

Also, I value Simon's opinion, his judgment. If we were the mob, he'd be my consigliere.

He gazes into his glass as if it holds the secrets of the world—and women. "Franny's not going to be happy."

"Give her something sparkly from the store."

Simon's family owns Barrister's, the largest department store chain in the world.

"Besides, you just spent an entire month together. You must be sick of her by now."

The secret to a long, successful relationship is frequent absences. It keeps things new, fun—there's never time for the inevitable boredom and annoyance to set in.

"There aren't any time-outs in marriage, Nick." He chuckles. "As you'll soon see for yourself."

I give him the finger. "Appreciate the sympathy."

"That's what I'm here for."

I drain my glass empty. Again.

"I've canceled our dinner plans, by the way. Lost my appetite. I told the security team we'll be heading to The Goat for the rest of the night."

The Horny Goat is the oldest wooden structure in the city. It's located in what used to be the palace proper—the village surrounding the palace where the servants and soldiers made their homes. In those days The Horny Goat was a whorehouse; today it's a pub. The walls are crooked and the roof leaks, but it's the best damn pub in the country as far as I'm concerned. I don't know how Macalister—he's the owner—does it, background checks or bribery, but not a single story has ever shown up in the press about me or my brother after a night at The Goat.

And there've been some wild ones.

Simon and I are already piss-drunk when the car pulls up to the door. Logan St. James, the head of my personal security team, opens the car door for Simon and me, his eyes scanning up and down the sidewalk for signs of a threat or a camera.

Inside, the pub air smells of stale beer and cigarettes, but it's as comforting as fresh biscuits baking in the oven. The ceilings are low and the floor is sticky—there's a karaoke box and stage in the back corner—with a light-haired girl swaying on it, belting out the newest Adele song. Simon and I sit at the bar, and Meg—she's Macalister's daughter—wipes it down with a rag and a sexy smile.

"Evening, Your Highness." Simon gets a nod but a less sexy smile. "Lord Ellington."

Then her light brown eyes are back to me. "Saw you on the television this afternoon. You looked well."

"Thank you."

She shakes her head just a bit. "I never knew you were a reader. Funny, in all the times I've been to your rooms, I haven't seen a single book."

Meg's voice has echoed off my walls and her moans have hummed around my cock—more than once. Her NDA is in my wall safe at home. I'm almost sure I'll never need it, but the first "talk" my father gave me wasn't about the birds and bees—it was about how it's always better to have a nondisclosure agreement that you don't need than to need one that you don't have.

I smirk. "You must've missed them. You weren't interested in looking at books when you were there, pet."

Women who live paycheck to paycheck can handle a one—or three—night stand better than those in my class. Noble ladies are spoiled, demanding—they're used to getting everything they want—and turn vindictive when they're denied. But girls like my pretty barmaid are accustomed to knowing there are some things in life they'll never be able to lock down.

Meg smiles—warm and knowingly. "What would you like to drink tonight? The usual?"

I don't know if it's the day full of interviews or the pints of scotch I've ingested, but suddenly adrenaline rushes through me, my heartbeat quickens—and the answer is so clear.

The Queen has me by the balls—and I'm going to have to bleach my brain for even completing that thought—but besides that, I still have time.

"No, Meg. I want something different—something I haven't had before. Surprise me."

If you were told that the world as you knew it—life as you knew it—would end in five months, what would you do?

You'd make the most of the time you had left, of course. Do everything you wanted to do—every*one* you wanted to do—for as long as you could. Until time was up.

Well . . . looks like I've got a plan, after all.

CHAPTER 3

Olivia

Days that change our life almost never happen to normal people. I mean really, do you know anyone who's hit the lottery, been discovered by a Hollywood agent at the mall, inherited a tax-free, move-in–ready mansion from a long-lost, dead great-aunt?

Me neither.

But—here's the thing—when those days do come along for the rare fortunate few, we don't even recognize them. We don't know that what's happening is epic, monumental. *Life-changing.*

It's only later—after everything is perfect or it's all fallen apart—that we look back, retrace our steps and realize the exact moment that split our histories and our hearts into two—the before and the after.

In the after, it's not just our lives that are changed. *We're* changed. Forever.

I should know. The day that changed my life was one of *those* days. The crappy kind.

Normal people have a whole lot of them.

It starts when I open my eyes—forty minutes later than I'm supposed to. *Stupid alarm clock.* It should know I mean *a.m.* Who the hell needs to wake up at four *p.m.?* No one, that's who.

Forget about self-driving cars; Google needs to move their asses on self-aware alarm clocks.

My day continues its downward spiral as I throw on the only clothes I wear these days, my work clothes—white blouse, faded black skirt, slightly ripped tights—then wrangle my mass of unruly black curls into a bun and trip my way into our mini-sized kitchen, eyes still partially closed. I pour myself a bowl of Cinnamon Toast Crunch—the best cereal ever—but when I turn around to grab the milk, my cereal is devoured by our devil-dog Bosco in three seconds flat.

"Bastard!" I whisper-yell, because my sister and father don't have to be up for a few more hours.

Bosco was a stray, a mutt, and he looks the part. The body of a Chihuahua, the wide-set eyes of a pug and the brown, stringy hair of a balding shih tzu. He's one of those dogs that are so ugly, they're actually cute. Sometimes I wonder if he's the odds-defying result of a kinky canine three-way. My mom found him in the alley behind our coffee shop when he was still a pup. He was a ravenous little thing back then and eight years later, he'd still eat himself to death if we let him.

I pick up the cereal box to refill my bowl—the *empty* cereal box.

"Nice," I tell the stealing stealer who steals.

He gives me the sad eyes as he jumps down from the counter he's not supposed to be on. Then he drops to his side, exposing his belly in contrition.

But I'm not buying it. "Oh, get up. Have some dignity."

After an alternate breakfast of an apple and toast, I grab Bosco's pink glitter leash that my sister bought—as if the poor thing didn't have enough reasons for a complex—and latch it to his collar.

Our building was built in the 1920s—it used to be a multifamily before the first floor was renovated into a restaurant around the time JFK was elected. There's a second set of steps that leads to the coffee shop's kitchen, but Bosco's not allowed in there, so I walk him out the front door and down the narrow, green-painted steps that lead out to the sidewalk next to the coffee shop entrance.

And holy shit icicles, it's cold!

It's one of those freak March days that come after a rash of mild weather has lulled you into a false sense of security that winter is over. You've no sooner boxed up the sweaters, boots, and winter coats in the crawl space than Mother Nature says, "Sorry, sucker," and dumps a frozen nor'easter on your ass.

The sky is gray and the wind is hair-whippingly bitter. My poor blouse, which only has two buttons fastened crookedly, never had a chance.

It bursts open.

Right in front of Pete the Pervy Garbage Man. My white lace bra is sheer as sheer can be and my nipples proclaim the arctic temperatures in all their pointy glory.

"Looking good, baby!!" he yells in a Brooklyn accent so thick, you'd think he was trying to make fun of people with Brooklyn accents. He wags his tongue. "Lemme suck on those sweet jugs. Could use a little extra hot milk to go with my coffee."

Ewww.

He holds onto the back of his truck with one hand while grabbing and rubbing his crotch with the other. *Jesus, guys are gross.* If this were half-decent revenge porn, he'd fall into the bin and the trash compactor would mysteriously turn on, crushing and slicing him into oblivion. Unfortunately, this is just my life.

But I'm a New Yorker, born and raised. So there's only one appropriate reaction.

"Fuck you!" I shout at the top of my lungs, lifting both hands above my head, middle fingers raised loud and proud.

"Anytime, sweetheart!"

As the truck rumbles down the street, I let loose every obscene hand gesture I know. The thumb-against-teeth flip, the chin flick, the horns, and the raised-fist bicep slap, also known as the Italian Salute—just like Grandma Millie used to make.

The only problem is, when I smack my arm, I also drop the leash, and Bosco takes off like a bat out of hell.

As I'm buttoning my blouse and trying to run at the same time, I think, *God, this is a crappy day. And it's not even five a.m. yet.*

But that was just the tip of the crapberg.

It takes me three blocks to catch the little ingrate. By the time I make it back, tiny snowflakes have begun to fall, like dandruff from the sky.

I used to like snow—love it, actually. How it coats everything in a sparkly diamond luster, making it all shiny-clean and new. Turning lampposts into ice sculptures and the city into a magical winter wonderland.

But that was before. Before there were bills to pay and a business to run. When I see the snow now, all I think about is what a slow day it's going to be, how little money is going to come in . . . the only magical thing is how all the customers will disappear.

A slapping, fluttering sound makes me turn my head to discover a paper taped to the outside of the coffee shop door. A foreclosure notice—the second one we've received, not counting the dozens of phone calls and e-mails that in a nutshell say, "Bitch better have my money."

Well, the bitch doesn't have any.

For a few months I tried sending the bank as much as I could, even if it was short. But when it came down to paying our employees and vendors or not, I stopped sending anything.

I tear the scarlet letter off the door, grateful that I got to it before any customers arrived. Then I walk up, toss Bosco just inside the apartment door, and head into the kitchen.

This is the real start to my day. I fire up the ancient oven, preheating it to 400 degrees. Then I slip my earbuds in. My mother was a huge fan of the eighties—the music and the movies. She used to say they'll never make 'em like that again. When I was little, I'd sit on the stool here in this kitchen and watch her do her thing. She was like an artist, creating one edible masterpiece after another, with female power ballads from Heart, Scandal, Joan Jett, Pat Benatar, and Lita Ford blasting in the background. Those same songs fill my playlist and pound into my eardrums.

There are over a thousand coffee shops in New York City. To stay afloat against the heavy hitters like Starbucks and The Coffee Beanery, us mom-and-pop shops need to have a niche—something that sets us apart. Here, at Amelia's, that something is our pies. Handmade from scratch, fresh every day, from my mother's recipes that were handed down to her from her grandmother and great-aunts in "the old country."

What country that is, we're not exactly sure. My mom used to call our nationality "Heinz 57"—a little bit of everything.

But the pies are what's kept us above water, even though we're sinking deeper and deeper every day. As Vixen sings about being on the edge of a broken heart, I mix all the ingredients in a massive bowl—a cauldron, really. Then I knead the sticky dough, squeezing and clenching. It's a pretty good upper-arm workout—no chicken arms for me. Once it's the right consistency and a smooth sable color, I turn the bowl on its side and roll the giant ball onto the middle of the expansive, flour-coated butcher-block counter. I flatten it into a big rectangle, first with my palms, then with a rolling pin, stopping every few minutes to re-flour. Once it's spread evenly thin, I slice it into six perfect circles. This will be enough for three double-crust pies—and I'll do this four more times before the shop opens. On Tuesdays, Thursdays, and Sundays, I mix up the regular apple, cherry, blueberry, and peach along with lemon meringue, chocolate, and banana cream.

With the bottom crust set in each of the six pans, I wash my hands and move to the fridge, where I take out the first six pies I made yesterday and put them in the oven to reheat to room temperature. These will be the ones I serve today—pies are always better on the second day. The extra twenty-four hours give the flaky crust enough time to soak up the brown sugar–sweetened juice.

As they reheat, I move to the apples, peeling and slicing as fast as the Japanese chefs at a hibachi restaurant. I've got mad knife skills—but the trick is, the blades have to be razor sharp. Nothing is more dangerous than a dull blade. If you want to lose a finger, that's the way to do it.

I pour handfuls of white and brown sugar over the apples, then cinnamon and nutmeg, and toss the contents of the big bowl to coat the slices. I haven't read the recipes or measured in years—I could do this with my eyes closed.

It used to be meditative, mindless, assembling the pies—tucking the fruit beneath the doughy blanket of top crust like it's settling in for a nap, fluting the edges, then scalloping a perfect, pretty pattern with a fork.

But there's nothing relaxing about it now. With every move there's the screechy worry—like a police car siren screaming in my brain—that these pies won't even sell, and the terminal water heater downstairs will finally throw in the towel and we'll be out on the streets.

I think I can actually feel the wrinkles burrowing through my face like evil, microscopic moles. I know money doesn't buy happiness, but being able to purchase some peace-of-mind real estate would be pretty great right now.

When the thick, buttery juice bubbles like caramel through the flower-shaped cut in the center of the pies, I take them out and set them on the counter.

That's when my sister bounces down the stairs into the kitchen. Everything about Ellie is bouncy—her long blond ponytail, her energetic personality . . . the dangling silver and pearl earrings she's wearing.

"Are those my earrings?" I ask, like only a sister can.

She plucks a blueberry from the bowl on the counter, throws it in the air, and catches it in her mouth.

"*Mi casa en su casa.* Technically they're *our* earrings."

"That were in my jewelry box in *my* room!" They're the only ones I have that don't turn my lobes green.

"*Pfft.* You don't even wear them. You don't go anywhere to wear them, Livvy."

She's not trying to be a jerk—she's just seventeen, so it's inevitable.

"And pearls like to be worn; it's a fact. If they sit in a dark box for too long they lose their luster."

She's always spouting off weird little facts that no one except a *Jeopardy!* contestant would know. Ellie's the "smart one"—advanced placement classes, National Honor Society, early acceptance to NYU. But book smarts and common sense are two different things. Outside of being able to run a washing machine, I don't think my sister has any idea how the real world works.

She slips her arms into a worn winter coat and pulls a knitted beanie down over her head. "Gotta go—I have a calc test first period."

Ellie skips out the back door just as Marty, our waiter/dish-washer/bouncer and consummate repairman, walks through it.

"Who the fuck forgot to tell winter it was over?" He shakes off an inch of white slush from his curly black hair, like a dog after a bath. It's really coming down now—a wall of white dots.

Marty hangs his coat on the hook while I fill the first filter of the day with freshly ground coffee. "Liv, you know I love you like the baby sister I wish I had—"

"You *have* a baby sister."

He has three, actually—triplets—Bibbidy, Bobbidy, and Boo. Marty's mom was still flying high when she filled out the birth certificates, a little mix-up with the meds during delivery. And Marty's dad, a rabbi from Queens, was smart enough not to quibble with a woman who'd just had the equivalent of three watermelons pulled out of her.

"You don't piss me off like they do. And because I love you, I feel entitled to say you don't look like you just rolled out of bed—you look like you just rolled out of a garbage can."

What every girl wants to hear.

"It was a rough morning. I woke up late."

"You need a vacation. Or at least a day off. You should've come out for drinks last night. I went to that new place in Chelsea and met the most fantastic man. Matt Bomer eyes with a Shemar Moore smile." He wiggles his eyebrows. "We're supposed to get together tonight."

I pass him the coffee filter when the delivery truck pulls into the back alley. Then I spend the next twenty minutes arguing with a thick-necked meathead about why I'm not accepting or paying for the moldy fucking Danish he's trying to dump on me.

And the day just keeps getting better.

I turn on the front lights and flip the CLOSED sign to OPEN at six thirty sharp. I turn the bolt on the door out of habit—it's been broken for months; I just haven't had the chance to buy a replacement.

At first, it doesn't look like the snow will be a total disaster—we get our coffee-craving, on-the-way-to-work local crew. Along with little Mrs. McGillacutty, the ninety-year-old woman from two blocks down who walks here every day for her "morning workout."

But by nine o'clock, I flick on the television at the end of the counter for background noise as Marty and I stare out the picture window, watching the snowstorm become the blizzard of the century. There's not even a faint pulse of customers—it's dead—so I call it.

"Feel like deep-cleaning the fridge and the pantry and scrubbing behind the oven with me?"

Might as well get some housekeeping done.

Marty lifts his coffee mug. "Lead the way, girlfriend."

I send Marty home at noon. A state of emergency is declared at one—only official vehicles are allowed on the road. Ellie bursts through the shop like a whirlwind at two, elated that school closed early, then twirls immediately back out to spend the storm at her friend's apartment. A few random customers stop in during the afternoon, stocking up for their pie fix while hibernating during the storm.

At six, I work on the bills—which means spreading papers, ledgers, and bank notices out at one of the tables in front and staring at them. The cost of sugar is up—*shitheads.* Coffee is up—*bastards.* I refuse to scrimp on fruit. I send Marty on regular weekly runs upstate to Maxwell Farms—they grow the best produce in the state.

By nine thirty, my eyes start doing that closing-without-realizing-it thing and I decide to call it a night.

I'm in the back, in the kitchen, sliding a plastic-wrapped pie into the fridge, when I hear the bell above the door jingle and voices—two distinct voices—come in, arguing in that ball-busting way men do.

"My fingertips are frozen, you know. Can't have frostbite—my fingers are Franny's third-favorite part of me."

"Your bank account is Franny's first-, second- and third-favorite part of you. And you sound like an old woman. We weren't even walking that long."

It's the second guy's voice that catches my attention. They both have an accent—but his voice is deeper, smoother. The sound of it feels like slipping into a warm bath after a long day, soothing and blissful.

I step through the swinging kitchen door. And I think my tongue falls out of my mouth.

He's wearing a tuxedo, the black tie hanging haphazardly around his neck, and the top two buttons of his pristine white shirt are open, teasing a glimpse of bronze chest. The tux hugs him in a way that says there are hard, rippling muscles and taut, heated skin beneath it. His jaw is chiseled—fucking *chiseled*—like it's made of warm marble. His chin is strong, beneath the planes of prominent cheekbones that a *GQ* cover model would kill for. His nose is straight, his mouth full and perfectly made to whisper dark, dirty things. Masculine eyebrows sit above gray-green eyes—the color of sea glass in the sun—framed by sooty, long lashes. His hair is dark and thick—a few strands fall over his forehead, giving him an effortless, edgy, I-don't-give-a-fuck kind of look.

"Hi."

"Well . . . hello." The corner of his mouth inches up. And it feels . . . naughty.

The man next to him—redheaded, kind of pudgy, with light sparkling blue eyes—says, "Tell me you have hot tea and my fortune is yours."

"Yes, we have tea—and it'll only cost you $2.25."

"You are officially my favorite person."

They pick a table along the wall and the dark-haired one moves with confidence—like he owns the place, like he owns the whole world. He sits in the chair, leaning back, knees spread, his eyes dragging over me the way a guy with X-ray vision would.

"Are you going to sit down too?" I ask the two men in dark suits who stand on either side of the door. And I'd bet my tip jar they're bodyguards—I've seen enough rich, famous people around the city to spot them—though these two are on the young side.

"No, it'll just be us," the dark-haired one tells me.

I wonder who he is. The son of some rich overseas investor, maybe? Or an actor—he's got the body and the face for it. And . . . the presence. That nameless quality that says, "Pay attention—you're gonna want to remember me."

"You guys are pretty brave to be out in this weather." I put two menus on the table.

"Or stupid," the redhead grumbles.

"I dragged him out," the dark-haired one says, his words slurring the tiniest bit. "The streets are empty, so I can walk around." His voice lowers conspiratorially. "They only let me out of the cage a few times a year."

I have no clue what that means, but hearing him say it may be the most exciting thing that's happened to me all day. Fuck, that's pathetic.

The redhead scans the menu. "What's the specialty here?"

"Our pies."

"Pies?"

I tap my pencil against my pad. "I make them myself. Best in the city."

The dark-haired one hums. "Tell me more about your magnificent pie. Is it delicious?"

"Yes."

"Juicy?"

I roll my eyes. "Save it."

"What do you mean?"

"I mean, you can save the pie innuendos." My tone drops, imitating the creepy lines I've heard one too many times. "'*Do you serve hair-pie, I'd eat your pie all night, baby*'—I get it."

He chuckles, and his laugh sounds even better than his voice. "What about your lips?"

My eyes snap to his. "What about them?"

"They're the sweetest thing I've seen in a very long time. Do they taste as good as they look? I bet they do."

My mouth goes dry—and my witty-comeback reflex flatlines.

"Pay no attention to this sorry mess," the redhead says. "He's been smashed for three days straight."

The "sorry mess" raises a silver flask. "And on my way to four."

I've seen my share of sloppy-drunk frat boys in the thrall of an after-party, late-night food binge. This guy hides it well.

The redhead closes his menu. "I'll have tea and the cherry pie. And peach. And hell, give me a blueberry à la mode as well."

His friend snorts, but he's unapologetic. "I like pie."

I turn to the other one.

"Apple," he says softly—managing to make the benign two-syllable word sound totally sexy. My pelvis swoons like a romance novel heroine who just saw her Brad Pitt circa *Legends of the Fall*–like hero riding toward her on horseback.

Either he's got a lust talisman for a voice box or I'm in serious need of a hookup. Oh, who am I kidding—of course I need a hookup. I punched my V-card when I was seventeen, with my high school boyfriend. Since Jack, there's been no one—it's distinctly possible my hymen has grown back. I'm not into one-night stands, and who has the time for a relationship? Not this girl.

The redhead's phone rings and when he answers the call on speaker, the conversation follows me into the kitchen while I get their order.

"Hello, darling! It feels like I've been waiting ages and I was frightened I'd be asleep when you finally called, so I called you instead."

The woman on the phone also has an accent—she speaks very fast and sounds very awake.

"How many energy drinks have you had, Franny?"

"Three, and I feel amazing! I'm going to have a bubble bath soon and I know how you love me in bubbles, so now we can FaceTime while I do!"

"Please don't," that sensual voice says sarcastically.

"Is that Nicholas, Simon?"

"Yes, he's here with me. We're grabbing a bite."

"Poo, I thought you were alone. The bubbles will have to wait, then. Oh, and I've made you two new shirts—they turned out marvelous. I can't wait for you to see them!"

There's a shrug in Simon's voice when he explains to his friend, "She's taken up sewing for a hobby. She likes to make me clothes."

And he replies, "Can she make herself a gag?"

Which Franny, apparently, overhears.

"Piss off, Nicky!"

After Simon gets off the phone, with a promise to bubble-bath together back at the hotel room, the two men continue to talk in a hum of lowered voices. I catch the tail end of the conversation when I back out of the kitchen door, teacup in hand and pie plates on my arms.

". . . learned the hard way. Everything is for sale and everyone has a price."

"My, but you're a delightful ball of sunshine when you're pissed—it's a shame you don't drink more often."

The sarcasm game is strong with Simon.

I feel those gray-green eyes watching me as I place the plates on the table. It's possible he's hotter now that I know his name. Nicholas—it's a nice name.

"What do you think, dove?" he asks me.

I slide his slice of pie in front of him and Simon digs into his blueberry.

"What do I think about what?"

"We were just having a debate. I happen to think that everything and everyone can be bought, for the right price. What do you think?"

There was a time when I was younger, stupider, and so much more innocent about life—like Ellie—when I would've said no way. But out in the real world, idealism is the first thing to go.

"I agree with you. Money talks, bullshit walks."

"Bloody hell, now you're both depressing me," Simon says. "I may need another slice of pie."

Nicholas smiles, slowly—gorgeously. It makes my head feel light and my knees feel weak. And he has dimples—how did I not notice them before? They're the perfect foil to his fuck-hotness, adding a playful, boyish handsomeness to his already devastating impact.

"I'm glad you said that, sweets."

And I'm a nanosecond away from giggling like a fool, so I start to beat it out of there. Until that voice—that I'd enjoy hear reading the phone book, if anyone still used a phone book—stops me.

"Ten thousand dollars."

I turn around, head tilting.

He clarifies. "Spend the night with me and I'll pay you ten thousand dollars."

"To do what?" I laugh, because he's joking, right?

"The bed is empty and large. Let's start there and see what happens."

I glance from him to Simon—to the two guys by the door. "Is this a joke?"

He takes another swig from his flask. "I never joke about money or sex."

"You want to pay me ten thousand dollars to have sex with you?"

"More than once and in a dozen different positions. I could," he makes air quotes, "'woo' you, but that takes time." He taps his watch. A Rolex, diamonds and platinum—easily $130,000. "And I'm pathetically short on time these days."

I snort, getting over the shock. "I'm not sleeping with you for money."

"Why not?"

"Because I'm not a prostitute."

"Of course you're not. But you're young and beautiful, I'm handsome and rich. The more applicable question is why aren't we fucking already?"

That is a strong argument.

Wait—no—no, it's not. It's a bad argument. A bad, dirty, wild—*crap!*

Nicholas seems to enjoy watching me think it over.

And, God, do I think about it. I'll be thinking about it on repeat down to the smallest—and most well-hung—detail after they're gone. But fantasies aside, I'm just not the kind of girl to go for something like this in real life.

"No."

"No?" He looks genuinely shocked. And disappointed.

"No," I repeat. "It would be wrong."

He rubs his finger along his bottom lip, sizing me up. Speaking of sizing, he has great fingers. Long, with just the right amount of girth, and with clean, trimmed nails. And freakily, Dr. Seuss pops into my head—*Oh the places those fingers will go.*

There's something very wrong with me.

"Do you have a boyfriend?"

"No."

"Lesbian?"

"No."

"Then it's the rightest thing you'll ever do."

My chin rises and my arms cross.

"My dignity isn't for sale."

Nicholas leans forward, eating me up with his eyes. "I don't want to put my cock anywhere near your dignity, love. I want to put it everywhere else."

"Do you have an answer for everything?"

"Here's an answer—twenty thousand dollars."

Holy shit! My jaw creaks open and if there were flies, I'd catch them all.

Those gorgeous eyes look deep into mine, pulling me right in. "You won't regret it, I swear."

And now thoughts of the money—all that cash—eclipse thoughts of all the sex. The things I could do with that much money . . . replace the water heater, make a dent in the mortgage payments, put some toward Ellie's second-semester tuition. Jesus, it's tempting.

But after the money was gone—and it'd be gone fast—my reflection in the mirror would still be there.

I'd have to look at it every day.

"I guess we were both wrong." I shrug. "Some things aren't for sale, for any price."

Simon claps. "Good for you, sweetheart. Optimism wins the day. This pie is fantastic, by the way—you make these yourself, you said? You should write a cookbook."

I don't answer him. Nicholas still holds my gaze—I can't look away.

"Or maybe I'm just trying to buy the wrong thing. Sometimes the cow's not for sale but the milk doesn't always have to be free."

Okay, now his drunk is showing, because that made no frigging sense.

"You want to explain what that means?"

He laughs. "What about a kiss?"

The breath leaves my lungs in one big swoosh. And what he says next makes it a struggle to replace it.

"If I don't get a taste soon, I'll go mad."

I've never thought much about my lips. They're nice, I guess, naturally plump and pink—and I use lip balm, raspberry flavored, sometimes shea butter—a couple of times a day.

"Five thousand dollars."

I would've kissed him for free. But there's something exciting—flattering almost, in a sick, twisted way—about him making the offer. Because he wants this bad enough to pay for it.

"Five thousand dollars? For a kiss?"

"That's what I said."

"With tongue?"

"It's not really a kiss without it."

I hesitate just a moment longer. Long enough for Nicholas to . . . ruin everything.

"Just say yes, pet. You obviously need the money."

I gasp before I can stop myself. I didn't think five words from a stranger could hurt so much. *What a dick.*

It's a thousand different things—the humiliation of having my circumstances thrown in my face, the disappointment that this man—this gorgeous, seductive man—thinks I'm some kind of charity case, the shame that comes along with struggling. In a flash, I get a bird's-eye view of the coffee shop: the chipping paint, the broken lock, the worn chairs and shabby curtains that stopped being chic years ago.

"For fuck's sake, Nicholas," Simon says.

But he just looks at me, waiting, those arrogant green eyes alight with anticipation. So I give him what he's waiting for.

"Hands under the table," I order.

He smiles wider, puts his flask in his pocket, and does what he's told.

"Close your eyes."

"I like a woman who's not afraid to take charge."

"No more talking." He's said more than enough.

I lean in, keeping my eyes open the whole time, memorizing every angle of that face, feeling his warm breath against my cheek. This close, I can see the shadow of stubble on his chin and for just a second, I let myself wonder what it would feel like scratching against my stomach, my thighs—everywhere.

Then in one move, I pick up his plate—and smash the apple pie in his stupid, handsome face.

"Kiss this, asshole."

I straighten up and slap the check down.

"Here's your bill; leave the money on the table. There's the door—use it before I come back with my baseball bat and show you why they used to call me Babe Ruthette."

I don't look back as I stalk toward the kitchen, but I hear a mumble.

"Good pie."

And as if I didn't know already, I'm sure of it now: men suck.

CHAPTER 4

Nicholas

There's a wall in Anthorp Castle that displays weapons of war used by the royal family through the centuries. Swords, sabers, daggers—some still have blood on the blades. One of those weapons is a flail, commonly known as a ball and chain—a two-foot baton attached with a chain to a heavy, spiked ball. It's an unwieldy mace that was actually rarely used in battle because of the danger to the wielder, and the long recovery time before one could strike again. However, when it was used, the damage it inflicted was deadly—the spikes pierced armor and embedded themselves in chests and skulls.

That flail is the first thing I think of when I pry open my eyes—because I feel like one has been planted in my brain. The bright sliver of white light seeping through the shades, in the otherwise dark room, makes agony explode behind my eyes. I moan, and a moment later the door opens, Simon's shadowed silhouette spilling in from the hall.

"You're alive then? For a time I wasn't sure."

"Thanks for your concern," I grate out.

Too loudly. Even the hushed words bounce around my skull like shrapnel. I try again, even softer this time. "What the hell did you let me drink last night?"

Simon laughs without sympathy. "Let you? You guzzled what you've been drinking since The Goat. Vodka—straight up. Barbarian."

Never again. I swear to my liver that if he just pulls through for me this one last time, I'll be kinder, smarter, from now on.

With sickening realization, I remember the black-tie fundraiser we attended last night to support a royal charity. "Did I make an idiot of myself at the gala?"

"No, you were very restrained. Quiet and aloof. I was the only one who could tell that you were lucky to still be standing."

Good. At least I don't have to worry about that.

I rub my temples. "I had the oddest dream last night."

"Was it flying pink elephants and Fergus in a ballerina tutu? That one always disturbs me."

I laugh—not the smartest thing, as pain reverberates through my bones.

"No," I tell him quietly. "I dreamed about my mother."

"Oh?"

"She was . . . scolding me. All sorts of riled up. She even yanked on the short hairs at the back of my neck. Remember how she used to do that when we'd misbehave in public?"

"I remember." Simon's voice is laced with nostalgia. "Until Henry ruined it for her in front of the press when he yelled, 'Ow, what'd you pull my hair for, Mum?'"

I chuckle again, despite the discomfort.

"What was she railing at you for? Did you know?"

"She said . . . she said I made the angel cry." I move my arm over my face to block out the light.

"Well, she did look like an angel and her pie was heavenly. I didn't see any tears, but you definitely hurt her feelings."

I drag my arm away and struggle to sit up.

"What are you going on about?"

"The waitress," Simon explains. "At the coffee shop we stopped in after you dragged me through the city because you could walk around without being mobbed by cameras and fangirls. Don't you recall?"

Images flicker through my head. I stop on one—the sound of a wounded gasp, and navy-blue eyes, the color of the sky at dusk, fighting back tears.

"That . . . that was *real?*"

"Yes, you bloody arse, it was real. You offered her twenty thousand for some rumpy-pumpy. She turned you down. Smart girl."

I run my palm along my jaw, feeling dry crumbs and leftover granules of sugar. The sweet taste of apples lingers on my tongue. And it all comes rushing back—every word.

"Fucking Christ—is the story online yet?"

I can see the headline now: PIMPING PRINCE HITS NEW YORK.

"No. Not a word." Simon checks his watch. "It's half past two in the afternoon, so you're probably safe. If the little bird was going to sing, I think it would've leaked by now."

"That's a relief, I guess."

But still . . . whether it's because of the dream or my own behavior, regret rises around me like steam. It seeps inside with every breath, clinging to my lungs.

"It's still coming down outside. Hell of a storm. You may as well finish sleeping it off; we won't be traveling today."

"Good idea," I murmur, already drifting off, with visions of delicious ripe lips and swirling dark hair dancing in my head.

Early the next morning I'm feeling almost human again—though still achy and fog-headed. I have a meeting upstate with the heads of a military charity organization, and we're scheduled to leave just before sunrise. The earlier we arrive at our destination, the less likely a crowd will be there to greet us. Thankfully, the damnable snow has finally stopped and if there's one thing I appreciate about this city, it's its ability to get up and running through any catastrophe. Although the roads appear passable, Logan trades out the limousine for an SUV. In the backseat, I straighten my tie and adjust my cuff links, while Simon mentions a craving for breakfast tea and a slice—or two—of pie to go with it.

I've been looking for a reason to return, not that I need an excuse. Because I haven't been able to stop thinking about the pretty waitress—and the way I treated her. After I nod, Simon gives Logan the directions, and we pull up in front of Amelia's a few minutes later. The streetlamps are still on and the sidewalk is empty, but the door is unlocked, so we walk inside, an annoying bell chiming above our heads.

It's quiet. I don't take a seat, but stand in the middle of the room amongst the tables.

"We're closed," she says, coming through the swinging door. And then her head jerks up as she comes to a halt. "Oh, it's you."

She's even lovelier than I remembered. Than I dreamed. Delicate midnight tendrils frame a face that belongs in a museum—with stunning dark sapphire eyes that should be commemorated in vibrant oils and soft watercolors. If Helen launched a thousand ships, this girl could raise a thousand hard-ons.

She's prettily made, the top of her head coming only to my chin, but fantastically curvy. Great full tits that strain the buttons of a wrinkled white blouse, shapely hips in a black skirt tapering to a tiny waist I could wrap my hands around and toned legs encased in sheer black tights finish off the whole package very nicely.

An unfamiliar anxiousness fizzes like soda in my gut.

"The door was open," I explain.

"It's broken."

Logan flicks at the lock. Security is his life, so a broken lock would annoy him like a puzzle with the final piece missing.

"What do you want?"

She has no idea who I am. It's in the defensive way she holds herself and the accusatory note in her voice. Some women try to pretend they don't recognize me, but I can always tell. Her ignorance is rather . . . thrilling. There are no expectations, no hidden agendas, no reasons to pretend—what she sees is what she gets. And all she sees is me.

My throat is suddenly a barren wasteland. I swallow, but it's difficult.

"Well, he's desperate for some pie," I say, hooking my thumb at Simon. "And I . . . wanted to apologize for the other evening. I don't normally act that way. I was on a bit of bender . . ."

"In my experience, people don't do things when they're drunk that they wouldn't do normally."

"No, you're right. I would've thought all those things, but I never would've said them out loud." I move closer, slowly. "And if I'd been sober . . . my opening bid would've been much higher."

She crosses her arms. "Are you trying to be cute?"

"No. I don't have to try . . . it just sort of happens."

Her brow furrows just slightly, like she can't decide if she should be angry or amused. I feel myself smiling. "What's your name? I don't know if I asked before."

"You didn't. And it's Liv."

"That's an odd name. Were you ill as a baby? I mean, is live what your parents were hoping you'd do or did they just not like you?"

Her lips fold like she's fighting a grin. Amused is in the lead.

"Liv, Livvy—short for Olivia. Olivia Hammond."

"Ah." I nod slowly. "That's a beautiful name. Much more fitting." I can't take my eyes off her. Don't want to in the slightest. "Well, Olivia, I regret my behavior when we first met and I hope you'll accept my apology."

There's the tiniest flinch of her features—a split second—but I see it. Then she moves to a table and fidgets with a clear-wrapped pie. "Whatever. I'm over it. It's not like you said anything that wasn't true. It is pretty obvious that I do need the money."

The self-deprecation in her voice—and knowing it's there because of me—makes my voice sharp. "Olivia."

She looks up, into my face. And my tone gentles. "I'm sorry. Truly."

That dark blue gaze holds onto mine for a few seconds before she says softly, "Okay."

"Okay," I return, just as soft.

Then she blinks and hands the pie to Simon. "You can have this—it's two days old, so I won't sell it. It might be a little dry, but it's on the house."

He smiles like a wolf that's just been handed a wounded sheep.

"You really are an angel, lass."

"Can he take a fork with him?" I ask. "So I don't have to listen to his stomach grumble the entire way."

Smirking, she hands over a fork.

And I go for the gold.

"Would you like to have coffee sometime, Olivia? With me?"

It's been years since I've asked a woman out on a real date. It's strange—exhilarating and nerve wracking at the same time.

"I don't like coffee. Never touch the stuff."

My eyes roll over the room. "You work in a coffee house."

"Exactly."

I nod. "Hmm, I see your point. It'll have to be dinner, then. Are you available this evening? I could pick you up on our way back."

She gives a jumpy laugh.

"I thought you didn't have time for," she makes air quotes with her fingers, "'wooing'?"

"Some things are worth making time for."

That catches her off guard, making her words stumble. "Well I . . . don't . . . date."

"Good God, why not?" I ask, horrified. "That's a bloody sin."

"A sin?"

"You're stunning, obviously clever—you should date often, and preferably with a man who knows how it's done." I rest my palm on my chest. "Coincidentally, *I* happen to be fantastic at it. What are the odds?"

She laughs again, quick and light. And it feels like when I pull myself up the last peak of a rock formation. Satisfying. More than a bit victorious. Before she can answer, a furry headache on four legs appears beside her, making a yapping, snarling sound.

"Ellie!" she yells over her shoulder. "Bosco can't be down here!"

"What is *that?*" I ask.

"It's my dog."

"No. No, I have dogs. Dogs are descended from wolves. That's descended from a rat." I look again. "An ugly rat."

She lifts the little monster into her arms. "Don't insult my dog."

"Not trying to—just telling the truth."

For once. And it feels fucking grand.

But the barking has to go. I make contact with its beady little eyes and snap my fingers, ordering, "Shh!"

And blessed silence fills the air.

Olivia looks from me to the animal. "How—how did you do that?"

"Dogs are pack animals; they defer to the leader. This one is smart enough to recognize that that's me." I step closer to her, detecting a clean, lovely scent—like fresh honey. "Let's see if it works with you." I snap my fingers. "Dinner."

She cocks her hip, annoyed and yet entertained against her will.

"I'm not a dog."

My eyes—filthy, deviant things that they are—slide over every beautiful inch of her. "No . . . you definitely aren't."

Her cheeks go pink, making her eyes appear almost violet. It's lovely.

But then another ball comes bouncing into the room—a small blond one, wrapped in a fuzzy teal robe with SpongeBob SquarePants slippers on its feet.

"Awwww, yeah . . . school's closed again." She does The Whip. "Ooh-ooh . . ."

Until she sees us—then she freezes.

And *she* definitely knows who I am.

"Hiiii. Wow." She points to Logan and says in a thin, mortified voice. "I like your tie."

He glances down at the tie in question, then nods his thanks.

And she seems to want to dissolve into the floor. But she takes the "dog" from Olivia instead, and confesses in a hushed voice, "I'm gonna go hang myself in my closet now."

After she's gone, I ask, "Is she joking?"

"She's seventeen. It depends on the day." Then she wipes her small hands down the front of her skirt. "Well, this has been fun. Thanks for stopping by." She waves to Simon. "Enjoy the pie."

He already is. He smiles, mouth full of peach crumble.

"See you around . . . I guess," she says to me.

I step forward and take her warm hand in mine, before brushing a kiss across her knuckles. "Count on it, love."

CHAPTER 5

Olivia

"*Count on it, love.*"

Wow. What the hell just happened? Walking up to the apartment, I feel like a James Bond martini—shaken—but also stirred.

Most of the guys I've known, Jack included, were laid-back and easygoing. Passive. *What do you want to do tonight? I dunno, what do you want to do? I dunno.*

But Nicholas is . . . different. Decisive. A *man.* A man who's used to being listened to. Seeing him sober, I can tell the difference. It was in the way he carried himself—wide shoulders back, long spine straight, his presence almost like gravity, pulling at everything in his orbit, making us all want to let him take us where he will.

Jeez—even Bosco listened to him, which definitely makes the little beast a traitor, but I get it.

It was fucking hot. I can still feel the press of his lips on the back of my hand. Who does that—kisses a woman's hand? No one I've ever met, that's for damn sure. The spot he kissed feels warm and tingly. Branded—but not in a skin-sizzling, gross, torturing way that happens on cable television shows. The good kind of branded. Marked.

"*Do you know who that was?*" Ellie shrieks, practically tackling me in the living room.

"Shh! Dad's sleeping."

She asks again, this time in a whisper-yell.

"Uh, a rich asshole with a friend who really likes pie?"

Her big blue eyes roll to the sky. "How are we even related?" She drags me into her bedroom and smacks me in the face with a six-month-old issue of *People* magazine. "That was Prince Nicholas!"

And there he is, on the cover—perfect mouth grinning, perfect arms folded across that broad chest, wearing a dark blue cashmere sweater over a white collared shirt. Looking like an Oxford University wet dream.

"Get out!" I deny it, even while ripping the magazine out of her hands.

That explains the accent I couldn't place—not British or Scottish, but Wessconian. And his attitude—he's not a leader of the pack, he's heir to a freaking throne! There are a dozen more pictures inside. A baby photo, his first day of school wearing a lacy collared shirt, a close-up of him as a teenager glaring at the camera, looking broody as hell. And more recent ones—one with his arm draped around a stunning, tall blond in a red dress at a dinner party, another with him sitting in a high-backed wooden chair during a session of Parliament.

And, *holy shit,* this one's gotta be a paparazzi shot—it's got a grainy, zoomed-in look to it but it's definitely him, walking out of the turquoise ocean off the Maldives Islands, skin glistening, dark hair slicked back . . . *naked.* The full monty parts are blacked out, but a dark, happy trail and the defined V of his pelvis are so very visible.

My tongue tingles with the raw desire to trace that groove. *Fuck,* I want to lick the picture.

A sidebar provides quick facts about his country and ancestry. He's a direct descendent of John William Pembrook, a northern British general who joined forces with the southern

Scots in the Wars for Scottish Independence. He married the daughter of Robert the Bruce, King of the Scots. After Scotland's defeat, Pembrook's coalition broke off from both mother countries and after years of battles, formed their own independent nation: Wessco.

Blood rushes to my cheeks and my head feels hot. He must think I'm an *idiot.* Did he know that I didn't know? Who am I kidding, of course he knew—*I threw a pie in his face.*

Jesus.

Ellie grabs her glitter-cased phone off the bed. "I am *so* putting this on Snapchat!"

My reaction is immediate and visceral.

"No." I cover her hands with mine. "Don't. Everyone will come here looking for him—it'll be a madhouse."

"Exactly!" She jumps up and down. "Business will be crazy. Ooh! We should name a pie after him! The McHotty—the king of pies!"

I know that would be the smart thing to do. The part of me that doesn't actually want to get kicked out on the street yells, *Sell, sell, sell!*

But it feels . . . wrong.

I'm still not entirely sure Nicholas isn't the dickhead he acted like the other night. I don't owe him a thing. And yet, selling him out, using him to bring in business, telling the world where he might show up next, feels like . . . a betrayal.

"He won't come back if you post that, Ellie."

"Did he say he was going to? That he's coming back?" This possibility seems to excite her more than a million social media likes.

"I . . . I think he will."

And electricity races up my spine, because I *want* him to.

Ellie and I use the rare day off as a do-it-ourselves spa day. We soak our feet, loofah our heels, and paint each other's nails. We glob Vaseline on our hands and put them in thick cotton socks, to moisturize. We rub a mixture of olive oil and raw eggs through our hair, then wrap our heads in plastic wrap, a *verrry* attractive look—if only Instagram could see us now. We put cucumber slices on our eyes and oatmeal masks on our faces—all with a VH1 The Big '80s: The Big Movies marathon playing in the background—*Ghostbusters, St. Elmo's Fire, Dirty Dancing.* We finish the beautification ritual by tweezing each other's eyebrows—the ultimate trust exercise.

At about four o'clock, our dad comes out of his room. His eyes are tired and bloodshot, but he's in a good mood. We play a few rounds of Hearts, a game he taught us when we were kids, then he makes Ellie and me tomato soup and grilled cheese sandwiches. It's the best dinner I've had in a long time—probably because someone else made it for me. After the sun goes down and I can see my reflection in the window, Ellie slips on her boots, throws her coat over her pajamas, and walks to a friend's house down the block. Our dad follows soon after—heading to the bar to "watch the game" with the guys.

And in my bed, alone, with a sandalwood and coconut candle burning on the nightstand, feeling soft and smooth and pretty, I engage in the activity I've been fantasizing about all day long.

I Google Nicholas Pembrook.

I have no clue if any of the information is true, but there's a ton of it. Everything from his favorite color (black) to what brand of underwear he prefers (Calvin's). Of course, he has his own Wikipedia page. He has an official website—and about ten thousand fan sites. His ass has its own Twitter handle, @HisRoyalArse, and it has more followers than Jon Hamm's Penis and Chris Evans' Beard put together.

The gossip sites claim he's screwed practically every woman he's spoken to—from Taylor Swift (she wrote a whole album about him) to Betty White (best night of her life). Nicholas and his brother, Henry, are close, sharing passions for polo and philanthropy. He simultaneously adores his grandmother the Queen—a gentle-looking woman, cute in that little-old-person kind of way—and is counting the days until she drops dead.

After a few hours, I feel like a stalker—and I'm convinced most of these writers are just making shit up. Before I log off, a video thumbnail at the top of the search list catches my attention—a news clip from the funeral of Prince Thomas and Princess Calista.

I click on it and am brought to a close-up of two coffins, both white and trimmed in gold, being pulled in a horse-drawn carriage. Throngs of crying spectators line the streets like a black curtain. The camera pans out, showing four people walking behind the carriage. The Queen and her husband, Prince Edward, are in the center; a young boy with light curling hair, Prince Henry, walks on the outside, and Nicholas, wearing the same coal-colored suit as his brother, is on the other side.

At fourteen, Nicholas was already his full height. His cheekbones are less defined, his chin smoother, shoulders narrower, but he's still a handsome boy. The newscaster's voice-over explains that it's Wessco tradition for the sovereign and heirs to walk behind the coffin of a royal family member as it's paraded through every street in the city, before arriving at the cathedral for the final service.

Miles. They had to walk miles before they could bury their parents.

Suddenly, Henry—he was ten then—stops walking, his knees almost buckling. He covers his face with both hands and sobs.

And I taste tears in the back of my throat, because he reminds me of Ellie, the day we buried our mother. How hard she cried—inconsolable—and that same devastation plays out on my computer screen. For several excruciating seconds, it's as if all the people are frozen. No one moves; no one tries to comfort him. *Water, water everywhere, but not a drop to drink.*

He might as well be standing in the middle of the street alone.

And then in three quick strides Nicholas is there, pulling his little brother against him, wrapping his arms around his small body like a shield. Henry's head only comes to the top of Nicholas's stomach—he buries his face and Nicholas gently strokes his hair. Then he glares up at the crowd and the cameras, a hooded gaze burning with resentment and grief.

After a few moments, Nicholas motions to a footman, and the broadcaster filming the event must have hired a frigging lip-reader, because there are subtitles.

"Have the car brought forward."

The man seems unsure and starts to turn toward the Queen—but the crack of Nicholas's words stops him in his tracks.

"Don't look at her. I am your prince—you will do what I say and you will do it now."

And in that second, Nicholas doesn't look like a fourteen-year-old boy; he doesn't look like a *boy* at all. He looks like a king.

The man swallows and bows, and a few minutes later a black Rolls-Royce creeps slowly up through the sea of people. Nicholas guides his brother into the backseat. Then with the door still open, he crouches down and wipes Henry's face with a handkerchief from his pocket.

"Mum will be so disappointed in me," Henry says, with a heartbreaking hiccup.

Nicholas shakes his head. "No, Henry, never." He brushes Henry's wavy blond hair back. "I'll walk for both of us. I'll meet you at the cathedral and we'll go in together." He cups his small jaw in his hand and tries to smile. "We're going to be all right, you and I. Yeah?"

Henry sniffles and works hard to give his brother a nod. When Nicholas takes his place beside the Queen, the procession continues.

As I close my laptop, my heart feels so heavy inside my chest, so sad for them. Henry was just a little boy and Nicholas—in spite of the money and the power and the gold-plated everything—Nicholas Pembrook hadn't been so different that day. Not so different from me. Just a kid, trying his hardest to keep the family he had left from falling apart.

The next day, the sun is shining but the air is still frigid, ensuring the snow piles outside won't be melting anytime soon. After the morning rush, I'm behind the register, cracking open a new roll of quarters, when a low, lyrical voice places an order.

"Large coffee, please. Milk, no sugar."

My eyes lift, meeting a gray-green gaze. And a spiky thrill zings over my skin, immediate and irrepressible. "You came back."

"Unlike some strange—but very pretty—people, I happen to like coffee."

He's wearing jeans, relaxed and worn, with a casual black button-down. And a baseball hat pulled low over his forehead. For some reason, the hat—seeing him in it—is funny. So *normal,* I guess, and a laugh weaves through my words.

"Nice hat."

He raises a fist. "Go Yanks."

"Do you really think it'll work as a disguise?"

He's surprised by the question. He glances around the room—only two other customers sit at the tables, and neither seems to notice him. He shrugs.

"Glasses always worked for Clark Kent."

Today the two men who shadowed Nicholas the other night are joined by a third. They sit at a table by the door, inconspicuous and casually dressed, but alert and watchful.

"Who told you? Did you figure it out yourself or," his finger flicks to the spot where Ellie did her celebratory jig yesterday morning, "was it the cherry bomb with an affinity for SpongeBob footwear?"

"My sister—Ellie—yeah, she spilled the beans." I thought it would feel different, seeing him again, now that I know who he is. But it doesn't—not really. Other than the sting of embarrassment for not recognizing him right off the bat, looking at him still stirs up the same feelings it did yesterday—heated attraction, magnetic fascination—not because he's a prince, but because he's him. Gorgeous, sexy, captivating.

Nicholas pays cash from a leather wallet and I pass him his coffee. "You must think I'm completely clueless."

"Not a'tall."

"Am I supposed to curtsy or something?"

"Please don't." And then the dimples make an appearance. "Unless you have the urge to do it naked, then, by all means, curtsy away."

He's flirting with me. It's a sweet, sliding, teasing dance—and more fun than I can remember having in a long time.

"You don't seem like a . . ." my voice lowers to a whisper, "prince."

Then he's whispering too. "That may be the nicest thing anyone's ever said to me." He rests his arm on the counter, leaning in. "Now that you know, have you reconsidered my invitation to dinner?"

I bet a guy like him—fucking *royalty*—is used to women falling at his feet. Literally. And I'm not used to seduction or head games, but working here all these years, growing up in the city, there is one thing I know how to do when it comes to men.

Play it cool.

"Why?" I scoff. "Because you happen to own a country? Like that's supposed to impress me?"

"It impresses most people."

And the dance goes on.

"Guess I'm not most people."

His eyes sparkle and his lips grin. "Apparently not." He angles his head toward a table in the corner. "Well, then—I'll be over there in case you'd like to join me."

"That's what you're going to do all morning? Stay here?"

"That's the plan, yes."

"Don't you have . . . stuff to do? Important stuff?"

"Probably."

"Then why aren't you doing it?"

He searches my face, those eyes falling to my mouth like he can't tear his eyes away.

"I like looking at you."

Whoosh goes my stomach and the whole world spins.

Nicholas casually strolls over to his table, looking so very satisfied with himself.

A few minutes later, behind the counter, Marty leans in close, his brown eyes wild. "Don't look now, but we've got a celebrity customer."

I start to turn, but he grabs me. "I said don't look! That's Prince Nicholas over there or my name isn't Martin McFly Ginsberg."

I think Marty's mom was kind of high when she named him, too.

I lay calming hands on his shoulders. "Yes, it's him—he came in the other night and yesterday morning."

He squeals like a teenage girl who just got her driver's license. "How could you keep this from me?!"

I invoke *Pulp Fiction*—it's his favorite movie of all time—and hope it's powerful enough to keep Marty from freaking out.

"Bitch, be cool. Don't make a big deal out of it."

"Bitch, be cool? You don't know what you're asking! That boy's picture hung on my wall for years. I always hoped he secretly played for my team."

I sneak a quick peek over my shoulder to see if Nicholas is watching.

He is. He waves.

Then I turn back to Marty. "I think I can say for sure that he doesn't."

He sighs. "That explains why his eyes are on your ass like a cat chasing a laser beam." He shakes his head. "Story of my life—all the good ones are straight or married."

CHAPTER 6

Nicholas

There's a perverse sort of pleasure in watching Olivia Hammond move. Peep shows have never really been my bag, but at the moment I have a whole new appreciation for the concept.

On the one hand, it's torturous—the teasing sway of her fine hips as she glides from table to table, the delectable offering of her arse when she bends over to pick up a dish, just waiting to be nipped and kneaded and worshipped. But there's a simmering enjoyment in it, too—in how her rosebud mouth slides into a welcoming smile, the sweet harmony of her voice, the feel of those exotic dark blue eyes as they drift back to me again and again.

I make a show of opening the newspaper—to at least try and be polite—but for the majority of the time, I stare. Openly. Hell, *rudely*. My etiquette tutor is rolling in her grave.

And yet, I just can't be bothered to give a damn.

I want Olivia. In my bed, on my cock, over my face. And I want her to know it.

You can also learn quite a bit about people by watching them. Olivia Hammond is hardworking. It's there in the way she rubs her neck and arches her back: she's tired, but pushes on.

Olivia is friendly, a characteristic that's clear when she approaches my security team and introduces herself. I chuckle when the lads give their names awkwardly—Logan, Tommy, and James—because they're not accustomed to being the focus of attention; it runs contrary to their job description. But then Tommy gives her a wink, and my chuckle cuts off.

Cheeky bastard—I'll have to keep an eye on him.

Olivia is kind. That's obvious when she hands over the prescriptions she picked up for her neighbor, Mrs. McGillacutty, then quibbles when the elderly woman insists on reimbursing her.

And Olivia is trusting—too trusting. I note this when she has a disagreement with an unpleasant, well-dressed customer who seems to have placed an order for fifty pies for a party she's canceling because of the weather. Though Olivia argues she's already put out the money for the ingredients—already made thirty of the fifty pies—the woman sneers that without a contract, that's Olivia's problem, not hers.

Just after two o'clock, a customer walks in who has a thick neck and HGH-infused arms that make his head look tiny. A pinhead, you could say.

He's wearing black bike shorts, so ball-stranglingly tight I adjust my own set in commiseration, and a ripped sleeveless shirt. He comes through the door like he's familiar with the place—with his arm over the shoulder of a bleached blond, Oompa-Loompa-colored girl, smacking bubble gum with engorged lips.

"Jack," Olivia greets him. "Hey."

"Liv! How's it going?"

"Uh, great." She leans against the counter.

He looks her up and down in a way that makes me want to jab his eyeballs out. "Man, it's been, like—five years? I didn't think you'd still be here."

Olivia's head bobs in a nod. "Yep, still here. What's up with you?"

"Things are awesome. I graduated from Illinois State last year and came back home to open up a gym in the neighborhood. With my fiancé—Jade." He turns to the woman clinging to his arm. "Jade, this is Liv."

"Hey!"

"Hi," Olivia returns. "Wow. Good for you, Jack."

He holds out a stack of business cards to Olivia. "Yeah, I'm just passing these out to all the local businesses. Could you could put them on the counter? Get the word out about the gym—we open in a few weeks."

Olivia takes the cards. "Sure. No problem."

"Thanks—you're the best, Liv." He starts to go, but then adds, "It's good to see you. I really thought you would've gotten out of here by now. But, hey—guess some things never change, right?"

What an obnoxious arsehole.

Olivia smiles tightly. "Guess not. Take it easy."

And he strolls back out the door.

Olivia shakes her head, almost to herself. Then she comes up to my table holding the coffee carafe. "Refill?"

I slide my mug over. "Thank you, yes."

I lean back in my chair, tilting my head as she pours.

"So . . . Jack. Ex-boyfriend?"

Her cheeks go slightly pink. I think it's an adorable reaction—my cock also goes rigid with approval.

"Yeah. Jack and I dated in high school."

"Well, if Jack's your only experience with dating, I understand now why you avoid it. He seems like a prat." I look up into her lovely face. "You can do better."

"Like you?"

"Absolutely." I point to the chair across from me. "Let's talk more about that—the you-doing-me part."

She laughs. "Okay, really—how do you get away with saying stuff like that?"

"I don't say things like that—ever."

"But you say them to me?"

She moves closer, leaning toward me, and my heart pounds so loud I wonder if she hears it. "Yes. I rather like saying . . . all kinds of things to you."

It's relaxed and easy, this newfound freedom I've allowed myself with her. The way I figure it, she's already seen me act like a tool—in for a penny, in for a pound. A dozen inappropriate, wonderfully dirty comments come to mind—but before I can whisper one, Olivia clears her throat and straightens back up.

She glances at the empty chair across from me. "Where's Simon?"

"He had to head home on an urgent business matter. The jet took off early this morning."

"What's his business?"

I bring the mug to my lips, blowing softly, and I catch her staring at my mouth as I do.

"He owns Barrister's."

"Which location—the one in Wessco?" Olivia asks.

"All thirty-seven of them."

"Of course." She laughs. "Silly me."

A bit later I get up to take a piss—four cups of coffee in half a day will do that to you. On my way, I pass the waiter—Marty, I think Olivia called him—a bag of trash over his shoulder, walking toward the back door. He nods his head in a friendly way and I smile back.

Then, when the rear door closes behind him, a deafening shriek—like a thousand hogs squealing in unison—resonates from the other side.

It's a typical reaction . . . and yet odd, every time.

When I walk out of the lavatory, the first thing that registers is the charged demeanor of my security team. Logan's jaw is tight, Tommy's fists are clenched on the table, and James is already half on his feet, ready to spring.

And it takes only a moment to understand why.

The dining area is empty except for one man—a small, bug-eyed man wearing a cheap suit and heavy cologne—standing too close to Olivia in the rear corner, practically boxing her in.

"That's not good enough, Ms. Hammond. You can't just ignore our notices."

"I understand that, but my father's the one you need to talk to. And he's not here right now."

He leans farther forward and her back touches the wall. "I'm tired of being jerked around. You owe us a lot of money, and one way or another you're going to pay."

Olivia tries to slip past him, but he grabs her arm.

Squeezing hard.

My composure snaps like a twig. "Get your hands off of her."

My voice isn't loud; it doesn't need to be. There's a brutal authority to it, a side effect of being obeyed my entire life.

He looks up—they both do—and he drops his hand from Olivia's arm as I approach. He opens his mouth to argue, but recognition makes the words pile up in his throat.

"You . . . you're—"

"It doesn't matter who I am," I bite out. "Who the hell are you?"

"I'm . . . I'm Stan Marksum of Willford Collections."

"I've got this under—" Olivia starts, but I push on.

"Well, Marksum, as the lady said, her father's not here, so I suggest you be on your way. Now."

He puffs his chest out, like some nasty little fish in the crosshairs of a very pissed-off shark. "My business is with the Hammonds. This isn't your concern."

He turns back to Olivia, but I move in front of her, cutting off his access.

"I've just made it my concern."

As I said before, most people are fucking idiots—and this prick is a prime specimen.

"Nicholas, you don't—"

It's the first time she's said my name. And I can't even enjoy it—don't get to savor the sound on her lips or see the expression on her face. And all because of this pissant in front of me. It's infuriating.

I snap my fingers. "Card."

"What?"

I shift forward, making him step back—see how he likes it.

"Business card."

He fishes one from his pocket; it's bent at the corner.

"I'll pass this along to Mr. Hammond. You're done here. There's the door—use it or I'll show you how."

When he's gone, I turn around to ask Olivia if she's all right, and I'd be lying if I said I wasn't expecting a little show of gratitude. Perhaps with her mouth, hopefully with her hands—and just maybe if she's really grateful, she'll bring some hip-grinding action into the equation.

She gives me some mouth, all right.

"Who the hell do you think you are?"

Her hands are on her hips, her cheeks are flushed and she's livid. Cock-stirringly stunning—but absolutely furious.

"Do you want me to list my titles?"

"That was none of your business! You can't just walk in here and . . . take over like that."

"I was helping you."

"I didn't ask for your help!" she rails. "I was handling it!"

"Handling it? Was that before or after he shoved you in the corner and grabbed your arm?"

My eyes are drawn to her forearm—and the angry, scarlet dots that now mar it. *Finger marks.* They'll likely bruise.

"Son of a bitch." Gentle but insistent, I take her wrist and elbow, looking closer. "I should've punched the bastard when I had the chance."

Olivia pulls her arm away.

"If he needed to be punched, I would've done it myself. I don't know what you think this is, but I don't need you riding in here on your white horse. I take care of my business—I take care of myself—just fine." She pushes her hair back from her face and puffs out a breath. "Your good deed is done for the day, so why don't you just go?"

And I choke. "Are you . . . kicking me out?"

There are women would give an ovary to keep me—half of them have actually tried—and this one's tossing me to the curb. Over *nothing.* What in the actual fuck?

"Yeah, I guess I am."

I hold up my hands. "Fine. I'm gone."

But I'm not—not just yet.

"You're crazy." My finger jams against my skull. "You've got a screw loose, love. You might want to have someone take a look at that."

She flips me off.

"And you're a royal dick. Don't let the door hit you on the ass on the way out."

It doesn't.

Bloody fucking hell, talk about schizophrenic—the woman is a complete nutter. She's gorgeous, sure, but she's got issues. And I make it a rule not to stick my dick into a girl who might want to chop it off right after.

I sit in the center row of the SUV, fuming on the way back to the hotel.

"Can I offer you a bit of advice, Prince Nicholas?" Tommy asks.

I may have been mumbling out loud.

"Shut up, Tommy," Logan says from the driver's seat.

Proximity breeds familiarity, and the lads in my personal security team have been with me for a few years. They're young, in their twenties, but their youthful looks belie lethal skills. Like a pack of German shepherd pups, their bark may not seem so dangerous, but their bite is vicious.

"It's all right." I meet Tommy's light brown eyes in the rearview mirror, where he sits behind me. "Offer away."

He scratches his head. "I think the lass was embarrassed."

"Embarrassed?"

"Aye. It's like my younger sister, Janey. She's a good-looking girl, but one day she had a zit on her forehead that was so big it made her look like a dickicorn. And she was walking—"

James, in the front passenger seat, reads my mind.

"What the fuck is a dickicorn?"

"It's an expression," Tommy explains.

James angles around to look at Tommy, his blue eyes crinkled.

"An expression for what?"

"For . . . someone with something big coming out o' their forehead that looks like a cock."

"Wouldn't it be a unicock, then?" James wonders.

"For Christ's sake," Logan cuts in. "Would you forget about the fuckin' unicorn or dickicock or whatever the hell it is—"

"It doesn't make any sense!" James argues.

"—and let Tommy finish his story? We're never gonna hear the end at this rate."

James throws up his hands, grumbling. "Fine. But it still doesn't make any sense."

For the record, my semantic vote goes to unidick.

Tommy continues. "Right. So, Janey's walking home from school with Brandon, a lad from up the street, who she'd been crushing on for weeks. And my da's home early from work, sittin' out on the stoop. So he says, 'Hey Janey, you want me to grab some cream from the pharmacy to kill that monster on your forehead?' And Janey goes crazy—screechin' like a banshee at my da, sayin' she'd never talk to him again, making him feel two cents worth o' shit. And my poor da—I mean, he was just tryin' to be helpful. But what I figured was, no girl wants her troubles rubbed in her face—Janey knew she was a dickicorn, she didn't need it said out loud. But she especially didn't want it said in front of a lad she likes."

He meets my eyes in the mirror. "It's a pride thing, ya know? It wasn't that Miss Hammond didn't want your help; maybe she was embarrassed that she needed it."

I don't go back to Amelia's the next morning. Not because I'm not thinking about Olivia, but because I have a prior commitment—a visit to The Boys' Home in the Bronx, one of many institutions funded by The Prince and Princess of Pembrook Charity. It's a private facility that takes in children who've been orphaned—an alternative to the overrun foster care system.

I meet with the director, an enthusiastic middle-aged man with tired eyes. He gives me a tour of the dorm room, the gymnasium, and the cafeteria. They do their best to cheer the place up with brightly colored paint and artwork on the walls, but it still resembles a prison for kindergarteners. The hollow-faced, curious glances of the children who live here follow my every move.

We venture out into the play yard, which consists of a fenced-in concrete paved square with a single basketball net. I tell the director to contact my personal secretary—because every child deserves to have a swing set.

My father used to say when it came to charities, helping people was the easy part—it was choosing whom to help first, allocating resources, that kept him up at night.

A few youngsters color with chalk on one side, while a group plays basketball on the other—but my eyes are drawn to one small boy in a red T-shirt who looks about seven years old, sitting on the sidelines. It's a view I'm familiar with. When I was a teen I had more "friends" than I'd ever need—everyone wanted a piece of me. But earlier, I was an oddity.

And children, like Mother Nature, can be breathtakingly cruel.

As I walk toward the boy, Logan reminds the group of staff members behind me, "No pictures today."

Big brown eyes that say they've seen more than they ever should regard me with interest as I sit down beside him.

"Hey."

"Hi." I hold out my hand. "I'm Nicholas."

He shakes it. "Freddie."

"That's a good name. My middle name is Freddie. It means 'peaceful ruler.'"

He kicks at the concrete with the tip of his worn sneaker. "Are you really a prince?"

"I really am."

"You don't look like a prince."

I pat the lapels of my gray suit jacket. "Must've left my crown in another suit. I'm always losing the darn thing."

I'm rewarded with a flash of white teeth and a giggle.

"Don't feel like playing today, Freddie?"

He shrugs.

"Do you like living here?"

I've seen the reports—mental health stats, graduation rates—but if you want the real story behind what goes on in a place like this, it's always best to go straight to the source.

"It's okay." He bobs his little head. "I used to live with my auntie—she was nice. But she died."

The sadness in those few words pierces like the prick of a steel nail.

"I'm sorry."

He nods, because he's heard the condolences before, but they don't change anything.

"The teachers here are nice; they smile a lot. But my auntie used to bake cookies. They don't give us cookies here."

"Smiles are good, but cookies are always better."

A spark of life flashes across his face. A connection.

"I know, right? Do you know what they make us eat for dessert?"

"What?" I ask, riveted.

"Fruit salad!"

I make a disgusted face. "Oh, no—not fruit."

"Yes!" he insists. "And not even with whipped cream! Fruit's not dessert." He wags his finger at me. "You should talk to someone about that. Set 'em straight."

"It'll be at the top of my list."

And then a thought comes to me. An impressive thought.

"Freddie—do you like pie?"

He looks shocked that I even asked.

"Well, yeah—everybody likes pie. There's fruit in it, but it's *pie*."

The director walks up to us. "How are we doing? Can I get you anything, Prince Nicholas?"

"Yes," I tell him, scanning the playground—counting. "You can get me a bus."

An hour later, I walk into Amelia's like the Pied Piper of Hamelin, trailing fifty children behind me. Behind the counter, Olivia's eyes flare round—surprised to see me—and to see the gaggle of little ones swarming her coffee shop like adorable locusts.

"Hey, what's going on?"

I gesture to the young man beside me. "Olivia, this is Freddie—Freddie, meet Olivia."

"'S'up?"

She smiles so sweetly. "Good to meet you, Freddie."

Out of the side of his mouth he says in a hushed tone, "You were right—she's really pretty."

"I told you so," I hush back.

Then I address her directly. "Olivia, we have a problem that needs immediate rectification."

"Sounds serious," she teases.

"Oh it is," Freddie pipes up.

"My friend Freddie here hasn't had a decent dessert in months."

"*Months!*" Freddie stresses.

My eyes meet Olivia's. "You wouldn't happen to have thirty extra pies around, would you?"

Warmth spreads across her face. And gratitude.

"As a matter of fact, I do."

A few hours later, after Olivia's stock has been completely demolished—and every pie paid for courtesy of the royal charity—Olivia and I stand side by side as the delighted, pastry-stuffed children waddle out the door.

Freddie high-fives me as he goes. "Catch ya later, Nick."

"Not if I catch you first." I wink.

When the last one is loaded on and the bus pulls away, it's just Olivia and I, alone.

"Did you do this just to impress me?"

I slide my hands into my pockets, rocking on my heels. "Depends. Are you impressed?"

"I am."

I can't hold back my grin.

"Good. But, in all honesty, I didn't just do it for you. The one perk of this job is getting the chance to make kids like Freddie happy. Even if it's just for the day."

She turns to me. "You're good with them. With kids."

"I like children. They haven't developed ulterior motives yet."

The air shifts between us, becomes thick with want and words not yet said.

"I'm sorry about flipping out on you yesterday," Olivia tells me quietly.

"It's all right."

"No." She shakes her head and a lock of hair falls from her topknot, drifting across her smooth cheek. "I overreacted. I'm sorry."

I catch the curl, rubbing it between my fingers. "I'll try to keep my nose out of your business."

And I just can't resist.

"I'll focus on getting it into your pants instead."

Olivia rolls her eyes, but she's laughing. Because exasperation is part of my charm.

After a moment, her smile stills and she takes a deep breath—the way a first-time bungee jumper would the moment before leaping.

"Ask me again, Nicholas."

It's a bit frightening how much I like the sound of my name on her lips. It could easily become my favorite word. Which is damn arrogant, even for me.

"I want to take you out, Olivia. Tonight. What do you say?"

Then she gives me a word I like hearing from her even more.

"Yes."

CHAPTER 7

Olivia

I have a date. *Holy shit.*

"How does this look?"

A date with a gorgeous, green-eyed, walks-around-like-a-sex-god man who's capable of making me orgasm with the sound of his voice alone.

"*Little House on the Prairie* called—Nellie Oleson wants her dress back."

Oh, and he's a prince. A real, live, actual prince—who kisses a lady's hand and makes orphans smile . . . and who wants in my pants. *Holy shit!*

He doesn't give off the white-horse-riding, 100 percent "nice guy" vibe, though. He definitely has some asshole tendencies. But that's okay. I like a little jerky in my men. Sue me. It keeps things interesting. Exciting.

There's only one problem.

"What about this one?" I hold up a hanger with a black pantsuit clinging to it.

"Great, if you plan on going to a Halloween party as Hillary Clinton from 2008."

I have nothing to wear.

Usually when women say we having nothing to wear, we mean we have nothing *new* to wear. Nothing that makes us feel beautiful or hides the few extra pounds we've put on because we've been hitting the salted caramel ice cream a little too hard lately. And is it just me, or do they freaking make *everything* in salted caramel flavor these days? It's my Kryptonite.

But anyway, that's not the case here, as my darling sister helpfully points out while rummaging through my closet.

"Jesus Christ, Liv, have you even bought any new clothes since 2005?"

"I bought new underwear last week."

Bikini style, cotton, in hot pink and electric blue. They were on sale, but I would've bought them even if they weren't. Because if I happen to get struck by an Uber driver or hit on the head in some freak scaffolding accident, there's no way I'm showing up in the emergency room in worn, holey panties. That's one rock bottom I refuse to reach.

"Maybe you should just wear the underwear and a trench coat." Ellie throws me a suggestive eyebrow wiggle. "I have a feeling His Hotness would like that."

I have a feeling she's right.

"Interesting idea . . . but I don't own a trench coat."

I wear a black skirt and white blouse to work—and I work *all* the time. Otherwise, I have a few pairs of jeans, old sweats, older T-shirts, a Confirmation dress I wore when I was thirteen and a pantsuit I graduated high school in.

I fall straight back on my bed, dramatically. The way someone would drop into a pool . . . or off a building ledge. Fitting.

"You could borrow something of mine," Ellie starts "but . . ."

But I'm five foot six. I have boobs—nice ones, actually—and while I'm not Kim Kardashian, I also have an ass. Ellie is five foot nothing and can still buy her jeans at GAPKids.

I scroll through the contacts on my phone, looking for the hotel number Nicholas saved there this afternoon. I noticed that he didn't put his cell number in, but he probably has to keep that a secret for national security or something.

"I'm just going to call him and be honest. Tell him, 'I don't know what you had in mind for tonight but we need to keep it jeans and T-shirt casual.'"

Ellie dives on me like I'm a grenade that's about to explode.

"Are you nuts?" She wrestles the phone from my hand and bounds off the bed. "If you want jeans and T-shirt you could go out with Donnie Domico from down the street—he'd give up a testicle to date you. Prince Nicholas doesn't *do* casual."

I'm the embodiment of informality. I have neither the time nor energy for fuss or muss. Nothing about me is Uptown Girl—but Nicholas is definitely interested in *doing* me.

Oh God, now I'm starting to sound like him.

I lift my head. "You don't know that."

Ellie opens the laptop on my dresser and a few key taps later, scrolls through image after image of Nicholas—wearing suits and tuxedos and more suits. In some of the pictures he's alone, but every time there's a woman beside him, she's wearing a gown—stunning, shimmery and divine.

"His casual is at least a cocktail dress."

She's right. And I have two hours before Nicholas picks me up—not nearly enough time to run out and buy something. Plus, that would require using the emergency somebody-better-be-bleeding-from-an-artery credit card. It's like I'm living an episode of reality TV—a full-fledged fashion fucking emergency. Except no camera crew and makeover-expert fairy godmother is going to pop out of my bathroom.

Although . . . I may have something better. I roll off the bed and sprint down the hall, through the living room, to the door that leads to the downstairs kitchen.

"Marty! Come up here!"

Five minutes later, Marty's standing in my bedroom, staring at the pile of clothes I just dropped in his arms. "What the fuck am I supposed to do with this? Salvation Army?"

I gesture to the clothes. "I need you to help me figure out how to turn this"—I swing around and point at the picture of Nicholas on the laptop with the tall blond wearing a bold fuchsia halter-dress—"into that."

I'm not stereotyping—I've seen Marty outside of work and he's an amazing dresser. Sophisticated, sleek, with a hint of flash.

He looks at the clothes, then dumps them on the bed.

"Let me explain something, baby doll. You are beautiful, inside and out . . . but I've known I like dick since I was twelve years old. Give me a tall, dark lumbersexual and I'll dress him so fine you wouldn't want to unwrap him even if it was the first night of Hanukkah." He traces the air around me. "But your squishy bits, I don't know what to do with."

I cover my eyes with one hand. What the hell was I thinking? Why did I agree to go out with Nicholas? It's going to be a total shit-show.

The last date I went on was at a Laundromat. Not even kidding.

Our washing machine broke and I spent four nights making flirty eye contact and small talk across the folding table with a super-cute guy. On the fifth night, he bought me a slice of pizza, then we made out on top of the heavy loaders during the spin cycle. It was only after, when I noticed the floral comforter, bras and panties in his colors wash, that he admitted to having a live-in girlfriend. *Bastard.* Six months later and I still can't look at a bottle of Clorox without feeling dirty.

Marty gently pulls my hand down from my eyes. He taps my nose—and smiles.

"But I know somebody who does."

Turns out, Bibbidy, Marty's oldest younger sister, has a new job as a receptionist at City Couture—a high-end fashion magazine. Which means she has the keys to the kingdom, also known as the Sample Closet: a mythical, magical, warehouse-sized room filled with dresses and gowns of every shade, size, and style, as well as shoes to match and every accessory known to man. All of which Bibbidy can use when she's on the clock—and after—as long as her "dragon-lady boss who makes Cruella De Vil look stable" doesn't find out.

She agrees to take the risk for me—and I'm not sure I'm okay with that.

But Marty assures me she owes him big time—something about making up for crashing his beloved-but-piece-of-shit Chevy Nova in high school.

And that's why Bibbidy Ginsberg shows up at our apartment forty minutes later, her arms laden with dresses and bags. And that's how, an hour after that, I end up wearing an Alexander McQueen light blue, sleeveless dress with a cut-out back that falls a few inches above my knee. It makes me feel pretty. Still me—comfortable—but an elegant, polished version of me.

Ellie flatirons my hair into a long, black shiny curtain, while I do my makeup—a bit of powder, a hint of blush, three coats of mascara, and a muted red lipstick that highlights the shape of my mouth Nicholas seems to like so much.

"These will be perfect!" Bibbidy exclaims, waving a pair of obsidian high-heeled ankle boots around like a magic wand.

"Mmm-hmm." Marty approves. "Fuck-me boots if I ever saw 'em."

"I can't wear those," I try to protest. "I'll break my neck. There's still snow on the ground."

"You're going from the coffee shop to the car," my sister counters. "You're not walking the Appalachian Trail, Liv."

Bibbidy points to my laptop—still open to Nicholas's delicious picture. "My brother wasn't messing with me—that's who you're going out with?"

I have to fight to not sigh like a dreamy schoolgirl.

"That's him."

She enjoys another look.

"Oh honey, you are *definitely* wearing the fuck-me boots."

And that settles that.

Twenty minutes later, I wait alone in the coffee shop—standing, so the dress doesn't wrinkle. The room is dim, illuminated only by the muted overhead lamp above the counter and a few twinkling battery-operated candles on the tables near the window.

I close my eyes. And swear to myself that I'll remember how this feels. This moment. This night.

Because I'm right on the edge—standing on that thrilling, wonderful precipice where everything is perfect. Where the dreams flickering through my head of how tonight will go are flawless—my witty, irresistible banter, Nicholas's sexy chivalry, our funny flirtations. We'll laugh, we'll dance—we'll share a good-night kiss. Maybe more.

I'm Dorothy gazing down at the Emerald City.

I'm Wendy rising in the air after my first pinch of pixie dust.

I'm . . . I laugh to myself . . . I'm Cinderella, stepping into her coach to go to the ball.

And even if this night is all there is, I won't forget it; I'll hold this memory close. Savor it, cherish it. It will make the hard times just a little easier, the lonely moments just a little less cold. When Ellie leaves for school, when I'm making pies before dawn in the kitchen day after day, I'll remember this feeling and I'll smile. This will get me through.

I open my eyes.

Nicholas is on the other side of the coffee shop door, watching me through the glass. His eyes are warm and wild, a heated jungle green. And then, slowly, he smiles, broad and big, dimples coming out to play. My chest constricts with unexpected emotion. And my own smile comes unbidden, easy—because it all just feels so good.

He walks through the door, stopping a few feet in front of me, both our gazes consuming each other. His black dress shoes are shiny—and I wonder if someone polished them before he came. I've never dated someone who gets his shoes shined. His slacks are charcoal and perfectly fitted—the shape of strong, lean thighs visible as he moves—with the hint of outline of what must be a magnificent cock teasing through the fabric.

I try to hide that I'm looking. But I am.

His tapered shirt is silver-gray—no tie—the top two buttons open at the neck, and my fingers rub together, itching to touch him there. A black sports jacket covers the shirt, sharp and expensive looking. There's a dusting of dark stubble across his jaw, and I want to touch him there too. The combination of five o'clock shadow and rebel strands of brown hair that fall over his forehead give him a roguish, wicked look that makes my bones feel liquid and my breasts suddenly heavy and tingling.

Our eyes finally meet—he's still staring at me, lips parted. And I can't get a read on his expression. As the moments stretch on, a bud of nervousness blooms in my stomach, its vine wrapping around my vocal chords.

"I . . . I wasn't sure what you had planned for tonight. You didn't tell me."

Those long lashes blink, but he doesn't say anything. I raise my hand toward the kitchen.

"I can go change if this isn't—"

"No." Nicholas steps forward, his hand up. "No, don't change a thing. You're . . . absolutely perfect."

And he's looking at me like he never wants to stop.

"I didn't expect . . . I mean, you're lovely . . . but . . ."

"Wasn't there a movie about a king who stuttered?" I tease him. "Was he a relative of yours?"

He chuckles. And call me crazy, but I swear Nicholas's cheeks go slightly pink.

"No, stuttering doesn't run in my family." He shakes his head. "You just knocked me on my arse."

And now I'm beaming.

"Thank you. You look pretty great too, Prince Charming."

"I actually know a Prince Charming. He's first-class prick."

"Well. Now that you've tarnished a precious piece of my childhood, this better be some date," I tease.

"It will be."

He holds out his hand to me.

"Shall we?"

My hand slides into his. Easily. Like it's the most natural thing in the world.

Like it belongs there.

CHAPTER 8

Nicholas

Olivia's nervous. Her hand trembles slightly in mine as I lead her toward the limousine, and I can see the rapid throb of her pulse at the base of her delicate neck. It stirs a twisted, predatory instinct in me—if she feels like running, I'll certainly chase.

Especially in that dress. And those fucking boots. For several moments all I could picture in my head was peeling the pale blue fabric from her body—slowly. The way her hands would dig into my shoulder blades and her nails would rake my back. The sounds she'd make—little whimpers and pants that I'd lick from her lips. And I'd lift her onto one of the tables in the coffee shop, then have her in every way I could think of—and probably a few that I haven't.

And I'd leave those boots on the whole time.

But her anxiousness draws out my protectiveness as well. The urge to wrap my arms around her and promise that everything will be all right.

I don't think she has anyone in her life who does that for her.

My thumb rubs small, soothing circles against her hand as James opens the car door for us.

Olivia waves to him.

"Good evening, Miss."

Inside the car she greets Logan and Tommy in the front seat.

Logan nods, and gives her a smile in the rearview mirror.

"Hello, Miss Olivia," Tommy replies—with another damn wink. *Tosser.*

I raise the privacy glass so it's just she and I alone. It's also mostly soundproof—she'd have to moan my name very, very loudly for anyone to hear, but I bet I could make it happen.

"You don't have to do that, you know." My chin lifts toward the front of the car.

"What, be polite?"

"They wouldn't think you were rude if you didn't say hello. They're good lads, Olivia, but they're also employees, and employees don't expect to be addressed. They're like . . . furniture, not really noticed until they're needed."

"Wow." Olivia leans back against the leather seat, regarding me. "Somebody's pompous tank is pretty full."

I shrug. "Occupational hazard. And as prickish as it may sound, it's still true."

She pushes her hair behind her ear, fidgeting, as if she doesn't wear it down often. Which is a shame.

"Are they always with you?"

"Yes."

"What about when you're home?"

"Security's there too. Or maids. My butler."

"So you're never just . . . alone? Can't walk around naked if you feel like it?"

I imagine Fergus's reaction to my bare balls resting on the sixteenth-century Queen Anne sofa—or even better, my grandmother's reaction. And I laugh.

"No, I can't. But the more important question is—do you walk around naked?"

She lifts one alluring shoulder. "Sometimes."

"Let's hang out at your apartment tomorrow," I tell her with an urgent, straight face. "All day. I'll clear my schedule."

Olivia squeezes my hand like she's telling me to behave, but the gentle flush on her cheeks says she's enjoying the conversation.

"So, the first night we met, if I'd gone back to your hotel room with you, they would've been there while we were . . ."

"Fucking? Yes. But not in the same room—I'm not into audiences."

"That's so weird. It's like the ultimate walk of shame."

She lost me.

"How do you mean?"

Olivia's voice lowers shyly, even though the boys can't possibly hear her. "They would've known what we were doing, maybe even heard us. It's like you live in a perpetual frat house."

"You're presuming they give a damn—and they don't." I raise her hand to my mouth, kissing the back. It's soft against my lips, like a rose petal. And I wonder if she's as soft all over. "When I head into the lavatory, on some level they realize I'm going to take a piss, but it's really not high on their list of things to think about."

She doesn't seem convinced. And if tonight is going to end like I'm hoping, she'll need to get over the security team. Challenge accepted.

I'm used to the curious stares and whispers of strangers when I go out in public—the way a lion at the zoo is used to annoying children banging on the glass enclosure, just waiting for the day it breaks. I don't notice them much anymore and, as we're led to the private room at the back of the restaurant, I don't notice them now.

Except Olivia does. And she takes exception to it—staring the patrons down for their rudeness, until they're forced to look away. Like she's defending me. Sticking up for me. It's very cute.

The overly friendly hostess leans closer than she should, flashing me an open invitation with her eyes. I'm used to that too.

Olivia notices as well, but, interestingly, seems less confident about how she should respond. So I respond on her behalf—resting my hand on the small of her back, possessively, and guiding her into the plush, cushioned seat. Then, after I've taken my own seat, I drape my arm across the back of Olivia's chair, near enough to stroke her bare shoulder if I want, making it clear that the only woman I'm interested in tonight is the one beside me.

After the sommelier pours our wine—Olivia prefers white because red "knocks her on her ass"—and the chef comes to our table to introduce himself and describe the custom menu he's created for us, we're finally left alone.

"So, you run the coffee shop with your parents?" I ask.

Olivia sips her wine, her little pink tongue peeking out to clean her bottom lip.

"It's just me and my dad, actually. My mom . . . died nine years ago. She was mugged on the subway . . . it ended badly."

There's an echo of pain in her words—one I'm familiar with.

"I'm sorry."

"Thank you."

She pauses a moment, seems to be debating something, and then confesses, "I Googled you."

"Oh?"

"The video of your parents' funeral came up."

I nod. "The search engines do seem to favor that one."

Her smile is small and flutteringly self-conscious. "I didn't watch it at the time, when it was on live, but I remember it being on TV all day. On every channel." She raises those stunning, shining eyes to mine. "The day we buried my mom was the worst day of my life. It must've been awful for you, to go through the worst day of yours with all those people watching. Filming it. Taking pictures."

Most people don't think about that part of things. They focus on the money, the castles, the fame, the privilege. Not the hard parts. The human parts.

"It was awful," I say quietly. Then I take a breath and shake off the sadness that's seeped into the conversation. "But . . . in the immortal words of Kanye, *that which don't kill me only makes me stronger.*"

She laughs, and like everything about her, it's delightful.

"I didn't think a guy like you listened to Kanye."

I wink. "I'm full of surprises."

Before our meal arrives, visitors stop by our table. I introduce Olivia and speak with them briefly about upcoming business. After they walk away, Olivia gives me an owl-eyed look.

"That was the mayor."

"Yes."

"And Cardinal O'Brien, the Archbishop of New York."

"That's right."

"They're two of the most powerful men in the state—in the country."

My lips slide into a grin because she's impressed. Again. At times like this, being me isn't so awful.

"The Palace works with both men on various initiatives."

She fidgets with the roll on her bread plate, tearing it up into tiny pieces.

"You can ask me anything, Olivia—no need to be shy."

Shyness has no place in my plans for this girl. I want her bold, wild, and reckless.

She munches on a piece of bread, head slightly tilted, watching—thinking it over. And I'm struck by the charming way she chews. *Christ, what a strange thing to notice.*

After she swallows and the pale, smooth skin of her throat ripples in an erotic way—well, a way *I* find erotic—she asks, "Why didn't you kiss his ring?"

I take a sip of wine. "I outrank him."

That makes her grin. "You outrank the Archbishop? What about the Pope? Have you ever met him?"

"Not the current one, but I was introduced to the former when he came to visit Wessco when I was eight. Seemed like a decent bloke—he smelled like butterscotch. He carried sweets in the pockets of his vestments. He gave me one after he blessed me."

"Did you kiss his ring?"

She's more relaxed now, the questions coming easier.

"I didn't, no."

"Why not?"

I lean forward, closer to her, elbows on the table—Grandmother would be appalled. But etiquette doesn't stand a snowball's chance against Olivia's sweet scent. It's roses tonight, with the slightest hint of jasmine—like a new garden on the first day of spring. I inhale deeply, trying to be discreet. Two points for me, because all I really want to do is rest my nose in the fragrant groove of her cleavage before sliding down, lifting her dress, and sinking my face between her smooth, creamy thighs. And that's where I'd stay, all fucking night.

And now my cock strains against my pants like a prisoner in a cage.

What was the question again?

I take another drink and run my palm over the bulge—adjusting—trying to get some relief. And failing.

"I'm sorry, Olivia, what was that?"

"Why didn't you kiss the Pope's ring?"

I've got a raging hard-on and we're talking about the Holy See.

One-way ticket to hell? Purchased.

"The Church teaches that the Pope has the ear of God—that he's closer to God than any other person on Earth. But kings . . . as least how the story goes . . . are *descended* from God. Which means the only person I bow to, the only ring I kiss, is my grandmother's—because she's the only person on Earth above me."

Olivia's eyes rake me up and down and one dark eyebrow rises playfully. "Do you really believe that?"

"That I'm descended from The Almighty?" I grin devilishly. "I've been told my cock is a gift from God. You should test that opinion tonight. You know . . . for religion."

"Very smooth." She laughs.

"But, no, I don't actually believe it." Olivia watches as I rub my lower lip. And give her my real answer. "I think it's a story—the kind that men have always made up to justify their power over the many."

She thinks on that for a moment, then says, "I saw a picture of your grandmother online. She looks like such a sweet little old lady."

I give her my real answer on that, too.

"She's a battle-axe with a chunk of concrete where her heart should be."

Olivia chokes on her wine.

She dabs at her mouth with her napkin and looks at me like she's got me pegged. "So . . . what you're saying is . . . you love her."

At my sardonic expression she adds, "When it comes to family, I think we only insult the ones we really love."

I dip my head closer and whisper, "I agree. But don't let that get out. Her Majesty will never let me live it down."

She taps my hand. "Your secret's safe with me."

Our main course arrives—salmon, colorfully plated with dashes and swirls of bright orange and green sauces with an intricate structure of purple kale and lemon rind on top.

"It's so pretty," Olivia sighs. "Maybe we shouldn't eat it."

I smirk. "I enjoy eating pretty things."

I bet her pussy is gorgeous.

Throughout the meal, the conversation flows as easily as the wine. We talk about everything and nothing in particular—my studies at university, the work I do when I'm not making public appearances, the behind-the-scenes details of running a coffee shop, as well as what it was like for her growing up in the city.

"My mom used to give me three dollars in quarters every week," Olivia tells me in a faraway voice, "so I wouldn't nag her about wanting to give money to the homeless people we'd pass when we were out. I'd try to spread it around. I didn't know how little a quarter was actually worth—I thought I was helping and I wanted to help as many as I could. But, if they had a pet with them—a sad-looking dog or cat—that always hit me hardest and I'd give them two or three quarters. Even then, I think I understood that people could be such assholes—but animals are always innocent."

When dessert is served—a frosted airy pastry in a bed of custard and caramel sauce—the topic turns to siblings.

". . . and my father put the money from my mother's life insurance policy into a trust. It can only be used for education expenses, which is good because otherwise it would've been gone a long time ago."

Like many of her fellow New Yorkers, Olivia is an animated talker—her hands flutter and weave like two graceful, translucent doves.

"There's just enough now for Ellie's first semester at NYU. I'll worry about the second semester when the time comes. She wants to live in the dorm—to get the 'full college experience.' But I worry about her.

"I mean, I think she could change the world—I really do—cure cancer or invent whatever comes after the Internet. What she can't do is remember where she put her house keys or understand that a checkbook has to balance once in a while. And she's gullible. Phishing emails were invented for people like my sister."

I lean forward, nodding. "I understand completely. My brother, Henry, has so much potential, and he's happily pissing it away. After that video you mentioned, the press christened him the boy who couldn't walk the walk. Who would never measure up. It's a prophecy he's gone out of his way to fulfill."

Olivia raises her glass. "To little brothers and sisters—can't live with them, can't have them banished from the kingdom."

We tap our glasses and drink.

After dinner, I suggest we go back to my hotel suite—*said the horny spider to the scrumptious fly*. And she agreed.

The ride in the lift to the top floor is silent, with James and Logan in front and Olivia beside me in the rear, giving me secret, sneaking glances. The doors open into the foyer of the penthouse and the hotel butler—David, I think his name is—is there to take our coats.

"Thank you." Olivia smiles and David gives her a silent nod.

As we step into the main living room, I watch her—the reactions and emotions that play over her features. How her lashes flare when she looks up, taking in the enormous crystal chandelier and the hand-painted, golden mural on the ceiling. The way the corners of her mouth rise with a bit of wonder at the furniture and marble floors—all the little signs of luxury. When she turns to the full wall of glass that offers a breathtaking view of the twinkling lighted city, Olivia gasps.

And lust surges through me like I've been struck by lightning.

She glides towards the window, gazing out. And damn, she makes a pretty picture—pale, bare arms, rivulets of long, black hair that fall just above the swell of a perfect, tight arse. I like the look of her here—in my rooms—amongst my things.

I'd like the view even more if she weren't still wearing her dress.

"Can we go outside?" Olivia asks.

I nod, then open the door to the large stone balcony. She steps out and I follow her. The temperature was milder today and the snow has been removed, of course. Olivia's gaze dances over the full potted evergreens that bookend the beige cushioned furniture, and the glow of the burning fire pits in the corners casts the area in a warm orange light.

"So this is like, your prison yard?" she teases.

"That's right. They let me out for fresh air and exercise—but only if I behave."

"Not too shabby."

I shrug. "It'll do."

We walk side by side along the walled edge, holding hands. And I'm reminded of my first social event—I'm all worked up and exhilarated, and at the same time mildly terrified of screwing up.

"So what's it like," she asks softly, "having everything set, knowing exactly what you're going to do for the rest of your life?"

"You have the coffee shop. It's not so different."

"Yeah, but my family needed me to run it. I didn't choose that."

I snort. "Neither did I."

She thinks that over, then asks, "But are you excited? Like Simba, are you all, 'I just can't wait to be king'?"

"Simba was a fool." I shake my head and push at the hair that brushes my forehead. "And considering me being king would mean my grandmother was dead—*excited* wouldn't be the word I'd use." I slip into interview mode. "But, I look forward to fulfilling my birthright and leading Wessco with honor, dignity and grace."

Olivia tugs my hand to a stop. Her eyes flicker over my face, her lips curled. "I call bullshit."

"What?"

"Total bullshit. 'Honor, dignity and grace,'" she imitates—accent included. "Those are pretty words, but they don't mean anything. How does it really feel?"

How does it really feel?

I feel like a fawn trying out its legs for the first time—wobbly and strange. Because no one's ever dug past my pat answer. No one's ever asked me for more. For real and genuine.

I don't know if anyone's ever actually cared.

But Olivia wants those answers—I can see it in the soft curves of her face as she waits patiently. She wants to know me.

And my chest tightens desperately—because I suddenly want the exact same thing.

"The best way to describe it, I guess . . ." I lick my lips. "Imagine you're in medical school, studying to be a surgeon. You've read all the books, observed the surgeries being performed, you've prepared. And for your whole life everyone around you has said what an amazing surgeon you'll be. It's your destiny. Your calling."

My eyes are drawn to hers. And I don't know what she sees in mine, but I find comfort in hers. Enough to go on.

"But then that moment comes—the day when it's your turn to go it alone. And they put the scalpel in your hand and . . . it's all up to you. That, I imagine, is quite a 'holy fuck' moment."

"I bet."

"That's what the idea of becoming king feels like. A 'holy fuck' moment."

Olivia takes a step forward but loses her balance, tripping on the pointy heel of her shoe, and I catch her. She collides with my chest, my arms around her, meeting at her lower back . . . and she stays just there.

With her gloriously soft breasts against my hard chest, we freeze—staring, breaths mingling.

"Frigging boots," she whispers, so near to my mouth.

A smile tugs at me. "I like the frigging boots. Seeing you in them—and nothing else—would really make my day."

And then my head is lowering and Olivia is reaching up, each of us drawing towards the other. Her silky hair slides over my fingers as I cup her cheek. My smile fades away, replaced with something more raw, more desperate.

Heat and hunger.

Because I'm going to kiss her now—and when the thump of her heartbeat quickens against my chest, I know she knows it.

Wants it, just as much as I do.

My nose brushes hers and those dark blue eyes close slowly . . .

And then Logan clears his throat loudly.

Meaningfully.

"Ahem."

I swallow back a curse and look up. "What?"

"Camera flash."

Fuck.

"Where?"

He lifts his chin. "Roof of the high-rise. Nine o'clock."

I turn my back on the city, keeping Olivia tucked against my chest. "We should head inside."

Olivia looks adorably dazed. She peeks over my shoulder at the dark sky, then lets me guide her inside. "Does that happen a lot?"

"Unfortunately. Long-range camera lenses—as accurate as rifles."

Back inside, Olivia's lips stretch into a long, wide yawn, and I try to stop the chain of indecent thoughts that follow. Damn, but her mouth is beautiful.

If I don't get in there soon, it may actually kill me.

"Excuse me." She covers her mouth. "I'm sorry."

"Don't apologize." I glance at my watch—it's after midnight. She was on her feet all day

and has to be up again in four hours. "I should've picked you up earlier."

She shakes her head. "This has been wonderful. I can't remember the last time I had so much fun. Not in forever, I think."

I want to ask her to stay. It would be so easy for her to slip out of that dress and into the magnificent bed just down the hall. But . . . she'd say no—I can feel it. Too soon.

And she wouldn't get a wink of fucking sleep anyway—I'd keep her up all night.

I gesture toward the door, like the gentleman I'm not. "Let's get you home, then."

Olivia's head rests against my arm the whole ride back to her place. Our legs are aligned and pressing, our hands entwined on top of my thigh. I turn my head just slightly and inhale the addictive jasmine scent of her hair.

There's a cable show, *My Strange Addiction*—one of the most insane things I ever saw, one episode was about a wanker who was obsessed with sniffing women's hair.

I'm sorry I judged you, wanker. I get it now.

"You smell fantastic."

She angles her head up, her eyes light and mischievous. Then she presses her face against my pectoral—and inhales so deeply she practically snorts my shirt.

"I like the way you smell too, Nicholas."

The car pulls up to the curb and rolls to a stop.

And I'm about to ask if I can sniff her again tomorrow, but Logan's voice comes through the speaker.

"Stay in the car, Your Grace. There's a vagrant outside Miss Hammond's door—Tommy and I'll take care of it."

Olivia jerks up away from me, going tense in an instant. She looks out the window, white-knuckling the armrest.

"Oh no . . ."

And her words barely register before she shoves the door open and dashes out.

CHAPTER 9

Olivia

"O*h no . . .*"

To little girls, fathers are heroes—at least the good ones are. Tall and handsome, strong but patient, with a deep voice that speaks the wisest truths.

My father was a good one.

A chaser-away of monsters under the bed, a sneaker of cookies before dinner, an encourager, a protector, a teacher of what a real man is supposed to be. His hands were big and callused—working man's hands—powerful, but gentle with us. He used to hold my mother's hand like she was a precious work of art. Oh, how he loved my mother. It was in every move he made, every word he said. His love for her was the light in his eyes and the breath in his lungs.

I look like him—his black hair, the shape of his eyes, his long limbs. It used to make me proud to resemble him because, like all little girls, I thought my father was unconquerable. Invincible. The wall that could never crumble.

But I was wrong.

One terrible day . . . one horrible moment on a subway platform . . . and all that strength just dissolved. The way a pillar candle melts down into a heap of wax. Into something unrecognizable.

"Daddy?" I kneel down.

Behind me, Nicholas's approaching footsteps stutter to a stop.

And the mortification nips at my heels as I imagine how this must look to him.

But I don't have time for that now.

"Daddy, what happened?"

His eyes struggle to find mine, to stay open, and whiskey fumes burn my nostrils.

"Livvy . . . hey, sweetie. Couldn't . . . somethin's wrong with the lock . . . couldn't get my key in."

He tried using the walk-up door to our apartment. He could have just gone through the coffee shop—but he doesn't know about the broken lock that I still haven't gotten around to fixing.

His keys slip out of his grasp. "Damn."

I scoop them off the cold sidewalk. "It's okay, Dad. I'll help you."

With a spine-straightening breath, I stand up, turn around and face Nicholas. And my voice goes straight to autopilot.

"You should go. I have to take care of this."

His gaze darts to my father on the ground, then back to me. "Go? I can't just leave you to—"

"It's fine," I grit out, teeth crunching and embarrassment creeping up my neck.

"He's three times your size. How do you plan to get him upstairs?"

"I've done it before."

In a nanosecond he goes from pitying to pissed. And he uses that voice again—the one that bent Bosco to his will, the one that says it's his way or his way.

"You're not doing it now."

I know what he's trying to do—and I hate it. He wants to be noble, helpful. Trying to be the hero. Isn't that what princes do? But it just makes me feel shittier.

I've been my own hero for a long time—I know how it's done.

"This is none of your business. This is my business. I told you yesterday—"

"If you fall down those steps you'll snap your fucking neck," Nicholas says harshly, leaning down. "I won't risk that because you've got more pride than sense. I'm helping you, Olivia. Deal with it."

Then he walks right past me. And crouches down.

His voice grows gentler. "Mr. Hammond?"

And my father slurs, "Who're you?"

"Nicholas. My name is Nicholas. I'm a friend of Olivia's. It looks like you're having a bit of trouble, so I'm going to help get you upstairs. All right?"

"Yeah . . . damn keys aren't working."

Nicholas nods, then motions Logan forward. They heave my father up, one on either side, his arms flung over their shoulders.

"Olivia, get the door," he tells me.

We go through the coffee shop because there's more room that way. And as I watch them carry my father through the kitchen and up the stairs—his head dangling forward on his neck like a newborn, his legs useless—I realize that this is a really, really bad night. The best I would have been able to do was drag him inside, get a pillow and blanket, and spend the rest of the night on the floor with him.

But even knowing that, it doesn't stop the humiliation that's burning under my skin.

And it only flames hotter when they move through our threadbare living room, messy with strewn shoes and papers because I didn't have time to straighten up. If things had gone the way I'd wanted, I would have made it look pretty—quaint—with fresh flowers and plumped throw pillows. Not like this.

In his bedroom, they put my father on the bed. I squeeze past Nicholas and get the dark blue blanket off the chair in the corner. I lay it over my father, tucking him in. His eyes are closed and his lips open, but he doesn't snore. There's more gray than black now in the thick stubble on his chin. Slowly, I lean over and kiss his forehead, because even though he's not my hero anymore, he's still my dad.

Silently, the three of us file back downstairs. My arms wrap around my middle, stiff and tight, and my skin feels prickly—too sensitive. In my head, I can already hear the words Nicholas will say:

I'll call you.

This was . . . nice.

Thanks, but no thanks.

He must be relieved to dodge the bullet—probably wondering what the hell he was thinking in the first place. The only baggage a guy like him is used to a woman having is Louis Vuitton.

"I'll, ah . . . I'll be at the car, Sir," Logan says when we reach the coffee shop's dining area. He nods my way, then heads out the door.

The silence is awkward. Uncomfortable. I can feel his eyes on me, but I focus on the floor. And I cringe when he finally splits the quiet, in that smooth, perfect voice.

"Olivia."

But I'm determined to rip the Band-Aid off first. Beat him to the blow-off punch. I'm a New Yorker and that's how we roll—if someone's getting kicked to the curb, you can bet your ass we're going to be the motherfucking kicker.

"You should go." I nod, lifting my face but still not meeting his eyes. "I want you to go."

His warm hand touches my bare arm. "Don't be angry."

"I'm not angry," I deny with quick, jerking shakes of my head. "I just want you to leave." My throat clogs, salty and wet. Because I like him so much. My eyes squeeze closed—a last-ditch effort to contain the giant, ugly tears hovering on my lashes. "Please just *leave*."

Nicholas's hand drops from my arm. And I wait—I listen—for the sound of him walking out the door. Out of my life. Where he was never really supposed to be in the first place.

But about thirty seconds later, what I actually hear is something entirely different.

"My grandmother talks to paintings."

My eyes spring open.

"What?"

"When I was younger I thought it was funny, in a freakish kind of way, but now I just think it's sad."

There's a prodding desperation in his eyes. Earnest, but . . . vulnerable. Like this is all new to him. Like he's taking a risk—going out on a limb—but he has to push himself to get there. Because he's not sure if the limb will hold or snap.

"She's almost eighty years old and the only person she's ever been able to talk to is my grandfather. He's been gone a decade and he's still the only person she can talk to."

He pauses for a moment, his brow growing weighted. When he speaks again, his voice is lower, hushed—like these are words he hasn't let himself think, let alone say aloud.

"My brother has been away on military service for the last two years. He was discharged three months ago and he hasn't come anywhere close to home. But even before that, he stopped taking my calls. I haven't spoken to Henry in six months and I have no idea why."

I think of the video—of the way Nicholas pulled his little brother into his arms, held him close and tight. Protected him, tried so hard to make him smile. And I know immediately how much this silence must hurt him. I can almost feel it in my own heart—the breaking of his.

"My cousins hate me," he goes on, in a lighter tone. "Like, 'I think they would literally try to poison me when they come to visit if they thought they could get away with it' kind of hate."

His mouth quirks up in an almost-smile and a snort that bubbles from mine.

"They hated my father, too . . . and all because his mother was born before theirs."

"Why are you telling me this?"

"Because if you think your family is the only one with dysfunction in it, you're wrong." His hand runs through my hair like he can't help himself, sliding the strands behind my ear. "Mine has that particular market cornered."

He's quiet after that. Waiting for me to take my turn—he doesn't say it, but I know. He wants me to crawl out on that shaky limb with him.

And if it breaks . . . at least we'll fall together.

"My father's an alcoholic."

The words feel awkward, strange. It's the first time I've said them.

"Not in a mean or violent way . . . He drinks when he's sad. And he's been sad every day since my mother died." I look around the coffee shop, my voice quivering. "This place was her dream—she was Amelia. If it goes under, if he loses this last piece of her . . . I don't know what he'll do."

Nicholas nods.

"He barely talks to Ellie. Some days he can't even look at her . . . because she reminds him so much of our mom. She tries to pretend like it doesn't bother her, but . . . but I know it guts her."

Quiet tears trickle from the corners of my eyes, and Nicholas brushes them away with his thumb.

"And she's gonna leave. She's gonna go and she'll never come back—and I want that for her, I do. But I'll still be here . . . all alone." I gesture to the door. "I think that's why I haven't gotten the lock fixed. Sometimes, I dream that I can't get out. I pull and pull on the door but I'm stuck. Trapped."

"Sometimes I dream I'm walking through the palace and there are no doors or windows," Nicholas says, roughly. "I keep walking and walking, but I don't go anywhere."

I move closer, resting my hands on his chest, feeling hard, solid muscle and the strong, steady thrum of his heart beneath my palm.

"Tell me something you've never told anyone," he asks. "Something no one else knows about you."

It takes only two heartbeats for me to answer.

"I hate pies."

Nicholas starts to laugh—but when I go on, it dies on his lips. "I used to love helping, watching my mom make them, but now I hate it. The way they feel in my hands, the way they smell—it makes me sick to my stomach." I look up into his face. "Now you. Tell me something you've never told anyone."

"I hate the bowing. Last month I met a World War II veteran who saved three of his mates in battle—he was wounded, lost his eye. And he bowed to me. What the fuck have I ever done that a man like that should bow to me?"

He shakes his head, lost in the thought.

The soft touch of my fingers along his jaw finds him again. And in that moment, something shifts . . . changes. My chest rises faster, my breaths come quicker, and the heart beneath my hand pounds just a little more fiercely.

Nicholas stares at my mouth. "If you could go anywhere, do anything, what would it be?"

This answer takes longer, because there isn't one.

"I don't know. It's been so long since doing anything else was even an option . . . I stopped imagining."

I lean in closer, inhaling his scent—spice and ocean and something decadently, uniquely him—a scent I would happily drown in.

"What about you?" I ask, the words rushing. "If you could do anything, right now, what would you do?"

His thumb slides across my bottom lip, stroking it slowly, gently . . . intently.

"I would kiss you."

The air leaves the room. All of it. Or maybe I just forget to breathe. I might pass out and I don't care, as long as Nicholas kisses me before the world goes black.

"Please," I manage, breathlessly.

He doesn't rush it. He takes his time. Savoring.

One arm wraps around my waist, pulling me sharply up against him. I feel him everywhere—the hard touch of his thighs, the flat planes of his stomach, the hot press of his thick, firm cock. My inner muscles clench around emptiness, needy. Seeking.

Nicholas's other hand slides up my spine, burying itself in my hair, and he cradles my head in his palm. And his eyes—the whole time, those simmering green eyes drag over my skin, consuming every inch they touch.

Slowly, he leans down. I taste his breath—cinnamon and clove—before I taste him.

And then Nicholas presses his mouth against mine.

Possessively. Boldly. Like he owns me. And in this moment he does. I follow his lead, moving my lips in time with his, relishing the feel, the sensation. He tilts my head, positioning me right where he wants me. And then I feel the warm, wet stroke of his tongue.

Holy fuck, does he know how to kiss.

I think I have an orgasm of the mouth.

A mouth-gasm. And it's amazing.

I moan deep and totally loud—not even a little ashamed. My arms curl around Nicholas's neck and his hands skim down to my ass, clamping and kneading. Then he's the one moaning—and it, too, is amazing.

"I knew it," he murmurs against my lips. "So fucking sweet."

Then our mouths fuse again, our tongues sliding and tasting. Nicholas pushes his knee between my legs, squeezes my ass and drags me up his leg. And the friction—the glorious fucking friction—would have me gasping yes if my mouth weren't wonderfully otherwise occupied.

But then a sound comes from above us—a thump that rattles the ceiling. We both hear it, looking up, lips retreating.

"I have to go—my dad might've fallen out of bed."

His hands tighten on my ass, almost reflexively—the way a child would grasp a favorite toy if it was threatened to be taken away. "Let me come up with you."

I look into his eyes, not embarrassed anymore. "No, it's better if you don't." My fingers comb his thick, soft hair before settling against his jaw. "I'll be fine, I swear."

Nicholas is still breathing hard and looks like he wants to argue, but after a moment of searching my face, he gives the smallest nod and slides me off his thigh.

"When can I see you again?" he asks. "Say tomorrow."

I laugh. "God, you're bossy. Okay, tomorrow."

"Earlier this time. We'll stay in at my hotel—I'll make you dinner."

"You can cook?"

He shrugs, and the adorable dimples make an appearance.

"I know how to make sushi, so technically, I can cut. But my cutting is top-notch."

I giggle again—feeling silly and light-headed. Possibly delusional.

"All right. Your place, tomorrow."

Then he's kissing me again. Sucking at my lips in a way that I'll feel in my dreams tonight.

"This is crazy," I whisper against him. "It's crazy, right? It's not just me?"

Nicholas shakes his head. "Bloody insane." His hands are on my ass again—a final quick grab. "And fucking fantastic."

CHAPTER 10

Nicholas

I'm going to have sex tonight. Lots of it.

I'm going to lay Olivia out on my bed and screw her sweetly, I'm going to hold her up against the wall and fuck her madly. No room or surface will be left undefiled.

Moves and configurations worthy of an Olympic gymnast—fantasies—play out in my head all damn day long. Leaving me hard and aching.

They make the interviews and charity luncheon I suffer through—awkward.

And it's all because of her. *Olivia.*

What a sexy, delectable little surprise she turned out to be.

Last night was . . . intense. I didn't mean to say all those things—they just spilled out. And, Christ, she didn't even sign an NDA—it's not like me to forget such a thing.

But it felt cathartic talking to her. Like we were in our own bubble, on a personal remote island—where no one else in the world could see us, touch us or hear us. Before I left for New York I'd planned to make the most of the freedom I have left—do things I never would've considered. And Miss Olivia Hammond certainly fits that bill.

I gave the butler a list of items I'd need for dinner and I told him to make sure the suite was stocked with condoms—

every room. *Cover your knobber before you bob her*—that's what my father used to say. Words every royal lives by.

Words I learned to never forget.

My leg jostles impatiently as the car pulls up in front of Amelia's just before sunset. I should've worked out, burned off some of this energy—or even better—I should've jerked off. I'm liable to jump her the second I see her. My balls feel like lead weights in my trousers.

Not very comfortable—in case you weren't sure.

I spot the CLOSED sign hanging in the window and smile. Closed means privacy. And just maybe I'll get the chance to act out the fantasy from last night—Olivia lying back on one of those dining tables, legs on my shoulders while I pump smoothly into her.

But those luscious thoughts are scattered to the wind when I walk inside. Olivia's not there to greet me—her little firecracker of a sister is.

Ellie Hammond is a tiny thing—pretty, with the same shade eyes as her sister, but rounder, less exotic looking. She's wearing a simple black T-shirt, snug across her chest, and jeans that look like they were chopped off at the knees with a hacksaw. Black square glasses perch over a pert nose and a streak of hot pink in her blond hair gives her a youthful, idealistic look—like a girl who'd be holding a sign at a college campus protest.

Ellie stands in front of me, then lowers gracefully into a perfect full curtsy.

"It's an honor to meet you, Prince Nicholas." She smiles.

"Have you been practicing that move?" I ask. "You do it very well."

She shrugs. "Maybe."

The tall, dark-skinned waiter approaches from the back. "We haven't been officially introduced. I'm Martin."

Then he curtsies too.

When he stands, I hold out my hand and he shakes it. "Good to meet you, Martin."

He pumps my arm enthusiastically. "I just want to thank you for all the hours of pleasure you've given me—you've been center stage in my fantasies for years."

And his gaze drags over me—not offensively, but like he's committing every particle to memory. For . . . later.

"Ah . . . you're welcome?"

He gestures to a nearby chair. "I'm just going to sit over here. And look at you." With a wink, Marty sinks into a chair, staring like he's trying very hard not to blink.

I wonder how long he can keep that up.

Ellie's hands fold together in front of her. "We should talk. Get to know each other—Prid Cocoa, Clarice."

I chuckle—cuteness runs in the Hammond family.

"Do you mean *quid pro quo?* It's Latin, meaning "something for something.""

She shakes her head with disappointment. "That was a pretentiousness test. You failed."

"Damn."

"Who speaks Latin anymore, anyway?"

"I do. As well as French, Spanish and Italian."

Her fair eyebrows rise. "Impressive."

"My language tutor would be happy you think so. He was a crusty sod who admired the beauty of language but detested actually speaking with people. And I made him miserable—I was an uncooperative pupil."

Ellie takes a seat at a table. "A bad boy, huh?"

I shrug, sitting down across from her. "It was a phase."

And suddenly the situation feels very familiar—like an interview.

"Would you get punished if you misbehaved or did they use a whipping boy?"

She's done research. Whipping boys were used back in the old days when corporal punishment was all the rage but princes were thought to be too sacred to be struck. So, an unlucky lad—usually poor—would be chosen as the prince's companion, and that child would take the beating in his place. The idea being that the prince would feel guilty watching an innocent boy receive his punishment.

Obviously the forefathers knew fuck-all about children.

"Whipping boy?" Martin pipes up, raising his hand. "I volunteer as tribute."

I laugh. "Whipping boys haven't been used for a few hundred years—how old do you think I am?"

"You'll be twenty-eight on October twentieth," Ellie replies.

Yes—she's definitely been a busy-researching-bee.

"So," she starts, leaning back. "What are your intentions with my sister, Prince Nicholas?"

If she only knew.

"I want to spend time with Olivia. Get to know her."

Intimately.

"My intentions are all good ones, I promise."

Very good. Orgasmic. The XXX-rated kind.

Ellie's innocent-looking eyes narrow, reading me, like she's a visual lie detector.

"You probably know a lot of people—rich people, famous people. Liv is good people. The best. She's given up her whole life to keep this place going—for me and my dad. She deserves to have fun—a good time—a hot fling with a former bad-boy prince who can talk dirty to her in five languages. I'm hoping you can give her that."

I know where she's coming from. I understand that protectiveness—the wish for happiness and joy for someone you care about so much your chest aches. It's what I feel for Henry every day.

At least, on the days he doesn't make me want to strangle him.

"That makes two of us, then," I tell her plainly.

"Good." With a rap to the table and a nod, little Ellie stands. She retrieves a pie server from a neighboring table and taps each of my shoulders with it.

Like she's knighting me.

"I approve you, Prince Nicholas. Carry on."

I try very hard not to laugh at her. And fail.

"Thank you, Miss Hammond."

And then she leans over me. "But just in case you get any ideas . . . if you hurt my sister," she tips her head toward Logan by the door, "delicious-looking security guards or not, I'll find a way to shave your eyebrows off."

And I actually believe she'd pull it off.

Ellie straightens up, grinning evilly.

"You feel me, Nicholas?"

I nod. "Loud and clear, Ellie."

That's when Olivia walks into the room. And just when I was sure my balls couldn't get any achier, she proves me wrong.

Her navy-blue tank top, beneath a light gray flannel, highlights her creamy skin, and tight dark jeans tucked into knee-high brown boots accentuate those long, slender legs. Her black hair is down, almost to the curve of her gorgeous arse, and simple silver and pearl earrings peek out between the glorious glossy waves.

"Hey." She smiles, making the room a little bit brighter and my cock a lot harder. "I didn't know you were here already. Were you waiting long?"

"It's all good, Livvy," Ellie says. "Marty and I kept him company."

Marty stands, wiggling his mobile. "Before you go, can I get a selfie? You know—for the spank bank?"

"Oh God." Olivia groans, covering her eyes.

Then she tries to get me off the hook.

"Nicholas doesn't like taking pictures, Marty."

I hold up my hand. "No, it's all right. A photo is fine." Then I lower my voice so only she can hear me. "But I'm going to need a deposit from you in my spank bank tonight."

She giggles, while Ellie watches us carefully, with something like approval in her eyes.

The ride to the hotel is pure, unadulterated torture—and an exercise in restraint. Our small talk is comfortable and benign, but our looks are intense and heated. I catch Olivia checking out the perpetual bulge in my trousers no fewer than three times. And I don't even bother trying to pretend that I'm not staring at her tits. Her scent—that clean, freshly shampooed, warm honey scent—fills the space of the limousine, making my nostrils flare, trying to absorb every trace of it.

Logan and Tommy flank us on the way through the lobby, with James taking the rear position. It's busier than it was last night—crowded with visitors on their way to dinner or a Broadway show—and we're the recipient of more than a few double takes. Once we arrive in the suite, the lads scatter. I've given David the evening off so that we have some privacy, and I guide Olivia into the kitchen.

Over a glass of white wine, she tells me about her day, about the poor, bedraggled young mother and her brood of five hell-raisers who visited the coffee shop. I convey the boredom of the Art Commission of New York charity luncheon—which is really just an excuse for politicians to hear themselves talk.

I take a chopping knife from the wood block on the counter, and the unpleasant, piercing sound that results from sliding it against the sharpening stone momentarily halts our conversation. Olivia comes up behind me, peeking over my shoulder as I slice the salmon and chop the celery into match-sized sticks.

"Where did you learn to do that?" she asks with a smile in her voice.

"Japan."

I look over my shoulder to catch her rolling her pretty eyes—because I suspect she already knew the answer.

Then she picks up a knife herself, stands next to me, and makes quick work of three carrots, chopping them just as well, if not better, than me.

Then she shrugs coyly. "Manhattan."

We both chuckle as she rests the knife on the counter and I wash my hands. As I dry them on a clean towel, I lean back against the sink—watching her.

Olivia runs her hand along the counter, observing the dishes of spices and rice, shrimp and salmon. She dips her finger into a small bowl of black soy sauce and seems to move in slow motion when she raises that finger to her mouth, and wraps those gorgeous fucking lips around it.

I've never come in my trousers, but I'm dangerously close.

A groan is trapped in my throat, because I want to be that finger—more than I want to breathe. Our eyes meet and hold. And the air is thick between us—filled with magnetic particles that draw us towards one another.

Dinner's going to have to wait.

Looking into her eyes, hearing the needy little puffs of breath that slip out between her glistening lips, I know for certain—we'll never make it that long.

Then there's a noise from the other room and Olivia jumps. Almost as if she'd been caught doing something naughty. She's all too aware of the security team's presence.

And that just won't do.

"Logan," I call, not taking my eyes off of her.

He pokes his head through the door. "Yes, Sir?"

"Go away."

There's a brief pause. And then, "Aye. Me and James and Tommy'll be down in the lobby and by the lift—to be sure no one comes up."

We wait, staring at each other . . . and when the elevator pings, proving that we are finally, perfectly, blessedly alone, it's like the starting shot of a marathon.

We move at the same time—Olivia springs forward and I pull her into my arms. Hands grasping, legs wrapping, mouths clashing. She squeezes my waist with her thighs and my palms flex against the taut swell of her arse. My teeth nip at those gorgeous fucking lips, scraping gently, before covering her mouth in a searing, wet kiss.

Yes, *yes,* this is it. It's everything I've been fantasizing about—only better.

Olivia's mouth is hot and wet and tastes like sweet grapes against my tongue. She moans into my mouth—a sound I could easily get drunk on.

I move us to the kitchen table, knocking over a chair. I perch her on the end, both of us breathing hard and heavy.

"I want you," I rasp. Just in case that isn't clear.

Her eyes are bright and manic—caught up in the same tsunami of sensation that grips me.

She tears the gray flannel from her arms.

"Have me."

Christ, this bold, daring girl—I *adore* her.

Olivia's pale arms wrap around my neck as we clash back together, kissing and grasping. I pull her hips forward to the edge of the table, grinding my erection that's hard as stone between her open, denim-covered legs. My hand dives through her soft hair, cupping the back of her head, holding her still so I can take and take from her mouth.

She moans again, sweet and long, and the sound pushes me right to the edge, making me shaky with want for her.

Then with her legs wrapped tight around my waist, she pushes against my shoulders, forcing me back, breaking our kiss. I catch her drift when she jerks at the hem of my shirt and I help her out—pulling it over my head. Her dark, enchanting blue eyes go wide as she takes in my bare torso, running smooth, petal-soft hands across my shoulders, over my chest, down through the grooves of my abdomen.

"Jesus," she breathes out softly, "you are so fucking . . . *hot.*"

And I laugh. I can't help it. Though I've heard such compliments before, there's a wonder in her voice, an awe, that's just too adorable. The chuckle still rumbles in my chest when I skim her tank top up and over her head. But I stop abruptly when I glimpse Olivia's breasts, covered in nothing but innocent white lace.

Because they are seriously, beautifully perfect.

I lean back in, my hips circling and grinding, lips skimming over her delicate shoulder to her neck—pausing to suck hard over her pulse, making her gasp. My teeth scrape the shell of her ear.

"I want to kiss you, Olivia."

She giggles, kneading my back. "You *are* kissing me."

I slide my hand between us, between her legs, rubbing where she's already hot and aching.

"Here. I want to kiss you here."

She goes languid in my arms, her head lolling, so my mouth can roam free.

"Oh," she moans on a breath, "oh, oh . . . kay."

I've pictured fucking her on the coffee shop tables a dozen times, but this kitchen table isn't cutting it. I need more room. And I want only softness and silk touching her back while I eat her.

In one move I scoop Olivia up and toss her over my shoulder, caveman style, heading for the bedroom. She squeals and laughs and squeezes my arse as I walk down the hall. I give hers a playful smack in return.

She lands in the center of the large bed with her eyes shining, her lips smiling, and her cheeks flushed. I stand at the edge of the bed and beckon her forward with my hand.

"Come here."

She rises to her knees and comes closer, but ducks her head when I try to kiss her—trailing her lips over my chest instead, in a dozen soft, worshipful pecks that turn my blood to fire. I cup her face in my hands, guiding her up to meet me.

And then I kiss her, slowly. Deeply.

And the teasing play, the joking spirit that surrounded us, dissipates, replaced by something more powerful. Urgent and primal. Olivia's mouth never leaves mine as my hands wander their way behind her back, releasing the clasp of her bra. I skim the straps down her arms and cup her soft, full breasts in my hands.

My thumbs drift back and forth over her nipples—hardening them to two dusty-rose peaks. She sucks on my neck and bites at my earlobe—getting rougher with desperation—and then I dip my head and my mouth takes the place of my thumbs.

I suck her in long, slow drags and quick flicks of my tongue. Olivia's spine arches, trying to get closer, and her nails sink into the skin of my shoulder blades—leaving half-moons I'll relish tomorrow. I move to her other breast, blowing first, taunting her just a bit, until she yanks my hair. My mouth suctions harder, bringing teeth into play, pressing against the tantalizing flesh.

When Olivia's hips begin to move in searching, seeking circles and frenzied, grunting gasps come from her throat, I lift my head from her sweet tit and guide her onto her back.

She looks into my eyes and I'm lost. Wrecked. Owned. There's no thought, no desire—

except to please her. Make her see stars and touch heaven.

Deft fingers open her jeans, peeling them down her legs as I straighten up.

I take a moment to enjoy the view—Olivia's flushed, heated skin almost bare in the middle of my bed. The way her pitch-black hair lies against the stunning, flawless flesh of her breasts. Her flat stomach, sculpted, and the way the thin straps of her pastel-pink underwear cling to dainty hips.

The triangle of fabric between her legs is lace—see-through. It shows a trim, pretty little bush of soft black curls. It's different—most of the women I've been with do their damnedest to have their vag imitate Mr. Bigglesworth, Dr. Evil's hairless cat.

I've yet to discover a thing about Olivia that I don't like—but this, I like very, *very* much.

I feel her eyes on me as I lick my lips and slide the pink lace down her legs—giving me an unobstructed view.

"Christ, you're a beauty," I groan. With a smirk, I crawl onto the bed, hovering over her. "Pretty enough to eat for breakfast, lunch and dinner—and still want more for dessert."

I raise her ankle to my shoulder—then I move upward slowly, kissing and sucking on the skin of her calf, behind her knee, to her taut inner thigh. Her breath hitches when I place her foot back on the bed and my palms against her thighs, spreading her wide. I lick two fingertips and run them through her cleft, rubbing, searching.

Olivia's eyes drift closed. "Nicholas."

Yeah, that's the spot.

My fingers circle Olivia's pretty clit—pink and swollen—and I drop down to my stomach. I kiss her thigh, sucking just hard enough to leave a mark.

"Say my name again," I murmur.

Olivia's chest rises and falls quickly. "Nicholas."

She pants and gasps as my mouth moves closer.

"Again."

Still rubbing with my fingers, my nose brushes those soft curls, every bit as fragrant and sweet as the rest of her. Maybe more.

"Nicholas," she moans, her voice raw and pleading.

Music to my fucking ears.

Then I give her what we're both aching for.

My mouth moves over her pussy, enveloping it in a heated kiss, and my tongue slides between those plump lips. With a loud whimper her hips rise, but I hold her steady. Focused and unrelenting in my need to make her climax.

Christ, her taste. The slick feel of her against my tongue. It's magnificent.

Enough to make my hips thrust against the bed, searching for relief.

I move my mouth to Olivia's clit, sucking hard while two fingers thrust, then pump, inside her. Oh, she's tight. And hot. And so wet it may drive me mad.

But she's so snug, I'm really going to need to take care with her.

The thought is chased from my mind when Olivia's back curves, her neck arches, and her mouth opens to whimper my name. And she comes. Stunningly. Fantastically. On my tongue, against my mouth, writhing with the sheer bliss of it.

When Olivia goes limp against the bed, I practically pounce on her. She doesn't seem to mind. In fact, after just a few minutes of kissing and humping, she pushes me back, rolling us over, to kiss her way down my chest.

She makes quick work of my trousers, tossing them on the floor. And she stares at me, with a secret smile on her lips—long enough for me to ask, "What?"

Olivia gives a tiny shrug. "The Internet was wrong. They said you wear Calvin Klein underwear."

They were very wrong—I don't wear underwear at all.

"Don't believe everything you read."

When she wraps her hand around my aching cock, it feels so damn good, I have no words—my eyes roll closed and my head digs into the pillow behind me. Olivia strokes me skillfully—once, twice—but that's all I allow.

It's all I can stand. If she keeps going, I'll fucking embarrass myself.

I jerk up, wrapping my arms around her, rolling her back under me and taking her mouth like a dying man takes his last meal. Blindly, my hand gropes for the night table drawer, for the condoms David put there. But when Olivia arches up—almost rubbing the tip of my cock against her slick entrance, I pull back fully. Quickly.

"Just a sec, love."

I rip open the condom with my teeth and Olivia's hands mix with mine, fumbling to roll it on as quickly as possible.

And then I'm there, over her, staring into those stunning dark blue eyes that caught me from the first moment. I breathe deep, silently begging for control, and then I press the head of my cock inside her. Gently and just the tip.

Olivia's mouth opens with the pleasure of it. And my heart pounds so fast and hard, I think I might be dying.

What a perfect bloody way to go.

She presses her palm to my cheek, reaching up for a kiss, drawing me in. Slowly, I slide inside her—the beautiful muscles fitting so snug and wet around me—stretching to make room. When our pelvises meet, when my heavy balls rest against Olivia's arse, I wait. Swallowing hard against a sandpaper throat.

Her eyes are closed, her lashes fanning out like tiny threads of black silk.

"Are you all right?" I pant.

Please, please say yes. Please let me move. Let me thrust and pump and fuck.

And then she does the simplest, most miraculous thing. She opens her eyes—and it feels like she's ripping my heart out—taking it for her own.

"Yes."

Definitely my favorite word.

I feel her squeeze around me—her hips pulsing upward, testing the feel.

"Oh God," she moans. "Move, Nicholas. I want to feel you. All of you. Now."

And those words are now my second favorite.

Keeping my weight on my arms, I pull back and thrust in slowly, with a guttural groan. Because it feels just that fucking fantastic. Indescribable. Olivia's arms wind around my neck and my hands slide beneath her shoulder blades, cradling her head as I ride her in even, steady strokes. Our panting breaths mingle, we kiss and taste, and the pleasure rises, tightens with every movement.

Until it peaks.

My hips move without thought, grinding and pounding hard now, rushing to catch the orgasm that's barreling down on us both. And then my mind goes white, blank—suspended in that perfect moment of deep, carnal pleasure. Olivia's there with me. She bites my shoulder but I don't feel it. All I feel is where we're connected, where I'm powerfully pulsing inside her, giving everything I have, over and over again.

Olivia lies in the crook of my arm, pretty and perfect, gazing at me as her hand runs down my chest, tracing the tic-tac-toe of my abdomen with her fingertips, then sliding back up to start all over again.

"You're beautiful when you come." I brush my knuckle against the rosy apple of her smooth cheek. "And after."

She bats her lashes up at me. "I try."

As my hand retreats, she catches my wrist, eyeing the bracelets that chronically encircle it. "You wore these the other night, too. Do they have any special meaning?"

I slip off the teakwood circle and pass it to her for a closer look. Her finger traces the etchings. "This was my father's," I tell her. "He built houses in Africa one summer when he was a teenager. One of the village women gave it to him—a blessing, she called it—for protection. He wore it almost all the time." My throat narrows. "After the funeral, our butler, Fergus, gave it to me. He said he found it on my father's dresser—didn't know why he hadn't taken it with him when they left for New York. I don't wear it because of superstition . . . I just like having something close to me that was close to him."

Olivia snuggles tighter against me and slips the bracelet back over my hand.

"And this one?" She fingers the platinum links circling the same wrist.

"It's Henry's." An easy smile comes to my lips. "Our mother had it made for him when he was eight and she was sure ID bracelets were coming back into style." I chuckle at the memory and Olivia lets out a small laugh. "He hated it, but he pretended to like it for her sake." And then I'm blinking against the burning in my eyes. "After they were gone, Henry never took it off. He had the links added when he outgrew it. He couldn't bring it with him to training, so he asked me to keep it for him until he came home."

Olivia presses a comforting kiss to my shoulder, and we lie against each other in relaxed silence for a few minutes.

But then she rolls over onto her stomach, her long, wavy hair scattering across my torso. "Hey, you know what else I am after I come?"

"What?"

"Thirsty."

I rub my eye and stifle a yawn. "Yes, I could go for a bottle of water too. There's a mini fridge just over there." I point to the far side of the room. "How about you go get us some?"

She burrows under the covers—her arms and legs wrapping like she's a koala and I'm her tree.

"But it's so cold. What do you have the temperature set to—arctic?"

"I like it cold. I tend to run on the hot side." I reach between us, tweaking her peaked, pink nipple. "And there are other benefits."

"You should go get the water—it's the gentlemanly thing to do."

I roll on top of her, nudging her legs open with my hips, settling comfortably between them, my cock already starting to harden again. "But there are no gentlemen here." My teeth scrape her lovely neck—gaining a whole new appreciation of vampirism. "And I want to watch you scamper across the floor." I shift my weight and cup one full breast. "See all these gorgeous parts jiggling along the way."

Olivia scoffs. "Perv."

She doesn't know the half of it.

"I have an idea," she suggests. "Let's play a game—a contest. Whoever tells the most embarrassing story gets to stay in the warm bed. Loser has to freeze their 'parts' off and get the water."

I shake my head. "Oh, sweets, you've just ensured that you're going to lose—no one has more embarrassing stories than I do."

I let Olivia roll us to the side, pushing me off her. She cocks her arm, resting her head in her hand. "We'll see about that."

"Ladies first—let's hear it."

Slight doubt shadows her features. "I hope it doesn't bother you . . . It has to do with . . . oral sex."

"Mmm, one of my favorite topics—tell me more."

And she's already blushing.

"All right, so, the first time I ever gave a . . . blow job . . . I didn't really know what it was. And since it's called a 'blow' job, I thought you were supposed to—"

She puffs her cheeks out, like she's trying to blow up an uncooperative balloon.

I fall back onto the pillow, howling. "Christ, you're lucky you didn't give the poor lad an aneurism!"

Her cheeks deepen to crimson and she pinches my side as punishment.

"Your turn."

I stare at the ceiling, deciding. There are so many stories to choose from.

"I shit in a bag once."

A shocked choke of laughter immediately bursts from Olivia's lungs.

"What?"

I nod. "I was on the rowing team at boarding school."

"Of course you were."

"And, we had a meet at another school, a fair distance away. On the bus back, there was an accident—congestion on the road—and whatever they'd served for lunch was fiercely disagreeing with me. So . . . it was either my pants or a gym bag. I went with option two."

She covers her eyes and her mouth, laughing in horror. "Oh my God! That's awful . . . and yet hilarious."

I laugh too. "It was. Especially after it hit the papers—bloody nightmare."

And suddenly, Olivia's not laughing anymore.

Not even a little.

"It was in the newspapers?"

I shrug. "Sure. The more embarrassing the story, the more the journalists will pay. My classmates were always looking for extra cash."

"But . . . but they were your teammates. Your friends."

I toy with her hair, tugging on a curl and watching it bounce stubbornly back into shape.

"It's like I told Simon, that first night at your coffee shop: everything's for sale and everyone—*everyone*—has their price."

Her eyes search my face, looking so very sad. I don't like it—not a bit.

I roll over on top of her again, nudging between her legs.

"Do you feel bad for me?" I ask.

"Yes."

"Do you pity me?"

Her fingers run gently through my hair.

"I think I do."

"Good." I smirk. "That means you get the water. And . . . when you get back . . . I want to test your blow-job skills. Make sure you've got it right—and if not, I'll happily instruct you."

That does the trick. Her mouth pinches to hide her smile and her eyes flash.

"So fucking bossy." She shakes her head.

But then she gets up to get the water—and I enjoy every second.

And when she crawls back into bed, Olivia gets right to work on that blow job.

And I enjoy that even more.

Eventually, hunger forces us out of bed. Olivia slips into one of my gray hoodies, which covers her to mid-thigh. I try out the "walking around the apartment naked" thing Olivia mentioned. This may be the only shot I have.

And she's right—it's rather fantastic. Freeing, everything just out and swinging. Natural—like Adam, if the Garden of Eden were a penthouse suite.

The hot, lusty look Olivia throws me makes it even better.

In the kitchen, neither of us is in the mood for sushi, so we scavenge for something else.

"You have Cinnamon Toast Crunch!" Olivia says, her voice excited but muted from inside the cabinet. She comes out smiling, holding the box like a found buried treasure.

I set two bowls on the table. "We have something similar in Wessco called Snicker-Squares. It's my favorite."

"Me too!" Then her blues eyes go light and soft as she sighs. "Just when I think you can't get any more perfect."

After a few minutes of sitting at the table, munching on cinnamon, sugar and squares that pretend to be whole wheat, words tumble out of my mouth without a second thought.

"This is fun."

Olivia grins at me over her bowl. "You sound surprised. Don't you usually have fun?"

"I do. But this is . . . more fun." I shake my head. "I can't really explain it, it just feels . . . good."

"Yeah, it does."

And then I gaze at her—that cute way she chews, the swipe of her tongue over the lower lip I can't wait to nibble on again.

She runs her hand over her forehead self-consciously. "Do I have something on my face?"

"No . . . I'm just wondering," I tell her quietly.

"Wondering what?"

I reach out my hand, tracing the slope of her cheek. "What in the world am I going to do with you?"

Our eyes hold for a few moments, and a spark of mischief lights in Olivia's. She takes my hand and kisses my palm lightly. Then she stands up, moves closer and sinks down on my lap—straddling me—her forearms on my shoulders, the slick heat of her pussy against my thickening cock.

"Do with me or do *to* me?" she teases.

"Either. Both."

Olivia runs her tongue along my top lip, sucking gently.

"How about you take me back to bed and we'll figure it out there."

My hands cradle her hips, holding her tight against me as I stand.

"Brilliant idea."

In the bedroom, I lay her back on the bed and lie down on top of her.

"Stay," I say between kisses. "Stay here with me."

"For how long?"

"For as long as you can."

Her hands slide up and down my spine. "I have to start things at the coffee shop at four."

I kiss her hard. "Then I'll drive you home at half past three. Yeah?"

She smiles. "Yeah."

CHAPTER 11

Olivia

Up until this point in my life, I would have described sex as . . . nice. My experiences with Jack were first-love sweet—in that hormone-driven, quick-and-over-just-when-it-starts-to-get-good kind of way that a seventeen-year-old girl thinks is romantic, because she doesn't know any better. She doesn't know there's *more.*

Sex with Nicholas is more-more.

It's fun. Like, John Mayer, "Your Body Is a Wonderland" music video kind of teasing and touching, rolling-around-the-sheets-and-laughing-in-bed kind of fun. We kiss and caress—not only as a warm-up to fucking, but because it feels good.

Sex with Nicholas is thrilling. Exciting in a heart-exploding kind of way. I didn't know having my wrists held down above my head could feel so amazing—not until he did it. I didn't know the slide of sweaty skin, drenched from hours of exertion, could be so erotic. I didn't know certain muscles could even be sore—or that everything still feels awesome when they are.

I didn't know I was capable of multiple orgasms—but glory be to God, I am.

I'm not uptight—or a prude. I know how to get myself off—a little rub and grind after a stressful day is the best and quickest way to fall asleep. But, after the grand finale, I've never tried going back for an encore.

Nicholas tries—and even better, he succeeds.

In the days that follow our first night together, we fall into an unspoken routine. I spend the day at the coffee shop and the night at his hotel suite. Sometimes he comes to pick me up, sometimes he just sends the car—trying to keep his frequent visits to Amelia's hidden from the public for as long as possible.

When I arrive, he sends the security guys out of the suite—going as far as to get them their own room one floor down. Logan grumbled the loudest, but went along with it.

The customer is always right, and apparently so is the royal.

We haven't gone out to dinner again—we order in or make something easy, like sandwiches or pasta. It's all surprisingly . . . normal. Some nights, we watch TV—try to binge on *American Horror Story*, season two, but we haven't made it past the second episode.

Because . . . sex.

Amazing, mind-blowing, I've-literally-had-to-change-my-panties-at-work-reminiscing-about-it sex. Marty noticed and was jealous. Then he teased me about it.

In bed, after the sex, we talk a lot—Nicholas tells me stories about his grandmother and his brother and Simon. And though I feel an intense growing tenderness for him that could quickly turn into something deeper, I make sure to keep it all casual and light. Un-clingy.

Nicholas already gets a whole lot of clingy from his day job.

The closest we've come to having "the talk"—the "Are we exclusive, where is this going?" talk—is when a story about him and a gorgeous blond he'd been photographed with in Wessco flashed across the television. "Wedding Watch," they called it.

Nicholas told me she was an old friend from school—*just* a friend—and that I should never believe anything any journalist said or wrote about him.

I mean, hey—they couldn't even get the underwear thing right. They obviously know dick.

Two weeks after that first crazy night, my growing tenderness toward Nicholas makes me do something I haven't done in years: take a Saturday off from the coffee shop.

Marty and Ellie cover for me.

And I do it because I want to do something nice for Nicholas. Not just to pay him back for all the fabulous orgasms—but just because.

What do you give a prince? A man with a country at his feet and the world at his fingertips?

Something only a New York girl can.

"I have a plan."

We're in the library of the suite. Nicholas is behind the desk, his hair falling still damp over his forehead from a recent shower, while James and Tommy stand near the windows.

"Take off your clothes," I say, dropping a stuffed backpack at my feet.

He stands, giving me a curious, dimple-flashing smile that makes my stomach tingle.

"I like this plan."

He pulls his shirt over his head—and at the sight of that gorgeous chest and ripped abs, I have to close my mouth to stop the flow of drool.

"Should I send the lads to their room?" he asks.

I toss him a Beastie Boys T-shirt and ripped jeans from the backpack. "They can stay—I'll get to them in a second."

Nicholas puts on the outfit, his disguise for the day. I hold up a thick gold chain with a dangling cross, and he dips his head so I can loop it over his neck. Then I squirt gel into my hand and reach up on tiptoes to rub it through his hair—mussing it at the top and slicking the sides.

Perfect.

"How do you feel about piercing your ear?" I ask, teasing.

He whispers, "Needles terrify me." Then he winks.

Nicholas's eyes are already sparkling with excitement—this next part is going to blow his mind. "Do you know how to drive a motorcycle?"

He mentioned the other night that he was a pilot during his stint in the military, so I made an educated guess.

"Sure."

"Perfect." I pull a helmet with a full, tinted face shield out of the backpack and hold it up. "Marty's bike is downstairs. He said to tell you: break it, you bought . . . a Ducati."

Logan steps into the room from where he was stationed just outside the door, lifting his hand, like a traffic cop. "Hold on, now—"

Nicholas takes the helmet. "It'll be fine, Logan."

"And . . ." I say cautiously, turning to the three big, strong, probably-have-a-license-to-kill boys. "I want Nicholas and me to go on this outing alone. You guys stay here."

Tommy says, "Jesus, Mary and Joseph."

James crosses himself.

Logan takes another route. "No fuckin' way. Not possible."

But the look on Nicholas's face says it really fucking is.

"No," Logan insists again, his voice straining with a faint hint of desperation.

"Henry used to slip his security detail all the time," Nicholas offers.

"You're not Prince Henry," Logan counters.

"I have an itinerary!" I jump up and down from excitement—like Bosco when he has to pee. "I wrote everything down for you, just in case—exactly where we'll be, every minute."

I take the sealed envelope out of the backpack and hand it to Logan. But when he starts to tear it open I put my hand on his. "You can't open it until after we're gone—it'll ruin the surprise. But I promise it will be all right. I swear on my life."

My eyes drift from Logan to Nicholas. "Trust me."

And I want him to—so much. I want to do this for him, give him something he hasn't had. Something he'll remember always: freedom.

Nicholas looks at the helmet, then at Logan. "What's the worst that could happen?"

"Ah . . . you could get assassinated and the three of us will hang for treason."

"Don't be silly," Nicholas scoffs. "We haven't hung anyone in years." He smacks Logan's back. "It'd be the firing squad."

Tommy laughs.

Logan doesn't.

James is Switzerland.

"Sir, please—if you'd just listen—"

Nicholas uses what I've now come to think of as "the voice."

"I'm not a child, Logan. I'm capable of surviving one afternoon without you. The three of you stay here, and that's an order. If I catch a glimpse of you or find out you followed us—and I will find out—I'll ship you home to guard the fucking hounds. Do I make myself clear?"

The guys nod, unhappily.

And just a few minutes later, he slips the helmet over his head so no one will recognize him while we walk through the lobby to the hotel's exit.

"Welcome to Coney Island!" I fling my arms out wide as Nicholas locks up the motorcycle. "Known for its epic roller coaster, just-clean-enough beaches, and hot dogs that might give you a spontaneous heart attack but taste good enough to risk it."

He chuckles. And holds my hand while we walk toward The Cyclone. No one gives us a second glance, but Nicholas keeps his eyes down or on me, just the same.

"So . . . how does it feel to be out . . . without them?"

He squints against the sun. "Strange. Like I've forgotten something. Like that dream when you show up to class without your trousers. But it's . . . exhilarating, too."

He kisses the back of my hand, the way he did that first morning—and it tingles all over again. After riding the roller coaster and eating hot dogs, we walk back to the bike to get the blanket I stowed there, and head toward the amphitheater.

"Kodaline is playing," I tell him. Nicholas has a bunch of their songs on his phone's playlist.

He stops walking and his face goes almost blank, but his eyes are the brightest green. Then in one move, he pulls me up against him and kisses me breathless.

He presses his forehead against mine. "This is absolutely the best thing anyone's ever done for me. Thank you, Olivia."

I smile—and I know it's radiant. Because that's how I feel. Right now—in his arms. Lit from the inside, like a luminous shooting star that won't ever dim.

Inside, as we stand on line for drinks, "Everything I Do" by Bryan Adams pours from the speakers. "I love this song," I tell him. "It was my prom song—but I didn't get to go."

"Why not?" he asks.

I shrug. "I didn't have time or a dress."

"Didn't your boyfriend . . . Jack . . . want to show you off?"

"He wasn't that into dances."

Nicholas makes a disgusted sound. "Definitely a ruddy tool."

After that, I notice that he keeps his head down, his chin tucked—trying to conceal his face.

I lift his chin. "This hiding-in-plain-sight thing only works if you don't act like you're trying to hide something."

He grins a little self-consciously—and the dimples show up. *Mmm.*

"Most of the people here would never think that you'd be here—and the few that do are probably too chill to make a big deal about it. New Yorkers are cool about celebrity stuff."

He looks at me like I'm nuts. "Not the ones I've seen."

I shrug. "They're probably from Jersey."

Nicholas laughs—a deep chuckle that makes me close my eyes in the hopes of hearing it even better.

But then, a voice comes from behind us—kind of gravelly, probably a smoker, definitely from Staten Island. "Oh my gawd, do you know who you look like?"

Nicholas's hand goes rigid in my mine, but I squeeze it because . . . I got this.

"Prince Nicholas, right?" I tell the aviator-glasses-wearing blond, letting my New York accent come through.

"Totally! You know, I heard he's in town," she points to Nicholas, "and you could so be him!"

"I know! I keep telling him we should move to Vegas—he could get work as an impersonator—but he doesn't listen to me." I jiggle Nicholas's hand. "Do the accent, baby."

With a soft look in his eyes, he speaks in his normal voice.

"I don't have an accent . . . baby."

I laugh loudly and the woman behind us goes crazy.

"Oh my gaaaawd, that's nuts!"

"Right?" I sigh. "If I'm lucky, I'll find out he's some long lost relative."

A register to the right opens up and I step towards it, telling the woman, "Take it easy."

"Have a good one," she says back.

Nicholas throws his strong arm around my shoulder and I lean in, pressing my nose against his shirt, smelling that awesome deliciousness that is him. Then I look up at him.

"See, told you."

He kisses my lips, nibbling in that way that makes me moan. "You're a bloody genius."

"I have my moments."

After we get our drinks—two beers each in red Solo cups—we walk on the grass until we find the perfect spot.

"Now what?" my I-think-he-could-be-my-boyfriend asks.

"Have you ever drunk cheap beer, listened to good music and made out on a blanket, surrounded by a couple hundred people in a field, under the warm sun all afternoon?"

"Never had the pleasure."

I lift one cup. "Today you will."

Nicholas

Olivia and I stumble through the revolving door into the lobby of the Plaza holding hands, stealing quick kisses, giggling like two randy teenagers ditching class for a quickie in the broom closet. Lying with her on the blanket throughout the afternoon, kissing her long and slow, without a care who was watching—because no one was—has made me desperate for her.

And hard. *Christ, so hard.*

So if heads turn our way or camera phones come out, I don't give a single shit. All I care about is my cock pressing against the confines of my jeans, thick and hot and aching.

Anticipation. Has there ever been a sweeter word? I've never had to wait—not really—not for this. I had no idea the buildup, hours of sizzling, teasing delayed gratification, could be such a heady aphrodisiac. My blood rushes and Olivia's eyes sparkle—with lust and playfulness and hunger. We make it into the lift and the moment the doors slide closed behind us, I pick her up into my arms, press her against the wall and ravage her mouth—tasting deeper than I was able to before. She moans around my tongue as I grind against her, relishing the pressure that won't bring any relief. But it's fine—thrilling even—because I know soon she'll be naked and spread out on my bed and I'll be able to drive into her tightness again and again, until we're both worn out.

Or we break the damn bed—whichever comes first.

As the lift rises, I lean back and look down, watching my denim-clad crotch thrust deliberately against her heated center. My cock slides exquisitely *right there*—against her soft, sweet flesh concealed beneath the thin fabric of her black cotton leggings. But I can *feel* it.

And it feels sublime.

With her fingernails biting into the back of my neck, Olivia pulls herself up, lips to my jaw, teeth scraping my stubble. "I want you to fuck me everywhere, Nicholas," she pants. "Come everywhere. Between my legs, on my chest, my mouth, down my throat . . . oh, *oh* it'll be so good. Everywhere, Nicholas."

"Fuck, yes," I hiss, feeling crazier with each word.

Note to self—cheap beer makes Olivia wild. Stock up on the stuff.

With a ding, the lift opens to the penthouse. *Home sweet home.*

Olivia locks her ankles at my lower back and I carry her, palming and kneading that luscious arse, across the foyer, heading for the bedroom. My journey is halted in the living room—by the head of my security team, waiting on the couch, stiff as an angry board and frowning.

And suddenly I don't just feel like a teenager—I feel like a teenager who's been caught sneaking in past curfew, stinking of sex and smokes and liquor.

"So . . . you're back, then?" Logan stands.

"Uh . . . yes. It was a grand show," I tell him. "No incidences occurred; no one seemed to recognize me."

He throws his arms out—imitating a fed-up mum now. He sounds like one, too.

"You could've called! I've been here all afternoon—goin' half out my mind with worry."

And I know it's rude, but the amazing day and the certainty that I'll be balls-deep in Olivia quite soon makes me too happy to care.

I chuckle. "Sorry, Mum."

Logan is not amused. His teeth grind so hard I think I hear it.

"This isn't funny, My Lord. It's dangerous." His eyes shoot to Olivia for an instant, then back my way. "We need to talk. Alone."

"All right, settle down, now. My hands happen to be exquisitely filled at the moment." I give Olivia's arse a squeeze, making her giggle and hide her face against my neck. "We'll talk in the morning, first thing—I promise."

His gaze darts between us, still looking unhappy. But he nods.

"Have a . . . pleasant evening," he grinds out, then marches toward the elevator.

Once he's gone, Olivia peeks out from her hiding spot. "I don't think he likes me anymore."

I kiss the tip of her pert little nose. "*I* like you." Then I push my hips forward while pulling her closer—letting her feel every hard inch. "Do you want me to show you how much?"

Heat rises in her cheeks. "Yes, please." Then she bites her lip and adds with a meek accent. "My *Lord*."

Hearing that from Olivia's lips does things to me. Makes me want to do filthy, dirty things to her. Without further delay, I carry her to the bedroom to get to it.

Olivia

Most of the time Bosco sleeps in Ellie's room. She rings him in with her and shuts the door—just to make sure our dad doesn't trip over him when he staggers in . . . or Bosco doesn't find a way to actually open the refrigerator door and eat until his stomach bursts.

But sometimes, Ellie gets up in the middle of the night to pee and forgets to close the door behind her. And on those nights, Bosco usually ends up in my room. If I'm lucky, he curls up quietly on the foot of my bed or burrows in close to me for warmth like a furry, ugly baby bird.

Usually, I'm not lucky. Because usually, Bosco is hungry when he finds his way into my room, and I'm the feeder. So he wants to wake me up. But he doesn't lick my face or bark to wake me up.

He stares at me.

With those black, beady little eyes he stares hard and long—and though it sounds weird, *loudly.*

And that's the exact same sensation I get later that night while I'm asleep next to Nicholas. Like someone or something is staring at us so intently, it's deafening.

I feel it before I open my eyes. But when I do, I see a woman in white standing at the foot of the bed, gazing down at us.

My lungs scrape to inhale shocked, terrified air. It's more than a gasp—it's a prelude to a scream.

But then I feel Nicholas's hand on my chest, under the covers. Steady, strong—pressing just enough to be meaningful. To tell me he sees her too and that I need to hold it in, hold it together.

The moonlight from the window casts the huge room in a bluish light, making the woman's skin shimmer in a milky glow. Her hair is dark, chopped in a bob to her shoulders, her face bony, with points at her chin and nose, but not unpretty. Her eyes are fixed on Nicholas, dark and shiny—and fucking loony-tunes crazy.

"You're awake." She sighs. "I've been waiting for you to wake up."

Nicholas's throat works reflexively, but his voice—that captivating voice—is smooth and reassuring. "Have you?"

"Yes. It's so good to see you again."

His fingers move just slightly against my sternum, saying it's okay—everything's okay.

"It's good to see you as well," Nicholas replies. "How did you get in, again?"

She smiles, and goose bumps rise all over my skin.

"It was just like we agreed. Work at the hotel, pretend to be a maid until you give me the signal. You always have those boys with you, so I knew, when you started sending them away at night, that was my sign."

Crap.

Her eyes jump to me, as if I said it out loud—but I didn't.

"Who is she?" she asks, sounding the same level of insane but not nearly as happy.

"No one," Nicholas says.

So coldly. So sure. It stops my heartbeat for half a second.

"She's no one."

Nicholas reaches down, grabbing his pants from the floor then slides into them as he stands up. "I want to hear about *you*. Let's go out to the living room and chat."

"But I want to stay here." She pouts. "In the *bedroom*."

"There's a bottle of Krug Vintage Brut chilling. And this occasion definitely calls for Champagne." Nicholas smiles easily.

He's really good. If the prince thing doesn't work out, he could totally be an actor.

"All right." The woman giggles, mesmerized.

Once they leave the room, I throw on the first thing my hands touch—Nicholas's button-down shirt—and dive for the phone on the nightstand to call for help.

But then there's a shattered scream from the living room—piercing and heartbroken.

"What are you doing? Let me go!"

I've never run so fast, or been so afraid.

In the living room, Nicholas has the woman pinned on her stomach on the couch, her hands behind her back.

When he sees me he says, "My mobile's on the bedside table. Dial seven—it'll put you through to security."

The woman cries and screeches like a wraith. "You're ruining it! You're ruining everything!"

And when she pulls against his hold on her hands, Nicholas tries to calm her. "There now, *shhh*. Don't do that—you'll hurt yourself. It's going to be all right."

I don't know why I don't move. It's like my brain's been disconnected from my feet.

"Olivia." The sharpness in his tone makes me blink. "Mobile."

"Right. Right." And then I sprint down the hall and do exactly as he says.

What seems like hours later, the woman is taken away and in addition to the regular security guys, there are policemen and hotel staff in the suite. Nicholas, dressed in a soft gray T-shirt and running pants, talks to them in the living room.

While I, feeling more put-together in my own clothes—jeans and an old peasant top—wait in the bedroom. With Logan.

Logan St. James, the head of Nicholas's personal security team, is the strong, silent type. But in this moment he doesn't really need to say anything—his eyes do all the talking for him.

They're deep brown, almost black, and they glare at me with the withering heat of a thousand dark suns.

I swallow nervously. Where's a trapdoor in the floor when you need one?

"This is my fault, isn't it?" I find the nerve to ask.

"You can't put ideas in his head about not needing security."

Well, that answers that.

"He's an important man, Olivia."

"I know."

"He has to have his wits about him. If anything happened . . ."

"I know that—"

"You *don't* know! You never would've pulled the shit you did today if you knew." Logan closes his eyes, breathing quick—like he's trying to rein in what I suspect is an explosive temper. "He can't afford to be screwed stupid by some New York gash."

Before the nasty words have time to register, Logan is hauled back by his collar and slammed up against the wall—hard enough to make the light fixtures rattle.

Because suddenly Nicholas is there, pressing his forearm right against Logan's throat.

"Speak to her like that again and you'll be picking your teeth up off the floor. Do you understand me?" When the answer doesn't come fast enough, he slams him again—making Logan's head bounce against the sheetrock. "Do you?!"

Logan stares him down, his proud jaw tense and stubborn. Then he gives a jerk of a nod.

Nicholas takes a step back, holding his hands open at his sides. "We both know the fault here is mine, so if you want to rail at someone, have at me. Get it off your chest."

Logan straightens the collar of his suit with a tight, resentful tug.

"Putting on a helmet doesn't change who you are—you can't walk about and pretend it does."

"Yes, I realize that."

Logan's lips purse and his thumb taps his thigh with agitation. "I wanna switch hotels. Quietly."

"All right."

"And I want more men here. I want someone at the coffee shop—it's insane that you come and go to an unsecured location so often."

Nicholas agrees, and Logan goes on.

"I want a tail on Miss Hammond and her sister. It's pure, dumb luck the press hasn't gotten a photo of them yet—and I want them covered when that happens."

"I agree."

"And no more nights in the suite, or afternoons at concerts or wherever the fuck without security. You want to get yourself killed, it won't be on my watch. You let me do my job the right way or you find someone else to do it."

Nicholas's eyes dim—the way an animal's do when it's locked back up in its pen.

"I shouldn't have put you or myself in that position. It was foolish and it won't happen again."

After a moment, Logan nods and then bows to Nicholas. He walks toward the door, but then stops and turns to me.

"I'm sorry. I should'na spoke to you that way. I don't lose my temper often but when I do, stupid shit comes out of my mouth that I don't mean. None of this is your doin'. Can you forgive me, lass?"

I nod my head slowly, still stunned by all of this. "Of course. It's all right, Logan. I . . . I understand."

He nods, gives me a quick smile and leaves, closing the door behind him.

With a weary exhale, Nicholas sits in the chair by the desk. He digs his palms into his eyes, rubbing. Then he lowers his hands—and opens his arm.

"Come here, love."

Greedily, I fly to him. Sitting in his lap, wrapping my arms around him, feeling pure relief when he returns the favor. I tremble against him—shaken to the core.

"Are you all right?" he asks, his breath warm against my neck.

"I think so. It's all just so weird." I straighten up in his lap, needing to sort my thoughts. "I can't believe that woman . . . the way she acted . . . like she was so sure she knew you. Has this ever happened before?"

"A long time ago, a man snuck into the palace, into my grandmother's private dining room."

My heart tightens with concern for a woman I've never met. But I realize that because she means so much to Nicholas, she already means a lot to me.

"He didn't intend any harm—it was similar to the lass tonight. Delusional."

I hold his strong, handsome face in my hands. "I think I'm only just really starting to get it. It's like Logan said—you're important. And I knew that, but . . . I don't think of you as Prince of Pembrook, heir to blah-blah-blah . . ." My eyes touch every inch of his face. "To me, you're just Nicholas. This amazing, sexy, sweet, funny guy . . . who I really care about."

His thumb brushes my bottom lip. "I like that you look at me that way."

Then he clears his throat and glances away. "And I know it's been a hell of a night, but . . . there's something I have to tell you, Olivia, before this goes any further. Something . . . we have to talk about."

Well, *that* doesn't sound good.

But after this, how bad could it be?

Stupid, stupid, stupid last words.

I play with the hair at the back of Nicholas's neck, combing my fingers through the thick, dark strands.

"What is it?"

Nicholas's arms tighten like two bands of iron—holding on like he doesn't want me to get away. And a second later, I know why.

"I'm getting married."

CHAPTER 12

Nicholas

I probably could've phrased that better. *Damn.*

Olivia stiffens in my arms, looking at me with big, dark eyes in a gray face. "You're *engaged?*"

"No. Not yet." She tries to rise, but I hold her close.

"Do you have a girlfriend?"

"Let me explain."

She struggles harder. "Let me up and then you can explain."

I squeeze her tighter. "I like you where you are."

Her voice turns to stone—the kind that's been sharpened into a shank.

"I don't give a flying fuck what you like right now—I want to get up. Let me up, Nicholas!"

My arms drop and she springs away from me, breathing fast, staring like she doesn't know who I am. Like she never did.

And it's as if a civil war wages across her face—half of her wanting to bolt, the other half wanting to hear what I have to say. After a few moments of indecision, the latter has won.

She crosses her arms and sits down on the edge of the bed, slowly. "Okay. Explain."

I tell her the whole story. About my grandmother, the list—about all the birds that need to be killed and how I'm the stone that gets to do the deed.

"Wow," she murmurs, afterward. "And I thought I was the one with baggage." She rocks a bit, shaking her head. "That's . . . crazy. I mean, it's the twenty-first century and you have to do the arranged marriage thing?"

I try to shrug. "It's not as arranged as it used to be. The first time my grandparents were alone in a room together was their wedding night."

"Wow," Olivia says again. "Awkward."

"I at least have the chance to get to know the woman I'll marry. I get to decide—but there are certain requirements that have to be met."

She leans forward, elbows to knees, her silky hair falling over her shoulder. "What kind of requirements?"

"She has to be nobility, even distantly. And she has to be a virgin."

Olivia grimaces. "Jesus, that's archaic."

"I know it is. But think about it, Olivia. My children will govern a country one day, not because they've earned it or were elected—just because they're mine. Archaic rules are the only thing that makes me who I am. I don't get to choose which ones I'll follow." I shrug. "That's life."

"No, it's not," Olivia says quietly.

"It's *my* life."

As she stares at me, her expression hardens and her eyes turn steely, pinning me to the wall. "Why didn't you tell me? All these nights, why didn't you say anything?"

"There was no reason to tell you . . . at first."

She stands up fast, voice rising. "Honesty is a reason, Nicholas. You should have told me!"

"I didn't know!"

"You didn't know what?" she sneers prettily.

"I didn't know it would feel like this!" I shout.

The scorn fades from her face along with the anger. Replaced with rising surprise, maybe a bit of hope. "Feel like what?"

Emotion coils inside me—so new and unfamiliar, I can barely put it into words.

"I have just over four months. And when I walked into that coffee shop, I didn't know that I would end up wanting to spend every single day of it . . . with you."

The corners of her eyes crinkle and her mouth pulls up in the tiniest of smiles.

"You do?"

I cup her cheek and nod. "Talking to you, laughing with you, looking at you." Then I smirk. "Preferably being buried deep in some part of you."

She snorts and pushes at my shoulder.

And then I sober. "But that's all I have to offer. When the summer ends, so do we."

Olivia combs her hand through her hair, yanking a bit.

I sit back down in the chair, adding, "And there's more."

"Oh, Jesus, what? Is there a long-lost child out there somewhere?"

I flinch—even though I know she's joking.

"Logan was right about the press. It's just dumb luck that they haven't snapped your photo yet—a matter of time. And when they do, your life is going to change. They'll talk to everyone you've ever known, dig around into the financial situation of Amelia's, comb through your past—"

"I don't have a past."

"Then they'll make one up," I snap without meaning to.

It's out of frustration—frustration that time is short . . . and the walls are closing in.

"It not easy being my friend; it's even more difficult being my lover. Think of me as a walking exploding bomb—anything near to me will eventually become collateral damage."

"And you seemed like such a catch," she jokes, shaking her head.

Then she stands and turns her back to me, thinking out loud. "So, it'll be like . . . like *Dear John,* or Sandy and Zuko in *Grease?* A summer fling? An affair? And then . . . you'll just leave?"

"That's right." I stare at her back, waiting.

My stomach rolls with nerves. Because I can't remember wanting anything as much as I want this—as much as I want *her.*

When a minute passes without a word, I offer, "If you need time to think about it, I—"

Olivia moves quickly—spinning around, cutting off my words with the urgent press of her mouth, her sweet lips hot and demanding. My hands automatically find her hips, pulling her forward between my knees.

Then she straightens, and runs her finger over her lips, gazing down at me. "Did you feel that?"

The spark, the electricity. The desire that feeds on itself, relishing the relief of contact but always wanting more.

"Yes."

She takes my hand and places it over her breast—where her heartbeat throbs wildly in her chest. "And do you feel this?"

My own chest pounds with the same rhythm.

"Yes."

"Some people go their whole lives without feeling that. We'll get to have it for four months." Her eyes dance with moonlight. "I'm in."

A few days later, I'm scheduled to attend a dinner in Washington, DC—a benefit for the Mason Foundation—and Olivia agrees to accompany me. When she worries that she doesn't have anything to wear, I arrange a shopping trip at the Fifth Avenue Barrister's, after closing.

Because I'm not a gentleman, I help her in the dressing room when the saleswoman is otherwise occupied—giving her a hand, and a finger, getting in and out of all that binding clothing—mostly getting out of it.

She settles on a deep, jewel-tone plum-colored dress that clings to all the best places, and gold strappy heels. They show her a simple diamond necklace that would look fantastic with the outfit. But Olivia won't let me buy it for her. She says Marty's sister has something more suitable she can borrow.

After we leave, it nags at me, though—the necklace. For purely selfish reasons. Because I want to see her wearing it. It—and nothing else.

Talk about prime spank-bank material.

But when the night of the dinner arrives, and I see Olivia for the first time at the helipad, I forget all about the necklace—because she's a vision. Her lips are dark rose and shiny, her midnight hair is swept up elegantly, her tits are high and stunning.

I take her hand, kissing the back. "You look amazing."

"Thank you." She beams.

Until her eyes settle on the helicopter behind me. Then she looks ill.

"So, we're really doing this, huh?"

I fly whenever I have the opportunity, which isn't nearly as often as I'd like. And Olivia's never flown at all—not in a plane or a helicopter. It's exciting to be her first.

"I told you I'll be gentle."

I guide her towards the custom craft that the CEO of an international bank who's friendly with my family was kind—and shrewd—enough to loan me for the evening. "Unless you're in the mood for a rough ride?" I wink.

"Slow and steady, cowboy," she warns. "Or I'll never *ride* with you again."

I help her into the soft leather seat, buckle her harness, and carefully put her headset over her hair, so we can talk during the trip. Her eyes are round and terrified.

Does the fact that that turns me on make me a sick bastard? I'm a little afraid that it does.

With a quick kiss to her forehead, I walk around and climb in. Tommy rides in the back; Logan and James drove ahead earlier to confirm security details and will meet us when we land.

With a thumbs-up to the ground crew, we lift off.

Olivia freezes next to me. Like she's afraid to move or speak. Until we bank to the right. Then she screams bloody murder.

"Oh my God! We're tipping!" She grabs my arm.

"Olivia, we're not tipping."

"Yes we are! Lean! Lean this way!" She shifts her weight away from window—in the opposite direction of our embankment.

And Tommy, trying to be helpful, leans with her.

I level us off, but her grip on my arm doesn't let up.

"Look at the view, sweets. Look at the lights—they're like thousands of diamonds on a bed of black sand."

Olivia's eyes are squeezed shut so tightly, they almost disappear into her face.

"No thanks, I'm good like this."

I pry her hand from my arm, one finger at a time. "All right, here's what we're going to do. You're going to put your hand on the stick and fly the helicopter."

Her eyes spring open. "What?"

"You're afraid because you feel out of control," I tell her calmly. "This will make you feel better."

"You want me to touch your stick so I'll feel better?" she asks incredulously. "Sounds like a line."

I laugh. "No line. But . . . my stick always makes everything better. You can't go wrong touching it." I take her hand and put it on the control, teasing her.

"That's it, grip it firmly, but don't strangle it. Don't stroke, just hold it for now—I know it's big—get used to the feel of it in your hand."

Olivia snorts. "You are a dirty, dirty man."

But she's forgotten to be afraid, just as I was hoping. And after a few minutes, I take my hand off of hers and she holds the control steady, all on her own, her face flushing with happiness.

"Oh my God!" she gasps—and that turns me on, too. "I'm doing it, Nicholas! I'm flying! This is amazing!"

We land about two hours later and drive to the Smithsonian, which has been decorated dramatically with crimson swaths between stone pillars and sweeping spotlights along the red carpet. As we pull up, I see the familiar flash of cameras.

"Front door or back?" I ask Olivia, turning to face her in the limo. I mean the question exactly as it sounds.

She looks at me with a hint of a dry smile. "Don't you think it's a little early to be talking about the back door?"

I smirk. "Never too early for the back door."

She giggles.

But then I turn serious. Because I know just how much I'm about to turn her life upside down . . . and then, in less than four months, I'm going to walk away. Olivia doesn't understand yet, not really.

"If we go in the front door, they take your picture, they find out your name and the world goes mad—but it's our decision. If we use the back door, we may buy a little more time but we won't know when or where or how the discovery will come. Just that it will." I smooth my hand over her knee. "It's up to you, love."

She angles her head, gazing at the window, watching the throng of photographers—seeming more curious than anything else. "What will we say?"

"Nothing. We don't give them anything. They'll write what they want and take their pictures whenever, but we never confirm or deny. And the Palace doesn't comment on the personal lives of the royal family."

She nods slowly. "Like when Beyoncé and Jay Z got married. It was all over the papers: the flower delivery, gossip from the caterers—everyone knew, but until they actually confirmed it, no one really, really *knew*. There was always that shred of possible doubt."

I smile. "Exactly."

After a few moments, Olivia takes a deep breath. And holds out her hand to me. "Sorry to disappoint you, Your Highness, but there won't be any back-door action tonight—front door all the way."

I take her hand and kiss her—sweet and brief.

"Let's go, then."

Olivia does well. She waves and smiles and ignores the questions that get thrown at us—like rice at a wedding. She's concerned that she'll have "fish face" in every photograph—I'm not exactly sure what that is, but it doesn't sound good. And there are spots before her eyes for a long while—I tell her next time to look down, below the flashes, not at them—but otherwise she gets through her first experience with the American press unscathed.

In the ballroom, with a glass of wine in my hand and my palm on the small of Olivia's back, we're greeted by our hosts, Brent and Kennedy Mason.

Mason's several years older than I, but there's an air of youthfulness about him. He doesn't seem like the type to take himself—or anything—too seriously.

They bow—a feat Kennedy Mason struggles with because of her large, round, heavily pregnant midsection. Then we shake hands and I introduce Olivia.

"We're honored to have you here, Prince Nicholas," Mason says.

He means money—he's honored to have *my money*, here—because that's what these things are really about. Although I like the Mason Foundation; their overhead is low and they support programs that actually help real people.

"But we'll miss your grandmother," Kennedy remarks. "She was the life of the party last year."

"She does handle the center of attention rather well," I reply. "I'll give her your kind regards."

The four of us converse easily, until Kennedy puts a hand over her belly, covered by a royal-blue silk gown.

"How far along are you?" Olivia asks.

"Not as far as you'd think," Kennedy laments. "It's twins this time."

"How exciting," Olivia says with ease. "Congratulations."

"Thank you. Our daughter, Vivian, is thrilled. And I am, too—when I'm not too exhausted to feel anything."

Mason shrugs. "That's the risk you took when you married a man with superpowerful sperm."

Kennedy covers her eyes. "Oh my God, Brent, will you stop! You're speaking to a prince!" She turns to us. "Ever since we found out about the twins, that's all he's been talking about—his superhero sperm."

Mason shrugs. "This is the one case where I believe, if you've got it, flaunt it." He lifts his chin to me. "He gets it."

And we laugh.

After the Masons move on to greet the rest of their guests, I ask Olivia to dance—because I want an excuse to put my arms around her, lean in close, and smell her sweet skin.

"I have no idea how to dance." She eyes the large band and bustling dance floor. "Not like that."

I take her hand. "I do. And I'm an excellent lead. Just hold on tight, and let me take you where you need to go."

As with the helicopter, she's hesitant at first—but her adventurous nature wins out.

"O-kay . . . but don't say I didn't warn you."

I have a few drinks with dinner, so we decide to drive back to Manhattan in the limousine. Olivia nods off against my arm before we hit the halfway mark. By the time we arrive in the city, it's so late—or early, depending on your point of view—there's no point in heading to the suite, so I have Logan drive straight to Olivia's apartment.

It's a good thing she slept on the drive home—I don't think she'll be getting back to sleep tonight. Because outside the coffee shop door, over a hundred people are waiting.

For me—and now, her.

From the looks of the cameras, pictures, and posters, it's a mix of fans, autograph seekers, and photographers. It's safe to say Olivia's identity—and address and occupation—are definitely out of the closet.

"Holy shit." She blinks, looking out the car window at the crowd.

"Welcome to my world." I wink.

"Hey, Lo, when are those extra men coming?" James asks from the front passenger seat.

"Tomorrow," Logan replies.

"It's a good thing, lads," Tommy says. "'Cause like the Americans say, I think we're gonna need a bigger boat."

CHAPTER 13

Olivia

Have you ever wondered what overnight celebrity is like? Well, now I'm qualified to tell you. It's like when those technically dead patients on medical shows get zapped by the paddles after the hot, young doctor screams, "Clear!"

It feels just how that looks: jarring, jolting.

It's as if I've been knocked down a black hole into an alternate universe . . . knocked into someone else's life.

And in a way I guess I have—I've been knocked into Nicholas's.

It sweeps me up in its current, and all I can do is remember to breathe and try to enjoy the ride.

The beginning is the hardest. Isn't it always? The first morning I took Bosco out to pee and was surrounded by people I didn't know—asking me questions, taking my picture. James and Tommy stayed with me and I saw a different side to them. The way they moved and spoke—sharp and intimidating—backing the crowd up, just daring anyone to try to get past them.

It was hard for Nicholas to leave me that morning. His eyes were ravaged—because he wanted to stay, to be the lion who kept the hyenas at bay. But he knew his presence would just make it so much worse—turn the curious crowd into a frenzied mob.

The next day, Nicholas has his people—the Dark Suits, he calls them—contact the NYPD, to make sure there's no loitering on the sidewalk in front of Amelia's. We institute a "must purchase to stay" policy in the coffee shop, because most of the dozens and dozens of people who visit are more stalker than customer. In spite of that, there's a definite uptick in business, which is a double-edged sword. Ellie starts to pitch in after school, taking opposite shifts with me, which is a huge help. And Marty, as always, is a calm, hilarious rock I can always count on. They both bask in the chaotic attention, posing for pictures and even signing the occasional autograph when requested—though I just think that's weird. They're both also able to keep their mouths closed when questions are asked—confirming nothing about me and Nicholas.

On the third day after all hell broke loose, I come upstairs to the apartment, finished with my shift and so looking forward to a hot shower. Well, lukewarm—but I'll pretend it's hot.

But when I pass Ellie's room, I hear cursing—Linda Blair-*Exorcist*-head-spinning-around kind of cursing. I push open her door and spot my sister at her little desk, yelling at her laptop.

Even Bosco barks from the bed.

"What's going on?" I ask. "I just came up but Marty's down there on his own—he won't last longer than ten minutes."

"I know, I know." She waves her hand. "I'm in a flame war with a toxic bitch on Twitter. Let me just huff and puff and burn her motherfucking house down . . . and then I'll go sell some coffee."

"What happened?" I ask sarcastically. "Did she insult your makeup video?"

Ellie sighs, long and tortured. "That's Instagram, Liv—I seriously think you were born in the wrong century. And anyway, she didn't insult me—she insulted you."

Her words pour over me like the ice-bucket challenge.

"Me? I have like two followers on Twitter."

Ellie finishes typing. "Boo-ya. Take that, skank-a-licious!" Then she turns slowly my way. "You haven't been online lately, have you?"

This isn't going to end well, I know it. My stomach knows it too—it whines and grumbles.

"Ah, no?"

Ellie nods and stands, gesturing to her computer. "You might want to check it out. Or not—ignorance is bliss, after all. If you do decide to take a peek, you might want to have some grain alcohol nearby."

Then she pats my shoulder and heads downstairs, her blond ponytail swaying behind her.

I glance at the screen and my breath comes in quick, semi-panicked bursts and my blood rushes like a runaway train in my veins. I've never been in a fight, not in my whole life. The closest I came was sophomore year in high school, when Kimberly Willis told everyone she was going to kick the crap out of me. So I told my gym teacher, Coach Brewster—a giant lumberjack of a man—that I got my period unexpectedly and had to go home. He spent the rest of the school year avoiding eye contact with me. But it worked—by the next day, Kimberly found out Tara Hoffman was the one talking shit about her and kicked the crap out of her instead.

I'm not used to people hating me. And from the looks of it, thousands—make that *tens of thousands*—of people have signed up to do just that.

@arthousegirl47 says I have a fat ass. @princessbill thinks I'm a money-hungry slut. @twilightbella5 suspects my mother was an alien because my eyes are too big and weird. And @342fuckyou doesn't care what the rumors are—Nicholas is hers.

Oh, and look at that—I've got my own personal hashtag. #OliviaSucks.

Great.

I slam the laptop closed and back away like it's a spider. Then I dive for my phone on the bed and text Nicholas.

Me: Have you seen Twitter? I'm being Photoshopped in effigy.

He takes only a few seconds to respond.

Nicholas: Stay far away from Twitter. It's a cesspool.

Me: So you have seen it?

Nicholas: Shield your eyes. They're jealous. As they should be.

Me: There you go being modest again.

Nicholas: Modesty is for the weak and dishonest.

And just like that, my unease about the nasty comments starts to fade away, brushed from my mind like a hand through smoke.

This—this summer affair with Nicholas—is real and solid and here right in front of me. And with its expiration date looming, I'm not going to waste time, not a second of it, worrying about meaningless words from faceless ghosts that I can't change, and in the end, don't matter anyway.

Nicholas: Just avoid the Internet altogether. Television too. Go outside (bring security). It's a beautiful day.

If I had a nickel for every time my mother said those same words, minus the "security" part, I'd be as rich as . . . well . . . Nicholas.

Me: Okay, Mom.

Nicholas: Not working for me. But if you want to call me Daddy, I might be able to get into that.

Me: Ewwww.

Nicholas: Have to go in a minute, love. Meeting about to start. I'll tell Barack you said hello.

Me: SERIOUSLY???

Nicholas: No.

I shake my head.

Me: You're a royal ass, you know that?

Nicholas: Course I do. The Archbishop of Dingleberry certified it the day I was born.

Me: Dingleberry??? You're messing with me.

Nicholas: Afraid not. My ancestors were a sick, twisted bunch.

Me: lmao!

Nicholas: Speaking of asses, I'm imagining mine pumping between your spread legs right now. Can't stop picturing it. What do you think about that?

As soon as I read the words, I'm picturing it too. And *God* . . . heat coils low in my belly, unfurling and expanding until my thighs tingle deliciously. My hands tremble a little as I type back.

Me: I think . . . we should stop thinking and start doing.

Nicholas: Brilliant. Go to the hotel, the front desk will let you up. Be in my bed when I get back in two hours.

Excitement bubbles through me like freshly poured Champagne.

Me: Yes, My Lord.

Nicholas: If your goal was to have me meet the Sisters of Mercy sporting a stiffy—mission accomplished.

I hop off my bed, heading for the bathroom to freshen up and change. On the way, I type the only reply I can manage.

Me: Awkward. Xo

Days pass, and what was once jolting and new becomes . . . routine. A regular day. It's amazing how quickly that happens, how quickly we adapt.

I have a boyfriend—at least for the summer. A sexy, gorgeous, fun boyfriend, who also happens to be a royal. That complicates things, but what would probably be most surprising to the Twitterverse and Facebook commentators and reporters is how . . . normal . . . it all feels.

We go to lunch—surrounded by security, but it's still just lunch. We visit a children's ward in a hospital. The kids ask him about his crown and his throne, and I get a round of applause when I juggle for them—something my dad taught me in Amelia's kitchen years ago. I let Nicholas buy me clothes—casual but expensive clothes—because I don't want to embarrass him by looking shabby when we're photographed together. I wear my sunglasses whenever I'm outside and I barely hear the questions that get shouted by reporters anymore.

This is my normal now.

But just when I thought we'd fallen into a comfortable routine—everything changed with just one question: "Feel like going to a party?"

Lightning flashes in the sky and warm rain pours down around us as James holds the umbrella over our heads when Nicholas and I step out of the car. The club is sleek, all polished onyx lacquer and stainless steel, windowless, with soundproof walls so as not to ruffle the feathers of the more conservative and ultra-wealthy neighbors. There's a velvet rope outside the door, and a mammoth bouncer in a dark suit and sunglasses waits with his own umbrella. But there's no line to get in—and it's not because of the weather.

It's because this club is invite only. Every night.

Inside, "My House" by Flo Rida blares and it looks like it's a costume party—an eighties costume party. I see a Madonna, two Princes—the *Purple Rain* kind, not the Nicholas kind—and a bunch of Cabbage Patch dolls that are a whole lot sexier than any of the pictures I've ever seen. The main room isn't huge—a few velvet couches and a mirrored bar along one wall. And there's a stage, with colored overhead lights that flash in time to the music.

Ellie would say, it's *Lit*.

On the stage is Tom Cruise from *Risky Business*—a guy wearing sunglasses and a pink button-down and, yep, tighty-whities. He dances and waves his arms, getting the packed dance floor even more riled up.

"Do you see that guy?" I yell above the music, pointing toward the stage.

Nicholas' handsome face is tight. "Oh, I see him all right."

I take a second look. And then I choke.

"That's your brother?!"

The call Nicholas took in the suite library was from one of the Dark Suits in Wessco—letting him know his brother had arrived in Manhattan.

"That's him," Nicholas practically growls.

"Wow."

"He's a brat," Nicholas explains, shaking his head. "He's always been a brat."

"Okay, in the problematic younger sibling department, you win."

Nicholas speaks to a security guy—one of the new ones, whose name I don't know yet. The guy nods and rushes off, and Nicholas grasps my hand. "Come on."

We make our way around the dance floor, through the tight crowd of bodies. We pass a Debbie Gibson and a Molly Ringwald from *Pretty in Pink*, then stop on the side of the stage. When the song ends and a techno mix of Fetty Wap takes its place, the security guard talks to Tom Cruise . . . uh . . . Henry on the stage.

His head snaps up—staring at Nicholas.

And then, slowly, like he doesn't quite believe what he's seeing, he smiles.

It's a sweet little-brother smile that tugs at my heart.

He practically runs to us, jumping off the stage with feline dexterity and landing on both feet just a few yards away. His lips move—I can't hear him, but I can read what he says.

"Nicholas."

Then he's here. I step back so I don't get trampled, as Henry tackles his brother in a bear hug, lifting him off his feet. They hug for a few moments, smacking backs, then Nicholas pulls away—slipping the sunglasses off his younger brother, searching his face and reading his eyes.

And a concern shadows Nicholas's features at what he finds.

But he smacks his brother's cheek affectionately and says, "It's good to see you, Henry."

Henry's the same size as his brother, with the same broad shoulders and long legs. I see the resemblance in the cheekbones, but their coloring is different. Henry's hair is blond, shaggy-long and curling, and his eyes are a brighter shade than Nicholas's.

Like wild grass after a rainstorm.

But they have the same bearing—both stand tall and straight, with an air of authority around them like a halo. Or a crown.

"Did you forget to put on trousers?" Nicholas asks.

Henry laughs and flashes—with a big, all-encompassing smile that makes me want to smile too.

"It's a costume party." He steps back, framing Nicholas's suit-clad form with his fingers, like a cameraman on a movie set. "Let me guess . . . you are Charlie Sheen from *Wall Street?*"

And then, Prince Henry's attention turns to me. His *interest* turns to me.

"And who might you be?"

I quickly review my 1980s movie mental database and pull the hair tie from my bun, shaking out the curls. "I could be . . . Andie MacDowell from *St. Elmo's Fire*."

He brings my hand to his lips, kissing the back. "Quick on your feet—I like that. How are you on your knees, love?"

Oh yeah—he's definitely Nicholas's brother.

Nicholas shoves him, kind of playfully—kind of not. "This is Olivia."

"Is she my welcome-home present?"

"No." Nicholas scowls. "She's . . . with me."

Henry nods, and rakes his eyes over me, head to toe. "I'll trade you."

"Trade me?"

He points at me, then spins his finger around the room. "Her . . . for any girl here."

Nicholas shakes his head. "I haven't seen you in a long while—don't make me smack you right away. Behave yourself."

I step closer. "He's teasing, Nicholas." Then I take pity on the younger brother—and throw him a bone. "And you're not one to talk about behaving . . . considering the first night we met you offered me money for sex."

Nicholas flinches.

And Henry's jaw drops. "No! My brother did that? Mr. Prim and Proper in Public—I don't believe it." He nudges me with an elbow. "How much did he offer you?"

I grin evilly at Nicholas and he looks like he wants to strangle me just a little bit.

"Ten thousand dollars."

"You cheap bastard!"

"I was pissed!" Nicholas defends himself. "If I'd been sober, the starting bid would've been much higher."

And we all laugh.

Nicholas puts his hand on his brother's shoulder. "I'm in the penthouse at the Plaza . . . let's get out of here. Come back with us."

Henry's demeanor changes then. Like the thought of being in a quiet place for too long panics him . . . but he's trying to hide it with a forced smile. It's only then that I notice the gauntness of his cheeks and the dark circles below his eyes.

"I can't. I just got in—lots of people to see, shots to drink, lasses who'll be so disappointed if I leave without fucking them. You know how it is."

Nicholas's eyes narrow. "When can I see you, then? There's much to talk about, Henry. How about breakfast, tomorrow?"

Henry shakes his head. "I don't eat breakfast. Since I was discharged, I make it a point not to rise before noon."

Nicholas rolls his eyes. "Lunch, then?"

Henry pauses, then nods. "All right, Nicky. Lunch it is." He turns his head, looking into the crowd. "I have to go—there's a gorgeous little piece I promised to trade costumes with."

And he points to a redhead in a Little Mermaid getup.

Nicholas grasps his brother's shoulder, like he doesn't want to let go.

"Until tomorrow."

Henry pats his brother's back and nods to me, then disappears into the crowd.

In the limo, on the way back to the hotel, Nicholas is quiet, the sound of the pelting rain and occasional thunder filling the silence.

"Are you okay?" I ask.

He rubs his lower lip with his finger, thinking. "He looks awful. Like he's haunted . . . being hunted . . . hiding from something."

I don't want to tell him it will be all right; that's too flippant, too easy. So I give him the only thing I think will help—a hug.

While the rain smacks against the windowpane outside, Nicholas thrusts into me from behind, long and slow. His thighs are spread, bracketing my closed ones; I feel them tighten each time he pushes forward, pressing his chest against my back, his pelvis against my backside, like he can't stroke deep enough. But then, suddenly, he pulls out of me and the bed jostles as he straightens, rising up on his knees behind me.

He taps my back with his wet cock. "Roll over, love."

My languid limbs do his bidding without question and I watch as Nicholas strokes his fist up his thick hardness—taking the condom off and tossing it over the edge of the bed to the floor. He's very careful about the condoms. I started birth control a few weeks ago, and even though it's definitely effective now, he still uses them every time.

Nicholas taps against me with his erection—this time my stomach—then he shifts up my torso, keeping most of his weight on his knees.

And his eyes—God—his eyes smolder with lust, burn bright even in the dim light of the room, gazing down at me, planning his next move. I don't have to wonder long what that move will be.

Nicholas cups my breasts in each large hand, and a bolt of tingling sensation streaks a path to my pelvis. He pinches my nipples and I moan loudly, arching my back for more. I feel him shift above me, then his cock slides against my sternum. Oh God, I've never done this before.

But I want it—with him. I want to watch his hips piston, feel the thick heat of his come on my chest, hear his groans of pleasure.

And a moment later, Nicholas gives me everything I want.

He presses my breasts around his cock, gentle at first, then tighter, harder, like he's barely holding onto his control. I open my eyes because I have to see—I need to keep this picture in my mind forever. It's the hottest, most erotic image. His chiseled body moves faster, glistening with a fine sheen. His fingers dig into my flesh and little growls escape from deep within his throat. His eyes are the deepest green, hooded by those long, pitch-black lashes. They flare wide when my hands cover his, taking over for him. I don't want him to hold back. I want him to move, to grind on me. Take me. Take everything.

My hands push my breasts closer, tighter around the slick cock slipping between them. He grips the headboard and it shakes when he uses it for leverage as he fucks my chest. His jaw is clenched and his brow is soaked with sweat—little drops fall on my collarbone, surprisingly cold compared to the slide of his heated skin.

A burst of air puffs from his perfect lips. Air and the sound of my name. Falling, begging, demanding. "Olivia, *fuuuuck*—Olivia."

I've never seen anything more amazing—more intense—than this man moving above me. Making love to me in this dirty, thrilling way—giving us both more pleasure than I've ever known. The headboard beats against the wall once, twice, then Nicholas's back arches and his head tilts back and he roars. His come, warm and thick, splashes across my chest, trickling down my neck, mixing with my own perspiration.

The moment his beautiful dick stops pulsing, Nicholas stretches out on top of me, covering my body with his, pressing us together, taking my face in his hands and kissing me wildly. It's sticky and messy and perfect.

Later that night, there's a knock at the door, waking us both from a sound sleep. I don't know what time it is, but it's still dark outside and the rain has stopped. Nicholas slips into his robe and opens the door.

Logan stands on the other side, his face is lined with worry. "Sorry to disturb you, Your Grace—but you're gonna want to see this."

He picks up the television remote from the nightstand and turns on the news. I squint against the blaring light and it takes me a few seconds to focus, but when I do—*holy shit!*

"Son of a bitch," Nicholas curses, because he sees it too.

His brother, Henry, is being led into the police station in handcuffs, and the banner at the bottom of the screen reads: PRINCE HENRY & ENTOURAGE ARRESTED.

CHAPTER 14

Nicholas

C*ousin Marcus is an imbecile . . . Cousin Marcus is an imbecile . . .*

I force the thought to repeat in my head. As a reminder that I can't kill my brother when I see him. Wessco needs a backup plan and regardless of his most recent antics, Henry's still our best option.

What a fucking cock-up.

It's almost three in the morning when we reach the police station. Olivia yawns next to me, her hair wild, looking beautifully, wearily rumpled in a sweatshirt and denim shorts. Thankfully, there's a back entrance to the station, because the front is already mobbed. The arrest of a royal is big news—particularly in America, where the only thing they like more than building their celebrities up is tearing them down.

I shake hands with a burly, gray-haired officer who regards me with coarse sympathy. "Follow me."

He leads us down a corridor, through two barred gates that open with a buzz, then into a cubicle area with a desk and a younger-looking officer stationed there. Down the hall are bar-lined doors on the left and the right—holding cells.

I hear the distinct sound of my brother's voice. He's singing.

"Nooobody knows the trouble I'm in . . . Nooobody knows till tomorrow."

Cousin Marcus is an imbecile . . . imbecile . . . imbecile . . . imbecile. And Louis Armstrong is rolling in his grave.

The younger officer gives me some forms to sign. "The rest of the paperwork will be sent to the embassy," he says.

"Thank you," I tell them tightly.

And then Henry is brought in—he's drunk, unsteady on his feet, his hair in need of a cut and a comb—and I war between concern and condemnation. What the fuck is wrong with him?

He zeroes in on Olivia with a stupid smile.

"Olive. You're still here—I'm so glad. You can help me walk—I'm having a bit of trouble managing at the moment." Then he flings his arms around her, almost making her knees buckle.

I yank him away from her and toss him to Logan. "Help him walk."

Then I warn, "Behave yourself or you'll be wheeled out on a stretcher when I'm done with you."

He makes a face, mimicking my words like an eight-year-old, and my hand literally twitches to smack him. But I don't. Because we're in public—and while he has zero respect for his position in the world, I do.

Princes get the piss beaten out of them in private.

But I can't stop myself from hissing. "Cocaine, Henry? Is that why you're such a disaster, that what you're into these days?"

It was found in the car he was traveling in—without security—with several "friends," when they were pulled over for driving erratically.

He stands with Logan's assistance and his bleary eyes rise to mine. "No," he scoffs. "I wouldn't touch the stuff—I'm high on life." He rubs his forehead. "It was Damian Clutterbuck's. I met up with him while he was on holiday in Vegas and he came to New York with me. I didn't know he had it on him. He's a . . ." His brow crinkles as he looks to Olivia. "What's the word again? Pitz . . . patz?"

"Putz?" Olivia suggests.

Henry snaps his fingers. "That's the one. Damian's a putz."

"*You're* a putz." I lean down over him. "You're being deported."

"Oh well . . . thank God for diplomatic immunity, then." He shrugs. "I was thinking of visiting Amsterdam anyway."

"Oh no, little brother," I warn him. "You're going home. If I have to tie you like a hog and box you up in a crate to get you there, it's the only place you're going."

He inhales deeply, like he's about to announce something profound, but all he comes out with is, "You're very cranky, Nicholas."

I rub my eyes and shake my head. "Shut up, Henry."

And then we head out the way we came in.

Because of the time, I take Olivia home before I deal with Henry. We park around the back just in case—although, since the NYPD has been assisting us, the crowds outside Amelia's have been smaller. I walk her in, and Henry insists on tagging along.

I suggest locking him in the trunk, but Olivia—sweethearted as she is—overrules me.

And it looks like tonight is the night for little brothers and sisters, because when we walk into the kitchen from the alley, we find Ellie Hammond covered head to toe in flour and sugar. Her hair looks like a powdered wig from the Revolutionary period and "Pressure" by Billy Joel plays so loud in her earbuds, we can hear it across the room.

She bounces and sings to the music, tossing white powder on the counter . . . and everywhere else.

Then she turns around. And screams loud enough to wake the dead.

"Jesus Christ!" She yanks her earbuds out. "Don't do that to me—you took like ten years off my life!"

Olivia looks around the room, blinking. "What are you doing, Ellie?"

The little blond smiles proudly and lifts her chin. "I'm helping. I mean, I know I've been doing the afternoon shifts but I figured, all this time you've been doing all the morning prep by yourself. So I got Mom's recipes out and figured I'd help with that too. There's only a few months left until I leave for school."

Olivia's face goes soft and grateful. "Thank you, Ellie." Then she looks around the disaster area again. "I think."

She engulfs the sugarcoated blond in her arms. "I love you."

"I love you too," Ellie says into her shoulder.

When she lifts her head, she spots my brother, leaning against the wall. With wide eyes, she shakes the flour from her hair like a dog shuddering off water.

"Oh my God, you're Prince Henry."

"I am, pet. But the more important question is, who are you?"

"I'm Ellie."

My brother smiles salaciously. "Hel-lo, Ellie."

"She's a minor," I tell him.

And the smile drops. He pats her head.

"Goodbye, Ellie."

Henry turns around. "I'll go wait in the car, after all." He yawns. "I could use a nap."

The moment we walk into the suite, Tommy descends on us. "The Queen's on the line. On Skype, Your Grace." Anxiety rings in his voice like the ping of a tapped crystal glass. "She's been waiting. She does'na like to be kept waiting."

I nod briskly. "Have David bring me a scotch."

"Oh, me too!" Henry pipes up.

"He'll have coffee," I tell Tommy.

And I think Henry sticks his tongue out at me behind my back.

I head into the library and he follows, seeming marginally closer to sober—at least he's walking straight and unassisted now. I sit behind the desk and open the laptop. On the screen, my grandmother looks back at me, wearing a pale pink robe, hair in rollers and a hairnet, gray eyes piercing, her expression as friendly as the grim reaper's.

This should be fun.

"Nicholas." She greets me without emotion.

"Grandmother," I return, just as flat.

"Granny!" Henry calls, like a child, coming around the desk into view. Then he proceeds to hug the computer and kiss the screen.

"Mwah! Mwah!"

"Henry, oh, Hen—" My grandmother swats the air with her hands, like he's actually there kissing her.

And I do my damnedest not to laugh at them.

"Mwah!"

"Henry! Remember yourself! My gracious!"

"Mmmmmwah!" He perches, grinning like a fool, on the arm of my chair, forcing me to shift over. "I'm sorry, Grandmother—it's just so good to see you."

She doesn't say anything at first, but peers closer at the screen—and I know she's seeing all the same things I see about him. Something close to worry pinches her lips.

"You look tired, my boy."

"I am, Your Majesty," he says softly. "Very tired."

"Then you'll come home, so you can rest. Yes?"

"Yes, ma'am," he agrees.

Then her voice goes sharp. "And I never want to hear a whisper about you and narcotics again. Do I make myself clear? I am very disappointed in you, Henry."

And he actually looks contrite. "It was a friend's, Granny, not mine. But . . . it won't happen again."

"See that it doesn't." She turns her attention to me. "I'm sending the plane for you. I want you back at the palace in twenty-four hours."

My stomach plummets and it feels like my throat is closing in on itself.

"I have commitments here that—"

"Break them," she orders.

"No, I won't do that!" I snap back, in a way I've never spoken to her in my life. In a way I would knock another man on his arse for speaking to my Queen.

"Forgive me, Your Majesty, it's been a long night." I scrub my hand over my face. "I have commitments here that need to be handled delicately. I've . . . made promises. I'll need a bit more time to tie things up."

She glares back like she can see right through me—and I have no doubt that she can. She's definitely heard all about Olivia by now, if not from the Dark Suits then in the papers and online.

"Forty-eight hours and not a minute more," she says—her tone similar to the sound of a handler snapping the leash on his errant charge.

My hands fist on the desk, out of view. "Very well."

After we say our pleasantries, we disconnect and I close the screen. I boil in silence, until Henry speaks.

"So . . . what's new?"

And I smack him.

Open-palmed and so hard the sound bounces off the walls.

He reaches for the spot I'd struck. "Fuck! What the hell you'd do that for?"

He jabs me with his elbow. I punch him in the ear. And the next thing I know we're rolling on the floor, cursing and pummeling each other.

"Spoiled little fucker!"

"Miserable bastard!"

At some point during the scuffle, Logan pops his head in. "Never mind." Then he backs out and closes the door.

Eventually, we call a draw, both too bloody worn out to continue. We sit on the floor, breathing hard, leaning back against the wall.

Henry tests his lip where a trickle of blood drips. "You're really angry?"

"Yes, Henry, I really am. I was planning on staying the summer here, in New York. With Olivia. Thanks to your little stunt, I can't do that now."

He looks confused. "I thought you said she was underage."

And I pray for patience. "That was Ellie. Olivia is the dark-haired one."

"Oh." I feel him staring at me. "You really like her, then."

"Yes," I agree, my voice rough and raw. "I do. And when we leave, I'll never see her again."

"But, why not?"

And it's only then that I remember how long he's been away. There's so much he doesn't know.

I look my little brother in the face . . . and he does seem frighteningly tired.

"A lot's been happening. I'll explain tomorrow, after you've gotten a good night's sleep."

I stand up, brush my trousers off and straighten my collar. "I'm going to see Olivia. I'll be back in a bit."

Just as I reach the door, Henry calls my name. I turn around.

"I'm sorry, Nicholas. I'm sorry that I ruined all your plans."

And the bracelets on my wrist seem to hug tighter.

I walk back to him and crouch down. Then I roll up my sleeve, unclip the silver bracelet and pool it in his upturned palm. Henry's eyes mist over as he looks at it.

"You kept it safe for me."

"Of course I did." I rest my forehead against his, squeezing the back of his head with my hand. "It's good to have you back, Henry. Everything's going to be all right now, yeah?"

"Yeah."

It's just after sunrise when I pull up to the back alley behind Amelia's. Again. The sky is still pink and gray and I know the sign in the front window still reads CLOSED. I walk through the now spotless kitchen and follow the sound of soft music to the dining area.

Then I cross my arms, lean against the propped open doorway, and enjoy the show.

Dolly Parton and Kenny Rogers sing on the television—a song about islands in streams—and Olivia sweeps the floor with a broom, unaware of my presence.

But she's not just sweeping—she's dancing.

Arse-shaking, hip-swiveling, knee-bending, gorgeous dancing—occasionally sliding down and up the broomstick like it's a pole or a microphone.

Christ, she's lovely.

My lips stretch into a smile and my cock goes so hard it's painful.

Silently, I slip up behind her, wrapping my arms around her waist, making her squeak and the broomstick crack when it hits the floor. She turns in my arms, her hands locked around my neck—pressing against me, all warmth and goodness.

"I'm a much better partner than a broomstick."

She arches her pelvis, pressing and rubbing against my erection.

"And better endowed." Olivia reaches up and kisses my mouth so sweetly. "How's Henry?"

I stroke her hair and gaze at her face, feeling like a hole's opening up inside me. A barren, painful emptiness that's an echo of how it felt when they told me my mother was gone.

"I have to leave, Olivia. We have to go home."

She stops dancing. Her delicate hands grasp me tighter, and her mouth narrows into a sad little bud.

"When?" she asks in a soft voice.

"Two days."

Her gaze touches my eyes, my lips, my jaw, as if she's committing them all to memory. Then she lowers her head, resting her cheek against my chest, right over my heartbeat.

Dolly and Kenny sing about sailing away together . . . to another world.

"That soon?"

I press her closer. "Yes."

We start to rock together in time to the music—and suddenly the words just come out.

"Come with me."

Olivia's head pops up. "What?"

And the more I talk, the more brilliant the idea becomes. "Spend the summer in Wessco with me. You can stay in the palace."

"The palace?"

"I'll take care of everything. I'll show you the city—it's beautiful, especially at night. It'll take your breath away. And I'll take you to the seaside—we'll swim naked in the waves and freeze our arses off."

She laughs, and I'm laughing with her.

"It'll be an adventure, Olivia." I run my thumb across her cheek. "I'm not ready for this to be over yet. Are you?"

She leans into my touch. “No.”

“Then say yes. Come with me.”

Consequences be damned.

Her eyes are shiny with hope, her cheeks flushed with excitement.

She holds me close and tells me, “Nicholas . . . I . . . I can’t.”

CHAPTER 15

Olivia

It's not the answer he's expecting. It's not the one I want to give. But it's the only option. His holds me roughly, almost desperately.

"I want to, Nicholas—God, I want to. But I just can't leave."

There's a crash from the kitchen—the harsh gong of metal pans hitting the floor. And then my little sister literally falls into the room.

"Oh yes, you can!"

"Ellie, what are you doing?"

She picks herself up. "Eavesdropping. But that's beside the point—there's no way you're not going to freaking Wessco, Liv! For the summer! In a palace!" She spins around like she's in an imaginary ball gown. "It's a once-in-a-lifetime chance and you're not missing it. Not for me or for Dad or for this place. No way."

I love my sister. No matter how much of a pain in the ass she can be, when it counts, her heart is golden all the way. But, that doesn't change the fact that in this case, she's wrong.

"You still have weeks of school left. You can't run this place by yourself."

She crosses her arms. "Marty can be here when I'm not. Business is frigging rocking. Thanks to all the illicit publicity of your torrid royal affair, we can afford to pay Marty for the extra time. And we can finally hire a dishwasher!"

"It's not just about running the coffee shop, Ellie. There's the books to keep."

"I can do that."

"Ordering supplies and stock."

"*Pfft*—I can totally do that."

"Dealing with the vendors and delivery guys." I turn to Nicholas. "Some of them are total assholes." I look back and forth between them. "And a thousand other little things that you're too young and inexperienced to handle on your own."

Ellie has no comeback for that, but she looks like she's about to cry.

Until Nicholas raises his finger. "I have someone who can handle it with her."

The next afternoon, I'm in my room—packing—because I'm going to Wessco. Forget butterflies, there's a flock of sparrows flapping and swirling in my stomach—a strange brew of excitement and nervousness. I've never flown on a plane. I don't even have a passport, but Nicholas made some phone calls and got me an emergency one this morning. I've never been on vacation, not counting the occasional weekend trips to the shore with my parents. And this isn't just any summer vacation—I'm going to another country, with its prince! To stay in a palace!

Talk about "holy fuck" moments. This one's surreal.

And still, it would all be perfect—except for one thing.

My father. Sitting on my bed, following my every move with a worried, disapproving, guilt-heavy expression.

"I can't believe you're really doing this, Liv. It's insane. You don't even know this guy."

Defensiveness makes me jam my hairbrush into my duffel bag. "I do know him. You met him once too, though you probably don't remember."

"I'd expect this kind of thing from your sister—she's always been flighty. But not you."

In goes my favorite nail polish, bras and underwear, the rose and jasmine perfume Nicholas likes. "Exactly. I've always been the responsible one—carrying the water, holding down the fort. And now I have the opportunity to do something amazing." I can't stave off the hurt that seeps into my voice. "Why can't you be happy for me?"

His eyes, the same color as mine, cloud over. "We need you here. Your sister needs you—you can't push your responsibilities off on her."

"Ellie will be fine. I've made arrangements—she'll have all the help she needs."

Logan St. James and Tommy Sullivan, Nicholas's security men, are staying for the summer. Staying to watch over Ellie and the business, to make sure she's not taken advantage of and help her in any way they can. Nicholas asked them to do it for him—as a personal favor—and they both agreed. Tommy seems particularly eager to stay. The Brooklyn girls, he says, really like his accent. I've seen for myself that they're good guys—and Nicholas trusts them, so I do too.

"It's selfish," my father bites out, standing up.

And I almost fall over. "Selfish? That's rich, coming from you."

"What the hell is that supposed to mean?"

My voice rises and nine years of resentment comes screaming out.

"We loved her too! You're not the only one who lost her! The day Mom died, Ellie and I lost both of you. You . . . you just checked out, Dad. Mom didn't have a choice, but you did!"

He dips his head, not meeting my eyes. "This guy, Prince whatever-he-is . . . he's going to hurt you, Liv. When he leaves—and mark my words, he'll leave—it'll break you. I don't want to see that happen to my little girl."

I zip up my bag and throw it over my shoulder. "I know exactly what I'm getting into with Nicholas. We're going to have something wonderful for as long as we can. And when it's over, I'll look back and I'll remember that there was something special and amazing in my life . . . even if only for a little while. And then I'll come back and life will go on."

I turn at the door, looking in the eyes of the man who was my hero.

"I won't break, Dad. I'm not you."

Down in the coffee shop, Nicholas waits by the door, while Ellie, Marty, Logan, and Tommy stand shoulder to shoulder along the wall.

I approach Tommy and Logan first, touching both their arms. "Thank you for doing this. I know it's not your job, but I appreciate it so much."

Logan nods, his gaze steady. "Don't worry, we'll look after things here. We'll take care of her."

"And have fun in Wessco," Tommy says, smiling brightly. "Maybe you'll like it enough to stay."

Logan shakes his head, exasperated, making me think he knows more than he lets on. "Shut up, Tommy."

I move to Ellie and Marty. Ellie flings her vibrating self at me. "I'm going to miss you! But I want you to do everything—go everywhere!"

I squeeze her as tight as I can, and my heart breaks just a little bit.

"I'm going to miss you too. I know you can handle this, Ellie—you're going to do great. But be careful and listen to Marty and Logan and Tommy, okay?"

"I will."

Then Marty scoops me up, hugging me right off my feet. "Have the time of your life, girlfriend. And remember—pics or it didn't happen." He gives me a dirty wink and tilts his head toward Nicholas. "Take *all* the pics."

I laugh and move toward the door. But a voice behind me freezes me in place.

"Livvy."

My father appears in the doorway. He walks up to me slowly and then wraps his arms around me in a strong, solid hug.

Just the way he used to . . . before.

He kisses my temple and whispers in my ear, "I love you, honey."

And I feel the tears come and overflow. "I love you too, Daddy."

A moment later, I pull away. I hiccup and give him a smile. Then I walk to Nicholas's side.

As we turn to leave, my father calls out, "Nicholas. You take care of her."

There's a distinct edge to his voice when he answers.

"Yes. I will."

Then he takes my hand and leads me out the door.

The tears are still flowing as I climb in the limo—where Henry is waiting.

"Oh no, she's crying. I hate it when girls cry. What did you do, Nicholas?" Then he raises his glass—filled with amber-colored liquid and ice. "Don't cry, Olive. Drink!"

In the seat beside me, Nicholas tugs me closer. "Are you all right, sweets?"

"Yeah, I'm okay. I'm just really emotional." I wipe under my eyes. "And I'm scared about the plane."

Nicholas smiles, flashing his dimples. "You can hold onto my stick the whole time."

I giggle, and Henry makes a grossed-out sound.

"Is that a sexual reference? Bloody hell, it's going to be a disgusting summer."

On the runway, outside the big, scary plane, Bridget, Nicholas's personal secretary, greets us. She reminds me of a favorite aunt—in a cheery violet suit and with an attitude that's both playful and efficient.

"Oh my," she stutters when Nicholas first introduces me. "I didn't know you were bringing guests, Your Grace." Then she recovers—or at least tries to. "The Queen will be quite . . . surprised."

She gives my hand a firm, friendly shake. "It's a pleasure to meet you, Miss Hammond. If there's anything you need during your visit, please don't hesitate to ask."

I have a feeling taking my first flight on a private plane is going to ruin me for "normal" air travel forever. It reminds me of Old Rose in *Titanic* when she said, "*The china had never been used. The sheets had never been slept in . . .*"

The interior of *Royal I* is all royal crests, creamy leather, and shining, polished wood. There are two fully appointed bedrooms in the back, and not just any bedrooms—these are beds fit for a queen. Literally. There are also two marble bathrooms with showers. The main fuselage has a dark wood desk and a computer and phones, a long leather couch and groups of four reclining seats that swivel around with gleaming wood tables in between.

Two uniformed stewardesses are there to cater to our every whim—and they look like supermodels, both blond and tall, with little navy caps perched on their heads. The pilot bows to Nicholas before he enters the cockpit and I notice a change in Nicholas's demeanor—or maybe it's just a reaction to how the staff treat him—with supreme leader deference. Respect bordering on worship. He leads the way . . . and everyone else gladly follows.

Takeoff is . . . absolutely terrifying.

I keep my eyes closed the entire time and choke down the urge to puke. It's a good thing I hold Nicholas's hand instead of his "stick," because my grip is so strong I would've crushed it.

And it's one of my favorite parts.

In the air, after hot towels and cocktails, Nicholas asks Bridget about things at home. Political things. Her eyes skirt briefly to me and then Henry, and I wonder if this is classified information.

But then she tells Nicholas, "The Queen has doubled her efforts to persuade Parliament to pass the trade and jobs packages, but talks remain . . . acrimonious. They want concessions."

Henry sits up from the couch where he's lounged, plucking chords on a guitar—Nicholas told me once that Henry "fancied himself" the "rock star royal."

"What kind of concessions?" the younger prince asks.

"Concessions from the Queen," Bridget says uncomfortably. "And the royal family."

"Two years is a long time to be gone, Henry," Nicholas explains. "Things have changed since you were last home."

"Parliament has always been filled with a bunch of useless wankers." He scoffs.

Nicholas tilts his head. "Now they're worse."

A little later, Bridget instructs me on protocol. How to greet and behave around the Queen . . . and the heir apparent.

"You'll have to be mindful of your interactions when you're in public. Everyone knows the princes; you'll be observed constantly. And we are a conservative country. No 'PDA's' as you young people call them."

Huh. Sounds fun.

"We're not that conservative," Henry objects. "You and Nicholas will just have to find a nice shadowy nook to get your public freak on. Or, if you really need to stick your tongue down someone's throat, I'm always available."

Nicholas glares heatedly at his brother, who shrugs innocently. "Just putting it out there." Then his voice drops to whisper to me, "No one cares what I do."

"Of course they care," Bridget consoles him.

"You just don't care that they care," Nicholas says dryly.

And Henry plays the intro of "Stairway to Heaven" on his guitar. "One of the perks of being second born."

It's just before sunset when the plane lands in Wessco. A warm breeze, with a hint of ocean, fills the cabin when the plane doors are opened. There's a carpet on the steps leading down to the tarmac—purple, the color of royalty. Soldiers in full dress of red coats and shiny gold buttons and black boots gleaming in the fading sunlight line the path from the plane to the airport.

Nicholas steps out first—I hear a deep bellowing call to attention from an officer on the ground and the snaps of hard heels against the stone pavement as the soldiers salute. I take a minute when I step out behind him to look, take it all in, so I'll remember.

But then, as we get closer to the airport door, there's another sound, this one much more ominous. It's jeers and shouts—and it's coming from a crowd of people on the side of the building, cordoned off behind a fence. Some of them hold signs, and all of them look angry. And they're yelling and cursing—at us.

What starts as a roar of indecipherable disdain becomes more individualized as we get closer.

"I don't have a job and you're flying about in a fucking private plane! Bastards!"

"Fuck you! Fuck the monarchy!"

I stay close to Nicholas's back. He reaches behind, holding out his hand without turning, searching for me. I take it and he squeezes.

"Stick it up your arses boys, and your grandmother's too!"

Nicholas's back stiffens, but he keeps walking forward.

Henry has an altogether different reaction.

Though the security men try to keep him away from the fence, he swaggers right up to it and calls one of the men forward with a flick of his hand.

Then Henry rears back . . . and spits on him.

And the world explodes.

People scream, the fence rattles, soldiers close in around us—jostling and pushing us toward the door. Nicholas pulls me forward by my hand, tucking me safely under his arm as we're practically carried into the building.

Inside, after the shouts are drowned out behind the closed door, Nicholas turns on his brother.

"What the hell were you thinking?"

"I'm not going to let them talk to us that way! You didn't do anything, Nicholas!"

"No, I didn't!" Nicholas shouts. "Because what I do matters. My words, my actions, have consequence. Spitting on people isn't going to win them over to our side!"

Henry's green eyes flare and his cheeks are red with anger. "Fuck them! I don't need them on our side."

Nicholas rubs his eyes. "They're our people, Henry. Our subjects. They're angry because there aren't any jobs. They're terrified."

Henry glares at his brother, stubborn and unyielding. "Well, at least I did something."

Nicholas snorts. "Yes. You made it worse. Congratulations."

Taking my hand, he turns on his heel, telling James, "Olivia and I will ride alone in the first car. He can follow behind in the car with Bridget."

No one hesitates to follow the command.

And that is our welcome to Wessco.

In the limo, Nicholas pours himself a drink from the cool blue-lit minibar in the center console. He's all tense muscles and scowly jaw. I rub his shoulders.

"Are you okay?"

He scrapes out a sigh. "I will be. Sorry about that, love." He plays with my hair. "This isn't how I wanted to bring you home."

"Pfft." I wave my hand. "I grew up in New York, Nicholas. Protestors and crazy people on every corner. That was nothing—don't worry about me."

I want to bring the playfulness back into those eyes, that delicious, devious smirk to his beautiful lips. I think about sliding down to the floor between his knees and giving him a blow job. But, to be honest, with the driver in front and his brother and so many staff members following behind us, I just don't have the guts to follow through.

Instead, I squeeze up close to him, letting my boobs press against his arm. He kisses my forehead, breathing me in. And that seems to make him feel better.

About an hour later, we pull onto the road that leads to the palace. Nicholas tells me to look out the window to see—and I'm gob-smacked.

I've never used that word before: gob. *Gob-smacked.*

There was never a reason—but, holy shit, there's a reason now. I've seen pictures of the castle but seeing now is . . . unreal. The massive stone building is lit from the bottom up—practically a hundred beams of light illuminate the façade. More windows than I can count dot the front, framed by a giant black-and-gold-trimmed iron gate. I can't see clearly from here, but there seem to be intricate etchings, statues and carvings built into the stone. There's a lighted fountain in the center, shooting half as high as the castle itself. A tall, stately flagpole holds the waving burgundy and white Wessco flag. And flowers! Thousands, maybe millions, of flowers surround the front and the sides, bursting with color even in the night.

"It's a castle!"

Yeah, not the most astute thing I've ever said.

Nicholas just chuckles. So I grab his arm, shaking. "I don't think you understand—you live in a freaking castle!"

"Technically, it's a palace. Castles were built for defense, palaces more for the monarch to hold court in appropriate grandeur."

And Jesus, I want to stick my tongue down his throat.

"Have I told you how hot it is when you roll out the royal facts?"

His eyes light up. "No, but it's good to know. I know things that will keep you perpetually wet and quivering."

As sexy as that response is, I just have to look back at the palace as we get closer. "It has a moat, Nicholas!"

"Yes. Generally palaces don't—but my great-great-great-great-grandfather had it dug because he 'liked the look of it.' I went swimming in it once when I was eleven. Got strep throat—

lesson learned. But there is a lake in the back, so skinny-dipping is definitely on the agenda."

"How many rooms does it have?"

"Five hundred eighty-seven, not including the staff bedrooms." He leans up and licks the shell of my ear, making the wet and quivering plan come to fruition. His next words almost make me come on the spot. "And I want to fuck you in every one of them by the end of the summer."

"That's ambitious," I tease, nuzzling him. "Do you plan on stopping to feed me?"

His hand skims down my back, cradling my ass. "You'll be well taken care of, I promise."

I promise. You know what that is? Yep—Famous. Last. Words.

CHAPTER 16

Nicholas

My grandmother is a night owl. She requires only three to four hours of sleep. It's a common trait in leaders, captains of industry, top-notch executives—and psychopaths.

So, although it's past the dinner hour, I know she'll want to receive us the moment we step through the palace door. And I'm not wrong. Her personal butler, Alastair, ushers us into the gold receiving room in her private quarters. We gather there—me, Olivia, Henry, Fergus, and Bridget—and we wait.

No matter how long I'm away, a month or a year, the Queen never changes. She looks exactly the same. It's a comforting and frightening thought that strikes me when she appears in the doorway—gray hair perfectly coifed, demure pink lipstick, a light green skirt and jacket with a diamond and emerald broach pinned to the lapel.

And though she looks the same, she appears particularly unhappy at the moment. Her gray eyes are solid as they scan us—the color of a concrete wall. She settles on Henry first, calling him forward.

He bows. "Your Majesty."

She stares at him, taking him in—and for a moment, her cold stare cracks. "Welcome home, my boy. You've been gone too long."

"Yes ma'am," he says softly, giving her a weary smile.

She doesn't embrace him as some would expect—it's not her way. But she touches his shoulder, reaches up and pats his cheek, covers his hands with her own and squeezes. For a queen, that's a hug.

She moves Henry to the side and steps closer to us, eyes landing on me expectantly. I bow and bring Olivia forward, holding her hand.

"Your Majesty, may I introduce my guest, Olivia Hammond."

There's not a shred of doubt that she's already been informed of Olivia's presence. The Queen's eyes drag over her, from head to toe, the way someone would look at a shaggy, wet stray dog that showed up on their doorstep.

I bristle—but hold back. If I react too strongly it will only make things worse.

Bridget and I explained the proper protocol to Olivia on the plane. She's nervous, I can tell, stiff and frozen—but she tries.

"It's an honor to meet you, Queen Lenora." Olivia bows her head, bends her knees and dips—then pops back up quickly.

And my grandmother glares.

"What was that?"

Olivia glances back at me, unsure, then returns her attention to the Queen.

"It was a curtsy."

One sharp, gray brow rises. "Was it? I thought perhaps you had gas."

That's the trouble with monarchs—people rarely have the balls to tell them when they're being fucking rude. And even if they do—the monarch doesn't have to give a shit.

"She will not do," my grandmother says, her gaze slithering to me.

For Olivia's sake, I try to play off the comment. "Don't worry—I'll show Olivia around, introduce her to everyone . . . she'll *do* just fine."

And then I put an end to the shit-show, taking Olivia's hand and putting myself between her and the Queen. Relief washes through me when Olivia smiles up at me, unscathed by the disapproving claws.

"It's been a long flight, Olivia. Go upstairs to your room and get settled."

I already explained that decorum required Olivia to have her own bedroom, but I'm not concerned. I have my ways.

"I'd like a private word with you, Prince Nicholas," my grandmother says.

I give her a scathing smirk. "Just one? I thought for sure there'd be dozens."

"Fergus," I call, "take Olivia to Guthrie House, please. Put her in the white bedroom."

And it's like the air freezes in place—crystalizing with tension.

"Oh yes," my grandmother says softly. "There will be many more than one."

I ignore her, and pet Olivia's hair reassuringly. "Go on now, I'll be along shortly."

She nods, and then, because she is naturally polite, Olivia peeks around me and says to the Queen, "Thank you for having me here. You have a lovely home."

Henry lowers his chin to his chest, muffling a chuckle. And Fergus leads Olivia away.

After Henry goes off to his own quarters, Bridget exits with a bow to my grandmother and me—and then we're left alone.

In a staring contest.

Surprisingly, she blinks first.

"What are you playing at, Nicholas?"

"I'm not playing at all, Your Majesty."

Her voice slices the air, bordering on shrill. "You have a duty. We agreed—"

"I'm well aware of my duty and our agreement." My tone is no less sharp, but respectful. "You gave me five months—I have three left."

"You should be spending that time reviewing the list I gave you. Vetting the women who may one day take their place at your side. Becoming familiar with—"

"I will spend the time I have left as I see fit. And I see fit to spend it with Olivia."

Even when my parents died, I've never seen my grandmother lose her composure. And she doesn't entirely lose it now—but she's close.

"I will not entertain one of your whores!"

I take two steps closer to her, dropping my voice.

"Be very careful, Grandmother."

"Careful?" she says the word like it's foreign. A foreign, dirty word. "Are you . . . are you *warning* me?"

"I won't have her insulted—not by anyone. Even you." Our eyes clash like swords, throwing sparks. "I can make life very difficult for you. I don't want to do that, but understand—I will if you do not treat her with the respect I'm telling you she deserves."

And with that, I release a breath and turn to leave the room.

Behind me, the Queen asks softly, "What in the world has gotten into you, Nicholas?"

It's a decent question. I'm not feeling at all like myself lately. My arms rise at my sides, a helpless shrug. "The beginning of the end has gotten into me."

With a curt bow, I excuse myself and walk away.

I find Olivia in the white bedroom, standing in the middle of the room, turning slowly—gazing at the walls and curtains and furniture. I try to imagine how it looks to her. The drapes are a gauzy opal, light enough to lift on a breeze from the floor-to-ceiling windows. The dresser, vanity and four-poster bed shine in the light of the crystal chandelier with an almost silvery sheen, the wallpaper is soft white with a ribbon of satin overlay and the antique artwork on the walls is framed in bleached wood.

She startles a bit when she catches me watching her. "Jesus, you're like a ninja—give a girl some warning, will you?"

I knew she'd look beautiful in this room, that the color palette would accentuate all her exquisite features. But she's even more stunning than I imagined—stealing my breath. Her wavy hair is an even deeper shimmery black, her eyes a darker blue, shining at me like two sapphires on a bed of velvet.

"Do you like it?" I finally manage to ask. "The room?"

Her gaze climbs up and all around. "I love it. It's . . . magical."

I walk in closer.

"So, did you get reprimanded?" she asks, only half joking. "Your grandmother sounded just like my mom used to when she was waiting for our friends to leave so she could yell at us."

I shrug. "I survived."

"What's the deal with the white bedroom? When you said it, her face turned so hard I thought it'd crack."

I wander over toward the window, leaning on the sill. "It was my mother's. No one's stayed in here since her."

"Oh."

And I hear the way my words must sound.

"But don't take that in a creepy Norman Bates, mummy-issues kind of way—it's just . . . it's the prettiest room in the palace. It suits you."

Olivia nibbles at her bottom lip. "But your grandmother's not happy about that, is she? Is that why I'm here, Nicholas? Am I a big fuck-you to the Queen?"

"No." I wrap one arm around her waist, melding our bodies together. My other hand delves into her hair, holding it with my fingers, tilting her face up to look at me. "*No.* I want you here because I want *you.* And I'd still want you here even if my grandmother was thrilled about it."

"She doesn't like me."

I've never blown smoke up Olivia's arse—I have more entertaining ideas for that particular body part—and I'm not about to start now.

"She doesn't like anyone. Most days, she doesn't even like me."

That gets a smile out of her.

I step backwards, leading Olivia by her hands. "This room is magical in other ways, you know." I turn around to the bookshelf along the wall behind me. I give the corner a tug, and swing it open to reveal the passageway. "Look."

Olivia's eyes go round and excited, like a child on Christmas morning first glimpsing the presents under the tree.

"It's a secret passage!"

She ducks her head inside, flicking the light switch there, illuminating the thirty-foot corridor leading to the closed door on the other end.

"That's so awesome! I didn't know palaces really had these!"

Her joy makes me laugh, makes my chest feel light.

"They do. And this one leads to an even more magical place." I wink. "My bedroom."

She laughs and bites her lip. "Did you install it? Your parents?"

"Oh no, it's been here long before us. Most likely so visiting dignitaries or princes could have their wicked way with a mistress without giving the staff something to gossip about."

"So cool. It's just like in *Harry Potter and the Sorcerer's Stone*." Olivia sighs, glancing at the passage again.

"There's one more thing I want to show you." I lead her by the hand to the curtained balcony doors. "Besides the obvious benefits of the passage, I wanted you in this room," I open the doors and Olivia gasps, "because it has the best fucking view ever."

Her mouth goes slack as she stares out over the rear of the property, which resembles the utopian landscape of a fairy wonderland. The stone paths lit every few feet by thousands of hanging lanterns. The fountains, the mazes of greenery, the abundance of flowers of every shape and size—cherry blossoms and roses and tulips so large they hang over like colorful bells. In the distance is the pond, shining in the moonlight like a bath of liquid silver.

I stare at her stunned expression. "Not too shabby, huh?"

"It's the most beautiful thing I've ever seen."

I don't take my eyes off Olivia's face. "Me too."

She turns toward me, reaches up slowly, and we kiss. The touch of Olivia's mouth is soft and supple and tastes like homecoming. I lean down to deepen the kiss, until . . .

"Christ, you two are like piranhas constantly eating each other's faces. Can you detach for a moment?"

My brother walks in and helps himself to a full glass of brandy on the tray by the fireplace.

I give Olivia an apologetic smile. "What do you need, Henry?"

"My rooms are being renovated, so Grandmother said I'm to stay in one of your guest rooms."

Five hundred eight-seven rooms, and she puts him in Guthrie House. With us. Subtlety was never the Queen's style.

"And I'm bored," he whines. "Let's give Olive a tour—that'll be something to do, at least. And we can go see Cook—ask her to make the biscuits I like so much. I've missed them."

He means cookies, for you Americans out there.

It's not a bad idea. If Olivia's going to be here for the summer, I want her to feel comfortable, introduce her to the staff.

"Are you too tired for a walkabout?" I ask Olivia.

"No, not even a little. But I should unpack."

I wave my hand. "The maids will take care of that."

She taps the side of her head playfully. "That's right, the *maids*—how could I forget." She picks up my hand. "Then let's go. Show me your palace."

We start in the kitchen and work our way up. Cook, a large, sweet, boisterous woman who's worked at Guthrie House since my father was a lad, tackles my brother on sight. She admonishes him for being gone too long—and then gives him a whole tray of his favorite biscuits.

Then Cook greets Olivia with another engulfing hug. Her name's not really Cook, but Henry and I don't know her by anything else. She has the thickest brogue I've ever heard, and Olivia smiles politely and nods while Cook jabbers on—though I can tell she has no idea what she's saying.

Olivia's already met Fergus, but on the way to show her the ballrooms, we pass Mrs. Everston, the upstairs maid, and make introductions. We also run into Winston, the head Dark Suit—who's in charge, in control and in-the-know of every nook and cranny of the royal family inside and outside the palace. Henry once heard that he was an assassin in his early years, and based on his calculating, cold attitude, I believe it. We see Jane Stiltonhouse, the Palace travel secretary—a woman who reminds me of a human butter knife. She's thin, sharp, and has a shrill voice like the sound made when two pieces of silverware are rubbed together.

Olivia's eyes glow and her mouth is perpetually open in awe as we go from one gilded historic room to another. Our last stop is the portrait hall, a long corridor with framed oil paintings of past monarchs, their families and ancestors. Olivia gazes timidly down the shadowy hall, so long and dark, the end can't be seen—it just trails off into total blackness.

"You grew up here, in the palace?" she asks.

"I was sent to boarding school at seven—lived most of the year there. But vacations and summers were spent here."

She shivers. "Weren't you ever afraid that it was haunted?"

"The portraits are on the creepy side. But it's not scary once you get used to it—Henry and I used to scooter down this hallway all the time."

"How cute," Olivia says quietly. "Just like the kid from *The Shining*."

I laugh. "Minus the elevator filled with blood, but yeah, just like that."

Her eyes slide over my face, gleaming with naughty intentions. She whispers, so Henry can't hear, "When you laugh like that, those dimples show up—it makes me want to climb up your body and lick them."

I immediately grow thick and hard at the idea. "Feel free to lick anything you want, anytime."

Later that evening, Cook makes us a giant bowl of salted-caramel popcorn. I take particular joy in watching Olivia suck on her sticky fingers between bites.

I remind myself to kiss Cook tomorrow.

The popcorn is for the movie Olivia wanted to watch. Although we have a media room, Olivia preferred my sitting room, in our pajamas, in an oasis of pillows and blankets on the floor. Henry joins us.

"I can't believe you guys have never seen *Beauty and the Beast.* This place is just like the castle—Cook could be Mrs. Potts, Fergus could be grumpy Cogsworth," Olivia says, twisting her black locks into a messy bun on top of her head.

"The thing is, pet, we have cocks," I smirk. "Those of us so endowed really weren't interested in Disney cartoons."

"You've seen *The Lion King,*" she argues.

"Well, yeah . . . there's lions in it. And murder."

"And kings," Henry adds. "The title says it all."

We watch the film, or more to the point—Olivia watches the film, smiling gently the whole way through. I mostly just watch her. Because I'm happy that she's here. I almost can't believe it. Every time I let myself, a warm, gushy feeling surges in my chest—like my heart is melting. And I feel . . . content.

When the music soars and the credits start to roll, Olivia presses her pretty hands to her chest and sighs. "Never gets old—that will always be my favorite Disney movie."

Henry finishes his fifth brandy. "It was all right, but I prefer *The Little Mermaid.*"

Olivia raises a black brow. "I thought 'cocks' didn't like princess cartoons?"

"Have you seen Ariel?" Henry asks. "My cock likes her a whole bunch."

Olivia wrinkles her nose. "Gross. Although I did read a book once that said most guys like Ariel."

"I should read that book," Henry declares.

"Fantastic idea, Henry. Why don't you run along and find the book in the library?" I slip my finger under the strap of Olivia's flimsy little pajama top, rubbing the soft, smooth skin. I lower my voice. "I'm feeling . . . beastly at the moment."

Olivia meets my eyes and smiles. She likes the idea.

Unfortunately, Henry heard me, and he makes a disgusted face.

"Is that supposed to imply doggie-style?"

Since he already heard me loud and clear . . .

"Yes."

He throws off the blankets and stumbles for the door. "That position is ruined for me now—and I really liked it. Thanks a lot."

I lock the door behind him, and Olivia and I act out our own interpretation of *Beauty and the Beast* for the rest of the night.

CHAPTER 17

Olivia

In the morning, Nicholas has Fergus bring us breakfast in bed. I hide in the bathroom when he actually brings it in. Nicholas says I'm being silly, that I have to get used to the fact that Fergus doesn't give a shit that I'm in his bed or that we had crazy, fantastic, would-make-the-Beast-blush sex last night.

But I can't help it—I don't know if I'll ever get used to servants and the . . . intimacy . . . of having them around all the time. Besides, come September, there won't be anyone bringing me breakfast in bed or hanging my clothes. Maybe it's best that I don't get used to it.

After breakfast, Nicholas showers, and I perch myself on a cushioned bench in his huge bathroom to watch him shave—with a straight razor, of course. And there is something so deliciously manly—raw and sexy—about watching him shave that perfect jaw. Shirtless. With nothing but a fluffy towel around his hips.

It makes me want to lick him—over his chest, up his neck—*again.*

Then he gets dressed, in a navy suit and a burgundy tie, and goes to work—at the offices on the other end of the palace. He said his schedule was "mad" because of his extended stay in New York, but he'd be back to have dinner with me in the

Guthrie House dining room. And after, he was taking me to a party.

Speaking of which, Nicholas said I would have a "schedule" of my own today: a stylist and personal dresser would arrive at ten to take care of everything I'll need.

And that's where I am now.

In a chair, in the white bedroom, getting facialed and trimmed, polished and buffed, waxed and massaged. I glance in the mirror and realize I look just like Dorothy in *The Wizard of Oz*—getting worked over and beautified—by a gaggle of Emerald City beauticians.

Afterwards, my skin feels smoother and softer than I ever thought possible. My muscles are amazingly relaxed; aches and pains that I didn't even recognize have completely disappeared.

When the last of the beauty brigade zips up her enchanted bag and leaves, I look in the mirror again.

And—*wow*.

I still look like me—but a shinier, more elegant version of me. My eyebrows are clean and arched, my fingernails are gracefully painted, my skin glows even without a trace of makeup, my hair is gleaming and bouncy without a single speck of split ends.

I look cultured. Sophisticated. *Rich*.

Yep, that last one's the bull's-eye. This is why rich people always look put-together—because they can afford to hire a team that specializes in *putting them together*.

Just as I caress my cheek one last time, there's a knock at the door. I open it to find Fergus.

"The personal shopper is here, Miss Hammond." He kind of snarls, in a way that reminds me of Bosco. "Shall I send her up?"

I automatically look around the room, checking for strewn clothes—out of habit. But the maids who flit by every hour or so would never let that happen.

"Uh . . . sure, Fergus. Thank you."

He dips his head and walks down the hall.

A few minutes later, a tiny, chirping, beautiful French woman walks through my bedroom door. She looks young, maybe twenty, and reminds me of Ellie—if my sister had brown hair and spoke French. Her name is Sabine, but in my head I call her French Ellie.

Half a dozen male assistants carry in racks of clothes—dresses and pants and blouses and skirts. Then they go back downstairs and bring up bags of lacy undergarments—bras, panties, garters and stockings. Finally, a tailor's platform is carried in, I assume for me to stand on. By the time the last assistant leaves, the white bedroom isn't so white anymore, it's covered in fabrics of every color.

It's like the entire Women's department at Barrister's exploded in here.

Sabine holds up a piece of paper. "Bridget."

It's a list, from Nicholas's secretary, Bridget. A list of events that I'll need clothes for: the party tonight, a polo match, another party, brunch, afternoon tea with the Queen.

Oh Jesus. Not for the first time, I wonder what the hell I was thinking.

But then I stop—because I'm here. And while I am, I'm going to be *here*. Be unafraid. Do everything, see everything—with Nicholas.

Trying on clothes is exhausting. I never realized it—until I'd done it for two hours straight. Just as I'm ready to ask for a break, the bedroom door opens—without a knock—and Prince Henry glides in. Carrying long-stemmed glasses and two bottles of Dom Perignon. He's wearing a black cashmere sweater with a white collared shirt underneath and tan slacks. It's a neat, preppy look that stands in contrast to his wild, wavy blond hair and the tattoo on his forearm peeking out beneath his rolled-up sleeve.

Henry Pembrook is a walking, living contradiction.

"Everyone's working," he says, holding up the bottles and glasses. "I'm bored. Let's get day-drunk, Olive."

I look down at Sabine as she fixes the hem on a pair of trim black pants, smiling around the pins in her mouth.

When in Rome . . . *or Wessco . . .*

"Okay."

After the corks are sprung and the glasses full, Henry looks through the intimate apparel laid out on the bed. "This would look fantastic on you. And that one, there." He plays with the pink ribbons that tie the front of a daring black lace bustier. "Do these open? Oh, they do—definitely this one—my brother will jizz in his pants when he sees you in it."

He snatches a peach silk baby-doll nightie, shoving it in his pocket. "This color's all wrong for you."

"I don't think it's your size, Henry," I tease. "Have you always liked women's clothes?"

He smirks, reminding me of his brother. "I like women. I know women. I know one woman who would like this bit very much, and I would enjoy seeing her wearing it."

Then he moves to the rack of cocktail dresses, going through them one by one. "Crap, crap, crap . . ."

Sabine is offended. "This is a Louis La Cher original."

"Oh." Henry wiggles his eyebrows at me. "Expensive crap."

Then he stops at a sexy black satin number with lace trim. "This one. Definitely." He holds it up in front of me. "In silver. It was made for you. Are you're staying until the end of the summer?"

"That's the plan."

He glances to Sabine. "She'll need a ball gown, too. Preferably something in pale blue." Then he explains, "For the Summer Jubilee. It's a party held every year here at the palace—a true ball—all top hats and tails and heaving bosoms. Everyone attends."

"Then I guess I'll need a ball gown."

Henry approaches Sabine slowly, speaking in a string of rapid French. I have no idea what he's saying, but I understand the blush that comes to her cheeks and the enamored glaze in her pretty eyes when she smiles and says, "*Oui*, Henry."

While Sabine sorts the keepers from the rejects and sets up another round in the dressing area, Henry and I sit on the snow-white couch in the sitting room.

"So it's just that easy for you, huh?" I ask him—referring to whatever proposition Sabine just agreed to with the naughty prince.

"Yes, just that easy."

Then he downs his Champagne like a shot. And immediately refills his glass. In the sunlight, the planes of his cheeks cast shadows and his eyes, for a moment, take on a distant sheen. What were the words Nicholas used? *Haunted. Hunted.*

And the big sister in me opens her mouth.

"Are you okay, Henry? I know we just met, but . . . your brother . . . he's worried about you."

He forces a laugh. "Of course I'm okay. That's my job—my one job—to be okay all the time."

My hand finds his shoulder. "But it's all right not to be. I mean, everyone loses it once in a while—no one's okay all the time." I sip my Champagne and add, "Except, probably, serial killers. And nobody wants to be around them."

Henry laughs easier this time, and his soft green eyes drift over my face.

"I like you, Olivia. Truly. You're sweet and . . . naturally honest. That's rare around here." He guzzles half his glass, then takes a big breath and says, "So because I like you, I'm going to give you some advice, all right?"

"Okay."

"Don't get attached to my brother."

Everything inside me goes cold, as though my bones turn to hollow icicles. But my palms are sweating.

"He doesn't belong to you. He doesn't even belong to himself."

I swallow. "I understand that."

"See," he wags his finger, "you say that, but it doesn't seem like you understand it—not when you're looking at him."

When I don't reply, Henry goes on.

"I took a theology course in university—a discussion of the concept of heaven and hell. One theory is that heaven is being in the presence of God, having the light of his face shine down upon you. And hell is when he turns away and leaves you—and you know you'll never feel the perfection of that warmth and love again." His voice lowers. "That is what Nicholas is like. When he shines on you, the whole world is shining. But when he's disappointed—and because his standards are higher than God's, he will always, eventually, be disappointed . . . that is a fresh, cold hell."

It's hard to swallow. Nerves, I guess. Fear of the unknown.

So I cling to my truth.

"That's not the Nicholas I know."

"Yes, he is different with you. Happier. More . . . free." Henry rests his hand on my knee. "But you must remember—whether you know it or not—that's the man he is."

After dinner, another stylist shows up to get me ready for the party. She blows my hair out into long, silky tresses and coils the ends into big, bouncy curls. But I do my makeup myself—I don't like feeling too gooped up.

Nicholas doesn't seem excited about going—"required to make an appearance," he says. But he's very excited about my dress—a shimmery, gray slip-dress that swoops in front, offering a peek of cleavage.

Around nine, we pull up to a mansion on a hill. No, not a mansion, an estate—with a historic-looking house about half the size of the palace, but still enormous. Security swarms—secret service–type men in tuxedos wearing little wire earpieces, but Nicholas still brings his own men, with James now leading the pack.

Nicholas holds my hand—I'm not sure if that qualifies as "PDA," but he doesn't seem concerned. He leads me through a cavernous foyer, down a hall, through the open doors of a ballroom. And into a casino! A fully stocked, even better-than-Vegas, wood-gaming-tables, giant-betting-wheel casino. The room is crowded, with groups of elegantly dressed people, every one young and beautiful, shouting and laughing and drinking.

I'm surprised I'm able to spot him so easily, but I see Henry by the bar, looking not quite as dashing as his brother, but handsome in a black tuxedo—surrounding by a group of men and women hanging on his every word.

"So, what do you think?" Nicholas whispers against my ear, giving me goose bumps.

"I think . . . I know how Alice felt when she fell into Wonderland."

He winks. "We're all mad here."

A swirl of red silk flashes in front of my eyes—engulfing Nicholas is a cackling hug. She has thick, honey-colored hair and is as tall as Nicholas—like an Amazon woman and every bit as stunning. It's the girl from the "marriage watch" piece on television and the *People* magazine pictures—the "old friend" Nicholas mentioned.

"There you are, you bloody sod! I blink and you disappear to the States for two months. How are you, love?"

Nicholas smiles. "Hello, Ezzy. I'm very well."

Brandy eyes, as sparkly as the dangling rubies in her earrings, fall to me. "I see that. Aren't you a pretty little thing."

Nicholas introduces us. "Lady Esmerelda, this is Olivia Hammond. Olivia, meet Ezzy."

"Hi, Ezzy."

She shakes my hand in a friendly grip. "Lovely to meet you, sweets. Tell me, are you a virgin?"

Nicholas groans. "Ezzy."

"What? I'm just making conversation." She elbows him. "If you want a shot at this sorry sack, the V-card has to be in pristine condition. Is it, Olivia?"

I stand up tall. "Does anal count? If it does, I qualify."

Esmerelda's red lips open wide in a contagious laugh.

"I like this one, Nicky."

Nicholas laughs too, and something like pride glows in his green eyes.

"So do I."

He grabs two glasses of wine off a waiter's tray and hands me one.

But then another woman approaches us—another blond in a royal-blue gown, with soft, pretty features and ice-blue eyes. A sedate, uncomfortable silence falls over Nicholas and Ezzy.

"Hello, Nicholas." Her voice is delicate—like a wind chime.

Nicholas nods. "Lucy."

Her eyes fix on me. "Aren't you going to introduce me to your new toy?"

His jaw tightens. "No, I'm not."

She gives a tiny shrug. "No matter." She holds out her hand. "I am Lady Deringer, and you are?"

"Olivia Hammond."

"I heard about you. The coffee waitress." Her mouth purses and her gaze flicks to Nicholas. "You always did enjoy slumming it, didn't you, darling?"

It's the "darling" that gets to me—that pokes at the flesh of my heart like a thorn.

"That's enough, Lucy," Nicholas says sternly, in that deep, authoritarian voice.

It has no effect on her, at all.

"No, I don't think it *is* enough," she hisses like a cornered cat. "Not even close."

Her eyes slide back to me and she leans in.

"He'll crush you, you know. It's what he does. Breaks you, then crushes you into dust with the heel of his shiny shoe."

It's the way she says it that's most disturbing. Gently. And smiling.

"Oh for fuck's sake, Lucille, get over it," Ezzy barks, waving her hand. "Be gone before somebody drops a house on you."

She raises her glass to me. "Remember that I told you so."

And then she drifts away, like smoke after a blaze.

I take a big gulp of wine and decide not to get into whatever that was with Nicholas. At least not now.

"So . . . ex-girlfriend?" I ask, clearly unable to resist.

"More like ex–psycho stalker," Esmerelda answers for him. Then she takes my hand. "Forget about her. Let's go lose some of Daddy's money."

Nicholas takes a breath, nods, and we head off to the tables.

But I don't lose anyone's money. An hour later, I'm up eight black chips at the blackjack table. I think, I hope, they're worth a thousand each—if it's any more than that, I'll be too freaked out to touch them. My dad taught me to play the game when I was twelve. On his good days, we still play a few hands.

Nicholas's big, warm hands squeeze my shoulders, and he speaks close to my ear. "I have to head to the little lads' room."

I look at him over my shoulder. "Okay."

Our eyes meet and I know him well enough to recognize the look burning in his. He wants to kiss me—badly. He stares at my mouth like a starving man.

But then he pulls back, looks around the room, remembers where we are.

"Ezzy—mind Olivia for me a bit?"

"Yeah, sure." She nods and Nicholas walks away.

But fifteen minutes later, he still hasn't come back. And Esmerelda spots a group of friends she hasn't spoken to "in ages." With a pat to my arm, she says she'll "be back in a jiffy" and she heads off to them.

Leaving me alone in the center of the room, feeling like an alien surrounded by Martians who sweat money and shit gold.

I watch a white-gloved waiter slip through a swinging door—probably to the kitchen—and my feet itch to follow him. Because my home planet is behind that door—my people.

Dozens of curious, unkind eyes appraise me as they float past, in groups of chatting, laughing twos and threes. So I lift the hem of my shimmery dress and walk closer to the wall, to be less conspicuous. I slip my phone out of my purse and text Ellie, asking what she's up to. I talked to her and Marty last night, just after they'd finished closing the coffee shop. They sounded good. I sent them pics of my room and the palace grounds—Marty replied with so many emoji's, he probably broke the button. He's expressive like that.

When she doesn't respond a few minutes later, I put my phone away. And I don't want to smother Nicholas, but at the same time—where the fuck is he? Five more minutes pass and my stomach turns twisty and sour. He knows I don't know anyone here—why would he leave me alone?

Screw it. I put my Champagne glass on the tray of a passing waiter and set out to find him. Every room I wander through looks like the inside of a crystal chandelier—sparkling and glittery. And they're noisy, with pinging slot machines and cheering crowds.

Royals like winning money too—even when they already have it. Go figure.

One room is dark, black, except for colored strobe lights, a glowing dance floor, and the pounding club music coming from the DJ's speakers. I spot Henry's unmistakable blond head in the middle of the floor, surrounded by gyrating women, and I almost head over to him to ask if he's seen his brother.

But then—I can't explain why—a door on the far side catches my attention. It leads outside, onto a balustraded balcony. By the time I reach it, my palms are sweating and clammy. My heels click on the tiled stone outside—I only go a few steps—and that's when I see them, at the far corner of the balcony in the soft halo of a teardrop-shaped lamp.

Nicholas and . . . Lucy.

I taste bile in the back of my throat.

Her back is to me, her blond hair cascading, her head tipped up to him and her forearms resting on those broad shoulders I love to touch. I can't tell if he's pushing her away or pulling her closer—and the sour sensation in my stomach seeps into my bones.

Anger mixes with embarrassment—and flight kicks fight's ass.

When I pull the door, back open I think I hear my name, but the sound is drowned out by the pumping bass that rattles the walls. I walk quickly, through the dance room, back into the main gambling room.

I make it through the doorway—and then my arm is grabbed, encircled by an iron grip, like a shackle.

"Just where do you think you're going?" she asks, with a light Wessconian accent.

I look up at her and the breath literally whooshes out of me. Because she's the most breathtakingly beautiful woman I've ever seen. Half a foot taller than me, with shiny dark brown hair, onyx eyes, perfect doll-like features and pale, pristine skin.

"Huh?"

Nice recovery, Liv.

"Let me guess—you walked outside and saw Lucille and Nicholas, not quite kissing but not not-kissing either?"

"How do you know that?"

She snorts—and manages to make it sound adorable.

"Because Lucy is the most unoriginal bitch I've ever known." She taps my nose. "But you aren't going to run off—absolutely not. You can't give her the satisfaction."

She plucks two fresh glasses of Champagne off a passing tray, hands one to me, and clinks our glasses together.

"Drink up and smile—you're being watched."

I peek around the room. "Watched by who?"

"Everyone, of course. You're new and shiny and . . . poor. And you have your hands on what every woman here, except me and Esmerelda, wants—the royal family jewels." Her head tilts. "Are you really a waitress?"

Why does everyone keep asking me that? I drink my Champagne—really, I chug the whole freaking glass; I deserve it.

"Uh . . . yes."

"That idiot. I can't believe he brought you here."

She shakes her head, pitying.

"The world is full of cunts, dearie—some are just smellier than others. Remember that, and they'll never be able to hurt you."

I stare at her for a beat. "Who *are* you?"

Her smile makes her even prettier. "I'm Lady Frances Eloise Alcott Barrister . . . but you can call me Franny."

Franny.

"Franny! Simon's Franny—bubble-bath girl!"

Franny pouts. "Did he put the call on speaker in front of a full house? I'm going to have a strongly worded chat with that husband of mine."

"Strongly worded chat about what, dove?" Simon asks, coming up beside her, his hand sliding affectionately around her waist.

Franny grins at him. "Say the devil's name and he doth appear."

Simon makes devil horns on his red head with his fingers. Then he smiles at me, blue eyes dancing. "Olivia, it's a pleasure to see you again."

There's a warmth about him, a genuine sweetness that makes me feel . . . comforted—without him even trying. Simon Barrister is the kind of guy that would stop to help someone with a flat tire even in a downpour, or help an old lady carry her groceries, or make silly faces at a kid having a meltdown.

"Hello, Simon, it's good to see you too."

"How are you, my dear?"

"What a question to ask, Simon!" Franny swats him. "Look at the poor girl. She's overwrought. Lucille has been playing her nasty head games again."

Simon scrunches his nose. "You should ignore Lucy, Olivia—she's a bit of a vile bitch."

"She's a cunt," Franny reiterates. "My love is just too kind to say so." She pats my arm. "But I'm not."

The jittery, sick feeling starts to creep up on me again. "I think I just need some air."

"Brilliant," Franny says, taking my arm and guiding me toward the large French doors. "Let's go out on the veranda for a smoke. I just recently started the habit—trying to work off the pounds I gained from the honeymoon."

I suspect Franny might be a little crazy. The fun kind, not the scary kind. Outside, she smokes her cigarette while Simon talks business with a man beside him. Then she quickly stubs out her bud on the iron railing, her eyes trained on the open doors that lead into the ballroom.

"He's found you."

I turn to look. "Nicholas?"

She doesn't let me look. "Yes, he's coming this way." She claps her hands together. "Now, when he arrives, you should smile gracefully and pretend like nothing in the world is wrong."

"Why would I do that?" I ask.

"He won't know what to make of it. It'll drive him insane. A woman's weapons of mass destruction are indifference and confusion."

I feel like I should be writing this down.

"He's coming. Get ready." She smacks my lower back. "Chin up, tits out."

With a mind of their own, my chin lifts and my shoulders pull back, pushing my chest forward. And believe it or not, it actually makes me feel stronger. More capable.

"Olivia."

Right up until he says my name. I close my eyes against the sound. The way he says it—there will never be a day that I don't love the sound of my name on his lips.

Bracing myself, I turn Nicholas's way, but I don't actually look at his face—instead I look just over his right shoulder into the bright, glistening lights of a golden chandelier.

I feel his gaze on my face, watching me, reading me.

I don't have the chance to pretend that everything is fine. Because without another word, Nicholas grabs my hand and pulls me toward the steps that lead off the veranda to the gardens. "Come on."

He guides me down a winding dim path, to a white trestle gazebo. Garden lights ring the outside, casting a soft glow, but under the roof it's dark and feels private. I hold my dress as I climb the steps.

"Why don't you like Franny?"

He told me in New York that they didn't get along—that he couldn't stand her. But he's surprised by my question. "Ah . . . from the moment Simon met her, he was enamored, but she gave him the brush-off over and over again. The night he told her he was in love with her, she said she could never be with him—and when I came home, I found her in my bed. Naked."

Jealousy, hot and biting, bites at me. And shock.

"Did you sleep with her?"

"Of course not," he says, low and growly. "I would never do that to Simon. I told him about it, but he didn't care. He said they were 'working through their issues.' Shortly after, they were an item—and they got married a few months ago. I've given up trying to figure it out."

I sit down on the bench. "Jesus. She doesn't seem like someone . . . who would do that. She was nice to me."

Nicholas stands in front of me, his face partially hidden by the darkness. "I'm glad she was nice to you, but things here aren't always what they seem. I should've told you that, before." He pushes a hand through his hair. "I should've told you a lot of things, Olivia. But I'm not used to . . . saying things . . . out loud."

"I don't understand what that means."

He sits down beside me, his voice hushed. "I want to tell you about Lucy. I want to explain."

I want to be the bigger woman—the kind who says he doesn't owe me an explanation. We're just temporary. But my heart . . . my heart pounds loudly that he does.

"Why were you with her? Why did you leave me alone? Did you kiss her, Nicholas—it looked like you could've been kissing her."

His hand splays across my jaw. "I'm sorry you were on your own—I didn't mean for that to happen. No, I wasn't kissing her. I swear to you—on my parents—nothing like that happened."

Relief loosens the pincers on my heart. Because I know he would never mention his parents—not unless it was true.

"Then what did happen?"

He leans forward, resting his elbows on his knees, looking at the ground.

"I met Lucy at school—Briar House—when we were both in year ten. She was the prettiest girl I'd ever seen. Fragile in a way that made me want to keep her safe. We started dating . . . The media went into a frenzy and I was worried it would scare her away. But it didn't bother her, and I remember thinking she was stronger than I thought."

He takes a breath, rubbing the back of his neck.

"She became pregnant when we were seventeen. I was stupid—careless."

"Oh my God."

He nods, looking at me. "Pregnancy at that age is difficult for anyone, but add in—"

"The whole future-leader-of-a-country thing . . ." I finish for him.

"And it was a horror show. Her family wanted to start planning the wedding immediately, wanted the Palace to announce our engagement. My grandmother demanded tests and retests to confirm that she was really pregnant and that it was really mine."

And again I'm struck by the strangeness of Nicholas's life—the archaic rules that box him in.

"What did you want?" I ask—because I have a strong feeling no one else did.

"I wanted . . . to do the right thing. I loved her." He rubs his face. "In the end, it didn't matter. Just a few weeks after she found out, she lost the baby, a miscarriage. She was heartbroken."

"And you?"

He doesn't answer right away. Then softly, he says, "I was . . . relieved. I didn't want that responsibility. Not yet."

I rub his shoulder. "That's understandable."

He swallows and nods. "When the year ended, my grandmother sent me to Japan for the summer—a humanitarian mission. Lucy and I talked at first, texted . . . but I was so busy. When I came back to school in the fall, things were different. *I* was different. I cared for her, but my feelings had changed. I broke it off, as gently as I could, but she still took it . . . badly."

Sadness washes through me like a wave.

"How badly?"

"She tried to kill herself a week later. Her family sent her away to a hospital. A good place, but she never came back to school. And I've always felt . . . guilty about it all. Responsible. It stayed out of the papers—I don't know who the Palace had to pay off or kill to keep it that way, but there wasn't a single line written about it."

"Is that why you're so careful? About the condoms?"

"Yes."

With a tug, he gathers me in his lap, hugging me close. And I know this wasn't easy for him.

"Thank you for telling me. For explaining."

We stay just like that, shrouded in shadows and earthy-scented air.

Then I ask, "Should we go back to the party?"

He thinks about it. And gives me a little squeeze. "I have a better idea."

The Horny Goat.

It reminds me of a pub in New York—comfortable, familiar, and a little sticky. After Nicholas gathered Simon and Franny, Henry and a cute redhead that was clinging to his arm, the six of us ditched the casino house party and ended up at The Horny Goat for the rest of the night.

I did tequila shots with Franny. Henry sang karaoke. Simon and Nicholas insulted one another about their dart-throwing skills.

By the end of the night, in the early morning hours, Nicholas and I stumbled into his room, fell onto his bed—and fell asleep, fully clothed, wrapped around each other . . . and happy.

CHAPTER 18

Nicholas

The following week is blissfully uneventful. I address Palace business during the day, and share my nights with Olivia—which are so much more than blissful.

During the day, she relaxes like I want her to. She walks the grounds and has found a friend in Franny. They've had lunch together several times, which doesn't exactly thrill me, but at the very least, I know she's safe with Simon's wife. Franny, and her forked tongue, will protect Olivia from the Lucy types looking to wound her with their half-truths.

On the rare occasions my brother is sober, he becomes increasingly agitated—like he's unable to sit still, to stand his own company, or any sound that resembles silence. Finally he decides to throw a welcome home party for himself.

I'm in my bathroom preparing for his royal yacht party, just showered with a towel around my hips, scraping the last of the shaving cream off my jaw, when Olivia appears in the doorway.

I thought she was lovely from the first moment I saw her. But here, now—her bare, soft skin wrapped in a pink silk robe, her face glowing with well-rested happiness . . . she's magnificent.

"So . . . do you guys have like a gift shop or a convenience store around here?"

I laugh. "A gift shop?"

She holds up a light blue disposable razor. "I'm out of razors. This one's so dull I could run it over my tongue without drawing blood."

"Let's not test that theory. I like your tongue too much." I wipe my chin with a towel. "I can have the staff bring one to your room."

The devil on my shoulder—and the angel, too—smack me upside the head. And they whisper a much better idea.

"Or . . . I could help you out."

Her brows draw together. "Help me out? I can't use your razor."

"No, definitely not—you'd cut yourself to ribbons." I finger the sharp, heavy straight blade. "What I mean is . . . I could shave for you."

Her eyes darken, the way they do when she's right on the edge—right before she comes. And she moves closer to me.

"Do you . . . want to do that?"

My gaze drags down, down, over every sumptuous inch of her body.

"Oh, yes."

"All . . . all right," she agrees, intense and breathless.

The corner of my mouth drags up, as I gently skim the robe back over her shoulders and slide it down. Revealing pale, full curves and soft, mouthwatering swells. I scoop Olivia up under her legs and perch her on the vanity, her legs dangling off.

The cold marble makes her squeak and we both chuckle. Then she reaches up for a kiss—but I drag myself back. "Uh-uh, none of that now. I need to focus all of my attention . . ." I slip my hand across her thigh, cupping between her legs, ". . . here."

Olivia's eyes roll closed at the contact and her hips lift up against my palm just a bit. All I want to do is slip my finger into her wet, tight heat. To get her all needy and clenching for my cock.

I blow out a breath. This is going to be more fucking difficult than I thought.

I lick my lips as I mix the shaving cream into a warm, thick lather, feeling her eyes follow my every move. I run a hand towel under the warm water, ring it out, and wrap it around her calf, to heat and soften the skin.

And then I paint her with the cashmere brush. Dragging the bristles up her leg, over the grooves of her sculpted calf, leaving a trail of white cream behind. I breathe evenly, steadying myself when I reach for the razor, scraping it gently over her skin. I rinse the blade, then go back for more, repeating the slow movements again and again.

After both calves and her knees are done, I get to work on each thigh. Olivia pants and then gasps when the bristles tickle the delicate skin at the apex between her legs. When the razor traces the same path—reaches that juncture—she moans.

And all I want to do is rip the towel off my hips and fuck her endlessly on the bathroom counter. My cock is aching, weepy, and every muscle in my body is strung so tight it borders on pain.

I save the best for last. Her sweet, beautiful pussy. I repeat the process—warm towel first—resting it over her and rubbing her clit beneath it, because how can I not? She starts to shift—writhe—and I have to admonish her.

"Stay still. I have to stop if you don't sit still."

Yes, I'm teasing her—taunting. Because there's no bloody way in hell I could stop now.

Olivia grips the edge of the counter until her knuckles are white and she stares at me with shiny eyes glazed over with mindless lust.

Once she's covered in cream, I toss the brush into the sink. I press the razor against her flesh, at the bottom—those plump, perfect lips. And I pause, looking into her eyes.

"You trust me."

She nods, almost frantically. And I slide the razor up, removing barely visible tiny sprouts of hair. I move to her vulva, swiping downward in short, careful strokes—being sure to leave her pretty, soft bush that I enjoy so much.

When I'm done, I set the razor aside and pick up the still-warm towel. Then I kneel down in front of her. I clean any last remnant of shaving cream from her skin and then I look up into her eyes.

And I watch her watch me, as I lean forward and cover her pussy with my mouth.

"Yes, yes . . ." she hisses.

I suck and lick and devour her like a man gone mad—and maybe I have.

She's so slick and smooth and hot on my lips, against my tongue. I could stay here—do this to her—forever.

But—forever is much too long for my suffering cock.

Breathing hard, heart pounding out of my chest, I stand up and tear at the towel around me. I push Olivia's knees up, bracing her feet on the edge of the counter near her hands, opening her up to me. *So fucking pretty.*

I take my long, hot erection in hand and run the head through her wetness, teasing her clit with the tip, rubbing it over the pink bud.

And there's no worry, not a single thought of consequences or responsibility. Because this is Olivia—and that makes all the difference.

"Are you sure?" she asks.

I drag my cock down to her tight opening, gliding it around, feeling the call to thrust hard and deep.

"Yes, yes I'm sure."

Olivia nods and I dip inside her.

She closes tight around me, gripping and snug, making me moan loudly.

"Oh, Christ . . ."

The bareness—flesh to flesh—is amazing. More. The slick slide of tight heat that brings so much pleasure with it. I watch as I push all the way into her, feeling every gorgeous inch.

It's the most erotic sight I've ever seen. Olivia moans—we both do.

And I know without a shred of doubt that we are going to be very, very late for Henry's party.

Olivia

By the time we actually leave the palace, it's so late that Nicholas has Bridget call ahead to tell them to hold the gangplank for us. He says we'll just be cruising around the bay, but I hope Henry isn't pissed at us for delaying his party.

I shouldn't have worried. After we board, it's immediately apparent Henry is too drunk to notice—or care.

He hugs us both sloppily, like he hasn't seen us in weeks.

"So damn happy you made it!" he howls, throwing his arms out wide. "I love this fucking boat!"

Nicholas's eyes crinkle with concern. "It's actually a ship, little brother."

Henry rolls his eyes and almost falls over.

"Don't you ever get tired of correcting people? Have a fucking drink."

We do just that.

I tried to imagine what a royal yacht would look like, but just like practically every other experience on this wild trip, my imagination falls sadly short.

The "ship" has every luxury imaginable. It's a floating palace—and almost as large. Strings of lights dot the sky above the deck, and some of the guests—also drunk but not quite as bad as Henry—turn it into a makeshift dance floor. They grind and twist to the beat of the music coming from the DJ's speakers at the helm. Kanye West is playing—and I laugh to myself, remembering my and Nicholas' first date.

It seems so long ago. So much has happened.

So much has . . . changed.

With our drinks in hand, Nicholas and I mingle. He introduces me to aristocrat after aristocrat—dukes and barons and ladies and one marchioness, whatever the hell that is. We find Franny and Simon and stick pretty close to them.

About an hour later, we stand against the railing, a slight breeze blowing my hair but not enough to do any damage, while Simon starts to talk about his plans for expanding Barrister's. How he wants to branch out into other products.

I look over at Nicholas and my heart skips. Because he isn't listening to Simon—his focus is across the deck, at the opposite railing. I've never seen Nicholas look terrified before.

But that's exactly the emotion that's frozen on his face.

"Henry," he whispers, but only to himself.

And then he shouts it. "Henry!"

He rushes forward, running across the deck, and I turn just in time to see what's scared him to death. Henry's laughing, leaning too much on the railing at his side.

And then . . . silently . . . he goes over it.

Someone screams. Nicholas yells his brother's name again. A guard makes the mistake of trying to stop him—and he gets an elbow to the nose for his trouble.

When Nicholas reaches the spot where his brother just stood, he doesn't pause for a second, but grabs the railing of the ship and hops over, feet first.

And both of Wessco's princes have gone overboard.

Security men in black suits wait outside the door of the private hospital room. Someone brought Nicholas a dry change of clothes—jeans and a simple black T-shirt.

He changed after the head doctors gave him and the Queen's advisor an update on Henry. They believe he hit his head on the way down. A mild concussion, with all signs pointing toward no lasting damage.

But that doesn't make Nicholas feel any better.

He sits in the chair at the foot of the bed, leaning forward with his elbows on his knees, strung tight and tense, jaw clenched. His eyes never leaving his unconscious brother, as if he can wake him up with the intensity of his stare. The room is deathly quiet, except for the sounds of Henry's deep, even breaths and the blip of the heart monitor.

It's just the two of us, but I don't feel awkward or out of place. There's no desire to offer to get him something to eat or a cup of coffee. Because I know Nicholas only wants me, needs me, right here. So there's no place on Earth I'd rather be.

I put my hand on his shoulder, kneading the rock-hard tendon. He turns his head, and his eyes meet mine—and God, they're simmering. Awash with sadness and guilt and anger—like he can't decide if he wants to cry or beat the crap out of his brother.

I'd feel the same way if it were Ellie. I'd want to shake her and hug her and strangle her, all at the same time. So I give him a small smile and a nod.

And as if he can sense Nicholas's attention isn't solely on him, Henry stirs. His thick blond brows draw together and he moans, then slowly his eyes—so similar to the beautiful gray-green of his brother's—creak open. They're unfocused, slowly scanning the room before coming to rest on Nicholas, growing more alert with every second.

In a dry, cracked voice, he mutters, "Stupid fucking boat."

After a moment, Nicholas shakes his head, pinning his brother to the bed with his gaze, his words quiet and ragged.

"No more, Henry. We're all that's left of them, you and I. And you can't . . . No more."

Pain creases Henry's face, chasing away the cheery mask he always has glued there.

"What happened?" Nicholas asks. "I know something happened. It's eating away at you, bit by bit, and you're going to tell me what it is. Now."

Henry nods, licks his lips, and asks for a glass of water. I pour him a cup from the plastic pitcher on the side table. After a few long drags on the straw, he sets it aside and rubs his eyes. When he speaks, he looks away from his brother, down toward the far corner of the room, almost as if he's seeing the words play out in front of him.

"It was about two months before my service was up. They'd kept me far from anything that resembled action—it was like a garden party. You know how it is."

Nicholas explained this to me. "High-profile target"—that's what he and his brother were. Although their training was the same as the other soldiers', when they deployed they received special assignments, because they were under a special threat. Because the princes would make a very shiny trophy.

"And then one day, the Dark Suits said they had a morale mission—a publicity opportunity. They wanted me to visit an outpost, still in the safe zone, but outside the main installation. There was a group of men who'd been there for a while—and they needed a boost. A visit from their prince. A reward for service well done."

Henry scrapes his teeth across his lip—almost biting.

"We drove out and I met them, about fifteen in all. They were good blokes. One was like a crusty old bulldog—he wanted to set me up with his granddaughter. Another . . . he was only eighteen . . ."

Tears swell in Henry's eyes and his voice bends, then breaks.

"He'd never kissed a girl. And he was looking forward to getting back home, to change that."

He scrubs at his face, rubbing the tears into his skin.

"So I told some jokes, made them laugh. We took a bunch of photographs and then we headed back out. We were on the road maybe . . . seven minutes . . . when the first rockets came in. I told the driver to turn around, to go back, but he wouldn't listen to me. What's the point of all this if they don't *listen?*" he asks in a tortured voice.

"I punched the lad next to me, crawled over his lap and rolled out of the Humvee. And I ran . . ." Henry chokes on a sob. "I swear, Nicholas, I ran as hard as I could. But when I got there—there was nothing left. It was just . . . pieces."

I cover my mouth with my hand and I'm crying with him.

Henry gives a long, sniffling inhale, wiping at his face again.

"And I can't get past it. Maybe I'm not supposed to. Maybe it should eat at me bit by bit." He looks at Nicholas and his voice turns bitter. "Those men died because of me. They died for a photo op."

At first, Nicholas doesn't say anything. He gazes at his brother with a cauldron of feelings swirling across his face. And then he stands.

And his voice—that voice—is comforting, but firm. Demanding to be heeded.

"There are two men outside this door who would die for you. A hundred at the palace, thousands across the city—they would all die for you or me. For what we represent. That's our burden, the payment for the lives we get to lead. You can't change it. All you can do is honor those men, Henry. Try to—"

"Don't tell me to live for them!" Henry lashes out. "It's stupid—they're dead! I'll go mad if you say it."

"I'm not going to say it," Nicholas tells him softly. "We can't live for them. All we can do is try to be men worth dying for. We are who we are—when you die, your headstone will read 'Henry, Prince of Wessco.' And if you had gotten yourself killed tonight it would've said, 'Henry, Prince of Wessco—he fell off a fucking boat.' And it all would've been for *nothing*."

Nicholas moves closer, crouching down to look into his brother's eyes.

"There are so few people in the world who have the chance and the power to change it. But we can, Henry. So if you pick yourself up and do something amazing with your life, then those men will have died for something *amazing*. That's all we can do."

They both fall silent. Henry seems calmer, mulling over Nicholas's words.

"Have you contacted the families?" I ask gently. "Maybe . . . maybe it would help you to help them. Give them support, see how they are financially—"

"I'm not going to throw money at them. That's crass." Henry shakes his head.

"You only say that because you have money. When you're struggling—it's not crass at all, but a blessing. And I don't just mean the money. You could talk to them . . . become a friend . . . maybe start to fill the space they left behind. Not because you're a prince, but because you're a pretty cool guy."

Henry thinks about that a moment. Sniffling and drying his cheeks.

"I am pretty cool."

And I laugh. My eyes are still wet, but I laugh. Nicholas and Henry do, too.

Then Nicholas sits on the bed and leans forward—pulling his little brother tight into his arms. Just like that moment in the video, on the awful day of their parents' funeral.

Just like that day, Nicholas tells him that it's all going to be all right.

CHAPTER 19

Nicholas

The next week, there's a polo match Henry and I are expected to play in. He begs off, on physician's orders—because of his recent concussion. My grandmother doesn't give him a hint of shit about the "ship incident" even though it's been reported in the press as "Wild, Drunk Prince Henry At It Again." I think she senses he's struggling with something and that, playing or not, he's not up to a public appearance at a polo match.

I, on the other hand, have no reason to get out of it. And I don't mind so much. Polo is a challenging game—a busy game—strangely relaxing since you don't have time to think about anything else. Though it's sometimes called the game of kings, way back in the day it was used to train cavalry, because in order to play well, controlling the horse has to be automatic, second nature.

Another reason I'm feeling pleasant about attending is Olivia's reaction to my uniform. I enter her room through the bookcase and her eyes slide all over me—the black and white shirt hugging my biceps, the impressive bulge prominently displayed in my snug pants.

Without a word, Olivia turns, calf-length, summer-pink skirt flaring out. And she locks the door. It snaps into place with a resounding click and I know without a doubt I'm about to get lucky.

She saunters up to me and lowers to her knees, laughing as she pulls my shirt from the pants and yanks at the belt buckle. The riding boots present a problem, so she just leaves them on, working me over with those skillful, glorious lips and tongue, making me come so hard in her mouth I see stars. Possibly the light of God.

Yes, lucky indeed.

Spectators and press are all over the fields and stands—not only am I playing, but the Queen is here to watch. The silky skin peeking out from Olivia's white crop top makes it hard, but I force myself to maintain a platonic distance from her as we walk towards where she'll be sitting with Franny. Simon's playing too. En route to the stands, Olivia laughs, flashing her phone my way to show a text from Marty—a reply to a photo of one of the horses she sent. "Like looking in a mirror," it says with a red circle drawn around the horse's cock.

Once she's settled, I snap on my helmet. And then I slip my father's teak bracelet off my wrist, handing it her. "Keep this safe for me, will you?"

She's surprised at first, then her cheeks pinken beautifully. "I'll guard it with my life." And she slips it on her own wrist.

"Have a good game," Olivia says. Then, quieter, "I really want to kiss you right now, for luck. But I know I can't, so I'll just tell you instead."

I wink. "I got my good-luck kiss in your room. If it had been any better, I would've gone blind."

I walk away towards the stables with the sound of her laughter ringing behind me.

Though black clouds gather and the air is heavy with the threat of rain, we're able to make it through two games. My team wins both, which puts me in a good mood. Sweaty and smudged with dirt, I lead my pony to the stables. I brush her down myself, in her stall, cooing about what a pretty girl she is—because human or beast, every female enjoys a compliment.

Once that's done, I step out of the stall onto the main walk and come face-to-face with Hannibal Lancaster. Inside, I groan. We went to school together—he's not a cannibalistic killer like his namesake, but he is a sleazy, disgusting prick. His parents, on the other hand—his family—are good people. And powerful allies to the Crown.

Just goes to show that even a bushel of good apples can produce a bad seed.

They're completely unaware of Hannibal's dickishness, which forces the rest of us—me—to put up with him from time to time and not punch his face in.

He bows, then asks, "How are you, Pembrook?"

"I'm well, Lancaster. Good match."

He snorts. "Our number four was a useless fucker. I'm going to make sure he never plays at our club again."

And I'm ready to get the hell away from him. But it's not that easy.

"I wanted to ask you about the souvenir you brought home from the States."

"Souvenir?" I ask.

"The girl. She's exquisite."

Twats like Lancaster can have anything they want. Anything. Which is why, when they find something that's hard to get—or that belongs to someone else—it makes them want it even more. They go after it relentlessly.

I learned a very long time ago that the world is full of fuckers who want what I have, just because it's mine. And that the most effective way to keep their dirty hands off of it is to pretend I don't care, that I don't really want it that badly—that maybe it doesn't even belong to me at all.

It's twisted, I know, but it's the way of the world. *This* world.

"She is," I smirk. "But that shouldn't surprise you. I've always had exquisite taste."

"But I am surprised. You don't typically bring your slags home to meet Grandmother."

I eye the polo mallet in the corner—and picture crushing his balls with it.

"Don't think too deeply about it, Lancaster; you'll hurt yourself. I've just discovered the convenience of having ready-to-go pussy in-house. And she's American—they gush all over themselves about the royal thing." I shrug, and my stomach clenches tight and sick. If I don't get away from him soon, I'm going to vomit.

Lancaster laughs. "I want to try American pussy. Let me have a go at her. You don't mind, do you?"

Or fucking kill him.

My fists clench hard at my sides and I swing around. What comes out of my mouth isn't at all what I'm thinking.

"'Course I don't, but not until *after* I'm finished. Do you understand, Hannibal? If I catch you within sniffing distance of her before then, I'll nail you to the wall by your cock."

Maybe I say a little of what I'm thinking.

"Christ, you don't have to get medieval about it." He holds up his hands. "I know you don't like to share. Let me know when you're sick of the cunt. I'll keep hands-off until then."

I'm already walking away. "Give my regards to your parents."

"I always do, Nicholas," he calls after me.

And just a moment later, the clouds open, the thunder wails, and the rain pours down like every angel in heaven is crying.

"What do you mean, you don't know where she is?"

I'm in the morning room of Guthrie House and a young security guard stands before me, his eyes downcast.

"She went to the loo, sir. She seemed to be taking a long time, so I went in to check on her . . . and she was gone."

I had interviews after the polo match. Olivia was supposed to be driven back here, to meet me. But she never arrived.

While I was wasting time answering stupid fucking questions, talking to people I abhor, Olivia was . . . getting lost? Getting taken? A thousand gut-wrenching thoughts barrel through my head, making it pound.

My hand tears through my hair. "Get out."

Winston is on it. He'll find her—that's what he does; he's good at it. But I pace the room, because I want to be the one out there looking for her.

"It'll be all right, Nick," Simon tries, sitting on the couch beside Franny. "She'll turn up. She probably just lost her way."

Thunder roars outside, rattling the window, mockingly.

And then the phone rings. Fergus answers and turns to me with the closest thing I've ever seen on his face to a smile. "Miss Hammond just walked up to the South Gate, Your Grace. They're bringing her around now."

And it's like my whole body deflates with relief.

Until I see her—dripping wet, with big, wounded eyes. I cross the room and pull her against me. "Are you hurt? Christ, what happened?"

"I needed to think," Olivia says flatly. "I think better when I walk around."

My hands tighten on her arms as I lean back, wanting to shake her. "You can't walk around the city without security, Olivia."

She just looks at me with that same blank expression. "No, I can. *You* can't, but I can."

"I've been going out of my mind!"

Her voice is colorless. Drained. "Why?"

"*Why?*"

"Yes, why? I'm just in-house American pussy that you're not tired of yet."

Horror slams into me like a sledgehammer, punching the air from my lungs, choking off my response.

"Just a cunt your friend is welcome to have at, but not until you're finished because you don't share."

"Olivia, I didn't mean—"

"You didn't mean for me to hear? Yeah, I got that." She shakes out of my arms and backs away, her eyes hard and distrustful. "How could you say those things?"

"I didn't mean them."

"I don't care if you meant them, you said them! Is that how you talk about me with your friends, Nicholas?" She points at Simon.

And I don't give a fuck that we have an audience.

I approach her and hiss, "Lancaster is not my friend."

"He sounded like your friend."

"He's not! It's just . . . it's just the way things are here."

Olivia shakes her head and her voice becomes clogged, strained with the effort of holding back tears. "If that's how it is, then I'm going home. I thought I could do this, but . . . I don't want to anymore."

When she turns, I yell, "Stop!"

She doesn't bother to turn around. "Fuck off!"

I grab her arm. And then she does swing around. Slapping me so hard my head snaps to the side and my cheek throbs.

"Don't fucking touch me!" Olivia faces me, her feet shoulder-width apart, hands curved into claws, eyes darting—like a beautiful, wild, cornered animal—that's been wounded.

"Let me explain."

"I'm leaving!" she screeches.

My face goes hard, tight, and anger sharpens my words—because she won't goddamn listen.

"Clue in, love—the car's mine, the house is mine, the whole fucking country is mine! You're not going anywhere because I'll tell them not to take you anywhere."

She lifts her chin, shoulders back. "Then I'll walk to the airport."

"It's too far—you can't walk."

"Watch me!"

Franny's voice, musical and calm, like a preschool teacher's, comes between us.

"Children, children . . . that's enough of that."

She takes both of Olivia's hands in hers, turning her back to me. "Olivia, Nicholas is right—it's dreadful outside; you can't walk anywhere. And you look terrible—you can't go out like this!"

She turns to Fergus. "Fergus, have a bath drawn and bring a bottle of Courvoisier to Olivia's room."

Franny pushes Olivia's hair back, the way you would for a sad little child. "A nice hot bath, a good drink, and if you still want to leave in the morning, I'll drive you myself." Her dark eyes glare at me pointedly. "I have my own car."

Olivia shudders when she inhales, like she's on the verge of tears—and the sound is tearing at me.

"Go on now," Franny tells her. "I'll be up in a moment."

When Olivia leaves the room, I move to follow, but Franny steps into my path.

"Oh no, *you* stay here."

"Simon," I say with a scowl, "collect your wife before I say something I'll regret."

But Franny just tilts her head, appraising me. "I used to think you were a selfish bastard, but I'm starting to believe you're just a fool. A double-damned idiot. I'm not sure which is worse."

"Then I guess it's good that I don't give a turtle's arse-crack about your opinion of me."

The only indication that she heard me is the sharp lift of one side of her pink mouth.

"I think you like her clueless—it makes her dependent on you. And it keeps her innocent. Untainted by this cesspool the rest of us swim around in every day. But you've left her vulnerable. She doesn't understand the rules. She doesn't even know the name of the game."

"So, you'll what?" I growl. "Teach her to play?"

Franny's dark eyes blaze.

"Oh no, silly boy—I'll teach her to win."

Olivia

I've never tasted brandy before. When Franny handed me my first glass, she warned me to sip, not gulp. The first taste felt hot in my mouth and burned its way down my throat. But now—three glasses later—it's like drinking a melted peach in a glass, thick and sweet.

The combination of liquor and a hot bath has made me feel calmer. No, that's not right—I feel numb. I'm not sure if that's better or worse for me and Nicholas, but I'm not thinking about him right now. Because Franny has kept me busy.

I'm tucked into the snow-white couch, engulfed in an oversized cashmere robe, my hair down and wet—curling around me as it dries. I have Franny's iPhone in my hand, looking through the pictures on her Instagram account. It's a veritable who's who of Wessco's rich and famous, and Franny's been filling me in on their dirty not-so-secret secrets and sins.

"Meth-head Bitch." Franny paces behind the couch like a drill instructor. "She tried cooking up her own batch and almost burned her family's castle to the ground."

She's referring to a blond with her tongue hanging out and her right hand giving the finger to the camera. *Classy.*

I move to the next picture.

"Bulimic Bitch. Everyone thinks she's cured, but there's not a meal that passes through those lips that doesn't come back up. Rotted her teeth out. Those dentures are as fake as her tits."

They're all bitches, according to Franny. Illegitimate Bitch ("the butler's child, don't you know"), Bald Bitch ("anxiety disorder, compulsively pulls her hair out"), Itchy-twat Bitch ("I'm going to do her a favor and send her a crate of Vagisil for Christmas"). Apparently, even the guys are Bitches: Rancid Bitch ("flatulence—spend too much time in close proximity and your nose hairs will be singed"), Microscopic Bitch ("But he's a big guy," I say. Franny wiggles her pinky finger. "Not all of him").

I toss the phone on the cushion beside me and drop my head to the arm of the couch. "Why are we doing this, again?"

"Because this is how it's done. They hate you—even the ones you haven't met yet. If there's a chance you're going to stay, you need ammunition."

"But it's not like I'm going to walk up to Illegitimate Bitch and tell her I know who her father is, Darth Vader style."

Franny's rosy lips slide into a smile. "And that's why Nicholas adores you. Because you're not like any other woman he's known." She pats my knee. "You're nice.

"But," she goes on, "using this information isn't the point. It's enough that they know you know—their bitchy-senses will tell them the moment they see you. It'll be in how you carry yourself, how you look them in the eyes. Perception is reality. If you can control perception, you control the world. That's how things are here. That's what Nicholas was trying to do today."

I take a drink of the warm liquor as her words sink in.

Then, just for shits and giggles, I wonder, "What kind of bitch would I be? Poor Bitch?"

"Definitely."

"And my sister would be Tiny Bitch," I pinch my fingers, "because she's this big."

"Now you've got it."

I look at Franny's profile—her perfect skin, adorable nose, shining, exotic eyes with thick lashes that go on for days. She really is breathtaking.

"What would you be?"

Franny laughs—it's a throaty, boisterous sound. "I'd be Ugly Bitch."

"Uh . . . you mean Opposite Bitch?"

It takes her half a minute before she answers me. She lifts the sleeve of her silk blouse, checking the diamond-encrusted watch around her delicate wrist. "All right, dearie, settle in and Franny will tell you a bedtime story. Once upon a time there was a girl—the most beautiful girl in the whole wide world. Everyone told her so. Her mother, her father, strangers on the street . . . her uncle. He told her each time he came to visit, which was horrifically often. His 'pretty princess,' he would say."

My stomach drops and the brandy feels too sickly sweet in my gut, nauseating.

"I've always loved animals," Franny says, smiling suddenly. "They have a sixth sense about people, don't you think?"

"Yeah, I think so. I don't trust anyone my dog doesn't like."

"Yes, exactly." Then she turns her eyes back to the fireplace. "The girl's uncle was killed in a riding accident. Thrown from his horse and trampled—his head was crushed like a melon beneath the hoof."

Good.

"By then, the girl was dreaming about carving her face up, so it would match how ugly she felt inside. But she couldn't bring herself to do it." Franny goes silent for a moment, lost to the memories playing out behind her pretty, dark eyes. "So instead, she acted ugly. Cruel. A venomous little thing. She was very good at it. And she became the ugliest beautiful girl in the whole wide world."

Franny drinks her brandy.

"Until, one day, she met a boy. And he was silly and awkward and the kindest, sweetest man she'd ever known. The girl was sure she could never be with him—because once he knew how ugly she was inside, he would leave and she would fall apart. So she was heartless to him. Tried to chase him off every way she knew how. She even tried to seduce his friend, but nothing worked. The boy . . . waited. Not in a weak way, but with patience. How a parent lets a tantrumming child scream and cry and beat the ground, until the child is spent. And one night, that's what happened. The girl wailed and kicked and sobbed . . . and told him everything. All the ugliness."

"And he didn't just love her anyway . . . he loved her even more. He told her it wasn't her face that made him love her—he said he would love her even if he was blind, because it was the spark inside her that had captured him the moment they met. And she finally started to believe him. With him she felt safe . . . and good . . . and maybe just a little bit beautiful."

I reach up and hug Franny tightly, stroking her soft, dark hair.

Then I sit back and look up at her. "Why did you tell me that?"

"Because this place, Olivia, it's a pretty little shitheap—with a thousand bloodthirsty flies. But there is goodness here. I've felt it. I've found it." She covers my hand, squeezing. "And my Simon loves Nicholas like a brother. So if he loves him, I know he is one of the good ones."

There's a knock at the door. With a pat to my knee, Franny rises and opens it. And Simon Barrister gazes at her, not like she's the prettiest girl in the world—but like she's the center of his universe.

"Time to go, darling." He grins.

Franny waves. "Goodnight, Olivia."

"Thank you, Franny, for everything."

As they walk through the door and down the hall, I hear Franny say, "I'm very drunk, Simon—you're going to have to do all the work tonight."

"Good by me, love. That's one of my favorite ways to do it—along with all the others."

I set my brandy glass on the table and close the door. Then I turn the lights down, slip off my robe, and get into bed.

The room is dark and still. Quiet enough to hear the scrape of the wall as it opens, and the footsteps that move steadily across the room. Nicholas appears beside my bed, kneeling like the stained-glass saints in the windows of his cathedral—gazing at me through the darkness with ravaged eyes.

"Forgive me."

It's hard not to feel bad for him, when his remorse is so raw and real.

"The night we met," I tell him softly, "I heard your voice before I saw you, did you know that? It's beautiful. Strong and deep and calming." I swallow, tasting tears. "But now I keep hearing you say those awful things, in your lovely voice."

"Forgive me," he whispers, harsh and sad. "I was trying to protect you, I swear. Keep you . . . safe."

I do forgive him. It's just that easy. Because I understand now.

And because I love him.

My eyes have adjusted to the darkness and I see him clearly. The dim moonlight from the window highlights the angles of his face, the incline of his cheekbones, the arch of his stubborn chin, the sharp strength of his jaw, the swell of those full lips.

It's the face of an angel. A fallen angel with secrets in his eyes.

"I don't like it here, Nicholas."

His brows pinch, like he's in pain. "I know. I never should have brought you here. It's the most selfish thing I've ever done. But . . . I can't be sorry for it. Because you have come to mean everything to me."

I lift the sheet, beckoning him, and he slides beneath it, our arms searching for each other in the darkness. Nicholas' mouth covers mine, gentle but with an urgent press of desperation. I give him my tongue and he moans. The sound turns my limbs liquid and the sadness that lingered between us turns to need.

We need this.

With my heels, I push his pants off his hips, then I slide down his body, leaving kisses in my wake. His cock is already hard and beautiful. I didn't think a penis could be . . . beautiful . . . but Nicholas's is. It's perfectly shaped, thick and hot in my hand, so smooth and glistening at the tip.

I take him fully in my mouth—beyond the ability to tease. And he sighs my name as I suckle him, my tongue tracing the silken skin and tight grooves.

With a gasp, Nicholas lifts me back up. Devouring my lips, he rolls us over, lifts my nightgown and slides inside me. And there's still that stretch . . . that delicious feeling of being so perfectly full. He stops when he's fully buried—when we're as close and tied as two people could ever be.

His eyes shine in the darkness, and he strokes my cheek, just gazing down at me.

And I know I love him. It's right there—on my lips—just waiting for breath to say the words out loud. He kisses me, and I give them over to him, but silently.

Because it's all already so very complicated. And it feels like, once I say those words I'll cross a threshold I won't ever be able to turn back from. Walk away from.

Nicholas moves above me, inside me, deep and slow. Wringing out the pleasure from us both. My eyes close and I hold him, my arms around him, feeling the taut muscles in his back tighten with every thrust as my hands clutch his shoulder blades.

And I'm lost. Gone. Coasting in a stratosphere of searing bliss. It expands inside me, building, soaring . . . until I come with an opened-mouth cry. Pressing my lips against his neck, tasting him, breathing in the scent of his skin with every writhing gasp.

His thrusts quicken, becoming rougher as the intensity crests for him too. Until he pushes in deep one last time, and comes on a quiet gasp. I feel him inside me—hot and pulsing. And I clench around him so tight, wanting to keep him inside me forever.

Later, with my cheek on his warm chest and his strong arms heavy around me, I ask him, "What are we going to do?"

Nicholas kisses my forehead, holding on tighter.

"I don't know."

CHAPTER 20

Nicholas

"Piss off, you bastard! I never liked you!"

"The best part of you leaked out of your mother to the wet spot on the bed, you tosser."

"Sir Aloysius's cock was the smartest thing that ever came out of your mouth!"

Welcome to Parliament. And you thought the Brits got rowdy.

Although, I admit, it's not usually quite this bad.

"I'll kill you! I'll kill your family and I'll eat your dog!"

Okay, then.

Normally, the Queen attends Parliament only to open and close out the year. But, given the state of Wessco's economy, she called a special session. So both sides of the clearly drawn line could work out their differences.

It's not going well. Mostly because there's the royal family and the MPs who actually give a damn about the country on one side . . . and on the other is a great big bag of smelly dicks.

"Order!" I call out. "Ladies and gentlemen, for God's sake—this is not a football stadium or a backstreet pub. Remember who you are. Where you are."

In the hallowed hall where one of my ancestors, Crazy King Clifford II, once wore his crown—and nothing else. Because he was hot. We're not supposed to talk about him.

Finally, the shouting quiets down.

And I address the head prick. "Sir Aloysius, what is your stance on the current legislation proposed?"

He sniffs. "My stance remains unchanged, Your Grace. Why should we pass these packages of laws?"

"Because it's your job. Because the country needs this."

"Then I suggest Her Majesty agree to our demands," he tells me, sneering.

And suddenly the dog-eating doesn't seem so harsh.

I stare him down, my face as cold and hard as my voice.

"That's not how this works, Sir Aloysius. And you can take your demands and go fuck yourself with them."

There are a few random shouts of agreement and "here, here."

Aloysius snaps, "You are not King yet, Prince Nicholas."

"No, I'm not." And I look him right in his eyes. "But you should enjoy your position while you can. Because when I am, it will be my mission to make sure you lose it."

His nostrils go wide and he swivels toward the Queen. "Does your grandson speak for the royal house, Your Majesty?"

There's a light in my grandmother's eyes and a smirk on her face. Though she'd probably prefer it not be over something so serious, she loves this. The struggle, the battle, the confrontation—it's her playground.

"I would have chosen less incendiary words . . . but yes, Prince Nicholas expressed our thoughts quite accurately."

See? She wanted to tell him to go fuck himself too.

The Queen stands, and all rise with her. "We are done here, for now." She scans the room, her eyes touching the face of each Member of Parliament. "Our country is at a crossroads. Rest assured, if you cannot show that you are capable of choosing the right path, one will be chosen for you."

Then, together, we turn and walk out the large double doors, side by side.

In the hall, walking toward the car, she speaks without looking at me. "That was not wise, Nicholas. You made an enemy today."

"He was our enemy already. Now he just knows that we know it. I had to say something."

She chuckles. "You're starting to sound like your brother."

"Maybe he actually has a point."

Speaking of Henry, he's doing better. It's been a few weeks since the boat incident and he seems . . . purged. Calmer. He also reached out to the families of the soldiers, like Olivia suggested. Speaking and visiting with them seems to have brought him some measure of peace.

So, he's coming with Olivia and I to the seaside. For the weekend.

I don't mind—I mean, I'm driving in an open-topped convertible with a motorcade of security agents driving all around me, so it's not like Olivia was going to suck me off on the way there anyway.

That being said, it's forty minutes into the five-hour drive . . . and I'm starting to have second thoughts.

"Sobriety is tedious," my brother says from the backseat. "I'm soooo booooored."

Then he pops up, placing his forearms on our headrests and hanging his head between us. "Is this how the whole trip is going to be? You two making goo-goo eyes at each other? Do you see that tree over there, Nicholas? Drive towards it as fast as you can and put me out of my misery."

We ignore him.

Olivia takes her phone out and snaps a picture of a cliff that she says looks like Patrick from *SpongeBob*, intending to text it to her sister. She talks or texts with Ellie and Marty every day—to check in and check up on how things are going in New York without her. Last night Ellie told Olivia their father was "doing better," which eased some of her worries.

"Oooh, Ellie," my brother coos, looking over Olivia's shoulder. "Let's call her. Find out if she's legal yet."

"My sister's off-limits to you, buddy." Olivia frowns.

He flops back onto the seat. "This is so boring."

It's going to be a long drive.

But when we get to Anthorp Castle, which sits on a cliff overlooking the ruckus of whitewater waves below, it's anything but boring. Henry doesn't want to swim, but he's interested in cliff diving.

Thank Christ, I talk him out of it.

Olivia and I skip skinny-dipping because of security—and her bare bits are for my eyes only. But we do freeze our arses off in the water down on the beach—Olivia in a turquoise string bikini, me in swim shorts both of us splashing and swimming in the rough waves like randy dolphins.

The good part about cold water is eventually, everything just gets numb.

And the best part about old stone castles is the giant fireplace in every room. We warm up in front of the one in the great hall, on a rug made of rabbit pelts. Olivia dries her hair by the fire and I watch the flames reflect in her eyes, turning them a deep violet.

We eat delicious stew and fresh-baked bread for dinner.

And that night, in the giant antique bed, in view of the stars, Olivia straddles my hips and rides my cock with slow, deliberate strokes. I gaze up at her, like a sinner who's found redemption. The way the moonlight streaming in from the window bathes her skin in an illustrious glow—*fuck*, she's beautiful. I could almost weep with it.

But I don't. Because there are other, better, ways to show my adoration.

I lift up, my hands skimming her spine to cradle her shoulders. I guide her back—at this angle, I'm still buried fully, fantastically, inside her, but the weight of her upper body rests in my hands. Then I bring my lips to her breast—and I make love to those soft globes with my lips and teeth and tongue. Worshipping them like the deities they are.

She whimpers as I lick her, and her pussy clenches harder around me. It's fucking magnificent.

Things have changed between us since the day of the polo match. They're deeper, more intense . . . just *more* everything. We both feel it, know it, though we haven't spoken about it. Not yet.

Olivia's hips circle and grind as my balls tighten. I lift her back up, so we're face-to-face. With my hands on her shoulders, I rock up into her while she fucks down on me hard and perfect. And we come together—grasping at one another, moaning and cursing.

The acoustics of these walls aren't as good as the palace . . . but they're damn close.

The next day, on the drive back, we stop at a pub for an early dinner. It's a low-key place, known for its ploughman's sandwich and good whiskey. Since it's an unplanned stop, security goes in before us, does a sweep, and remains nearby while we eat.

Afterwards, as we stand up from the table, Henry squints at a curvy strawberry blond across the room, pressing a finger to his lips, then aiming it in her direction. "I know that girl. How do I know that girl?"

"Titebottum," I tell him.

"Yes, she certainly has that. Though I'm surprised you'd mention it in front of Olive."

Olivia folds her arms, looking for an explanation. And I chuckle at my brother because he's an idiot.

"That's her name," I tell them both. "She's Lady Von Titebottum's daughter, the younger one . . . Penelope."

Henry snaps his fingers. "Yes, that's it. I met her at Baron Fossbender's a few years back when she was still in university."

Just then, a long-haired brunette with glasses steps up beside Penelope, and I add, "And that's her sister . . . Sarah, I believe."

As we head towards the door, Penelope spots my brother, and from the look on her face she doesn't have any trouble recalling who he is. "Henry Pembrook! It's been forever—how the hell are you?"

"I'm good, Penelope."

Sarah and Penelope both curtsy, short and quick, then Penelope scowls dramatically at Henry. "Don't tell me you were here visiting and didn't think to look me up! I'll never forgive you."

Henry grins. "Drive back with us. I'll make it up to you."

She pouts. "I can't. Mother hates the city—too noisy, too crowded."

"And we have to bring home dinner. We're picking it up now," Sarah says in a soft, airy voice, clutching a leather-bound book to her chest.

"What are you reading?" Olivia asks.

The girl smiles. "*Sense and Sensibility.*"

"For the thousandth time," Penelope grumbles. "And she won't even read like a normal person—I got her an e-reader for her birthday but she doesn't use it! She carries all those books around in that satchel that's about to fall apart."

"An e-reader's not the same, Penny," Sarah explains quietly.

"A book's a book." Henry shrugs. "It's just . . . words. Isn't it?"

Sarah blushes deeply—almost purple. But she still shakes her head at my brother—pityingly. She opens the book and holds it up near his face.

"Smell."

After a moment, Henry leans down and sniffs the pages distrustfully.

"What do you smell?" Sarah asks.

Henry gives it another sniff. "It smells . . . old."

"Exactly!" She smells the pages herself, deep and long. "Paper and ink—there's nothing like it. The only thing that smells better than a new book is an old one."

Someone drops a tray of glasses behind the bar, and the shattering crash reverberates throughout the room. And Sarah Von Titebottum goes very still, her eyes blank and her skin whiter than the pages she's holding.

"Lady Sarah," I ask, "are you all right?"

She doesn't respond.

"It's okay," her sister whispers, but she doesn't seem to hear her.

Henry presses his palm to her arm. "Sarah?"

She inhales swiftly—gasping—like she hadn't been breathing. Then she blinks and looks around, slightly panicked, before recovering herself.

"Forgive me. I was . . . startled . . . by the crash." She presses her hand to her chest. "I'm going to get some air and wait outside, Pen."

Just then, a uniformed waiter brings the dinner order they're picking up. Penelope asks the waiter to carry it to the car for them and we say our good-byes.

On the way out, Penelope reminds Henry, "Ring me! Don't forget."

"I will." He waves.

Then he stares after them, watching them walk out the door. "She's an odd little duck, isn't she?"

"Who?" I ask.

"Lady Sarah. Pity—she could be pretty, if she didn't dress like a monk in drag."

Olivia clucks her tongue, like a disapproving, big-sister hen. "She didn't look like a monk, you jerk. Maybe she's busy with—interests, or whatever—and doesn't have time to spend on her appearance. I can understand that." She points up and down her luscious little form. "Believe it or not, I don't look like this in my real life."

I slip my arm around her waist. "Rubbish—you're beautiful no matter what you have on." Then I whisper in her ear, "Especially when you have on nothing."

"Still," Henry muses as we head for the door, "I wouldn't mind getting a peek at what's under Miss Sense and Sensibility's long skirt. With a name like Titebottum, it must be good."

CHAPTER 21

Nicholas

My mother once told me that time was like the wind. It rushes over you, passes you—and no matter how hard you try, how much you want to, you can't hold onto it, and you can't ever slow it down.

Her words echo in my head as I lie awake in my bed, in the gray dawn stillness, while Olivia sleeps soundlessly beside me.

Four days. That's all we have left. The time has flown by as quickly as turning the pages in a book. They've been glorious days—filled with laughter and kisses, moans and gasps, more pleasure in every way than I ever let myself dream about.

For the last month, Olivia and I have truly enjoyed our time together. We've gone biking around the city—with security nearby, of course. The people wave and call—not just to me, but to her as well. "A lovely lass," they say. There were picnics near the pond and trips to our other properties, Olivia's sweet voice echoing with joy down the aged halls. I taught her to ride a horse, though she prefers a bike. A few times she's gone clay-pigeon shooting with Henry and I—covering her ears at every pull of the trigger in the adorable way she has of doing things.

There hasn't been much reason for Olivia and my grandmother to come into contact, but when they have, the Queen has treated her civilly, if not frigidly. But one Sunday for tea, Olivia baked scones. It was the first time she'd baked since leaving New York and she actually enjoyed it. She made her own delicious recipe of almond and cranberry. My grandmother declined to try even one bite.

And I hated her a little bit then.

But that one, dark moment is extinguished by a thousand brilliant ones. A thousand perfect memories of our time together.

And now our time is just about up.

The seed of an idea has been planted in my mind for a while—months—but I haven't let it sprout. Until now.

I turn on my side, kissing a path up Olivia's smooth arm to her shoulder, burying my nose in the fragrant crook of her neck. She wakes with a smile in her voice.

"Good morning."

My lips drift to her ear. And I give voice to my idea. To my hope.

"Don't go back to New York. Stay."

Her reply comes a heartbeat later. In a whisper.

"For how long?"

"For always."

Slowly she turns in my arms, her navy eyes seeking, her lips just starting to smile.

"Have you talked to your grandmother? Are you . . . are you not going through with the announcement?"

I swallow hard, my throat rough.

"No. Canceling the announcement isn't possible. But I've been thinking . . . I could push the wedding off for a year. Maybe two. We would have all that time together."

She flinches. And her smile falls into oblivion.

But I push on—trying to make her understand. Make her see.

"I could have Winston look into the women on the list. Perhaps one of them has what we have. I could . . . come to an understanding with her. An arrangement."

"A marriage of convenience," she says in a detached tone.

"Yes." I cup her cheek, bringing her eyes to mine. "It's been done for centuries—because it works. Or maybe . . . I could marry Ezzy. It would make things easier for her . . . and for us."

Olivia's gaze touches the ceiling and her hand scrapes into her hair, tugging. "Jesus fucking Christ, Nicholas."

And my voice is raw with desperate emotion. "Just think about it. You're not even considering it."

"Do you have any idea what you're asking me?"

Frustration turns my tone cold. "I'm asking you to stay. Here. With me."

And hers bursts into flames. "Yes, stay and watch you announce to the world that you're marrying someone else! Stay and watch while you go to parties and luncheons and pose for pictures with someone else. Stay and watch you . . . give her your mother's ring."

I wince.

Olivia shoves me, rises, and scrambles off the bed.

"You are such an asshole!"

She heads for the bookcase, but I bolt off the bed, chasing her. I wrap an arm around her waist, locking her in place, my chest against her back—my hand in her hair, my scraping voice at her ear.

"Yes, I'm a fucking arsehole and a bastard, too. But I can't . . . bear it. The thought of you being an ocean away. The thought of never seeing you, never touching you again."

I close my eyes and press my forehead against her temple, breathing her in, holding her too tight but too desperate to loosen my grip.

"I love you, Olivia. I love you. And I don't know how to do this. I don't know how to let you go."

She shudders in my arms. And then she's sobbing into her hands. Great, heaving, heartbroken bursts that wreck me.

I should've left her alone. I should've walked away the moment I started to feel . . . everything. I had no business trying to keep her. It will forever be the cruelest thing I've ever done.

She turns in my arms and presses her face against my chest, wetting it with her tears. I hold her close and stroke her hair. "Don't cry, love. Shhh . . . please, Olivia."

Broken eyes look up at me.

"I love you too."

"I know." I stroke her face. "I know you do."

"But I can't . . ." Her voice quakes. "If I stay here, if I have to watch you . . . it'll be like being burned alive, one piece at a time, until there'll be nothing left of me . . . of us."

My ribs squeeze as if a snake has coiled around them, making every breath painful and hard.

"It was unfair of me to ask you, Olivia." I push at her tears, wiping them away. "Please don't cry anymore. Please . . . forget. Forget I said anything. Let's just—"

"Enjoy the time we have left," she finishes softly.

My finger traces the bridge of her nose.

"That's right."

Olivia

I wait outside the Queen's office. Her secretary, Christopher, told me she can't possibly see me today, but I wait anyway. Because I have to—I have to try.

When she walks into the room, brisk and efficient, I say, "I need to speak with you."

She doesn't even look at me.

"It's important."

She walks past me toward her office door.

"Your Majesty, please!"

Finally, she stops and turns her head. Her lips purse, looking me over. And that Christopher guy must have mental telepathy, because without a word, when the Queen proceeds into her office, he raises his arm and leads me in behind her.

I don't know how long she'll let me speak, so as soon as the door closes, I start right in.

"Nicholas needs more time."

Her words are clipped and dismissive. "Time will not make this better."

"He's not ready."

She walks behind her desk, scanning the papers there. "Of course he is. He was born for this—quite literally."

"He doesn't want this."

"But he'll do it. Because he is honorable and it is his duty."

"I love him!"

That makes her stop. Her hand pauses over a piece of paper, and her face slowly lifts, meeting my eyes.

And then, the Queen's expression goes softer—the lines around her mouth and eyes smooth out, making her look gentler. Like the grandma she's supposed to be.

"Yes, I believe you do. He loves you too, you know. When he looks at you . . . His father used to look at his mother the same way—like she was the Eighth Wonder of the World. These last months, Nicholas has reminded me so much of his father, at times it's been almost as if my son were standing right there."

She gestures to the sofa near the fireplace. "Sit."

I do, carefully, while she takes a cushioned chair, facing me. "I had a second child, after Thomas—a daughter. Did Nicholas ever tell you that?"

"No," I answer, all of the righteous heat leaching out of me.

"She was a sickly, beautiful creature. Born with a heart condition. We brought in all the specialists, doctors from all over the world. Edward was out of his mind with grief. And I would have given up my crown to save her . . . but there was nothing to be done. They told me she wouldn't last a month. She survived for six."

She seems lost for a moment, in the memory. Then her gray eyes blink out of the reverie. Her gaze falls back to the present—back to me.

"That is when I learned that hope is cruel. A pitiless gift. Honesty, finality, may seem brutal—but in the end, it's mercy." And then her voice turns to steel. "There is no hope for a future between you and my grandson. None. You need to accept that."

"I can't," I whisper.

"You must. The law is clear."

"But you could change the law. You could do that for us—for *him*."

"No, I cannot."

"You're the Queen!"

"Yes, that's right, and your country has a president. And what would happen if your president announced tomorrow that elections would be held every eight years instead of every four? What would your government do? What would your people do?"

I open my mouth . . . but nothing comes out.

"Change takes time and requires will, Olivia—there is no will in Wessco for this kind of change. And even if there were, now is not the time. Even monarchs are bound by the law. I am not God."

"No," I bite out, on the verge of totally losing it. "You're a monster. How can you do this to him? How can you know how he feels about me and make him do this?"

She turns to the window, looking out. "A mother burying her child is the only thing that could make one truly long for death—if only for the sliver of hope that she might glimpse her child again. Thomas got me through it the first time. Because I knew he needed me. And when I had to bury him and Calista, it was Nicholas and Henry who pulled me through, because they needed me even more. So, if you wish to think of me as a monster, that is your right. Perhaps I am. But believe me when I tell you, there is nothing—*nothing*—I would not do for those boys."

"Except let them live their lives. Let them marry who they want."

She scoffs at me, shaking her head. "If I am a monster, then you are a naïve, selfish girl."

"Because I love Nicholas? Because I want to be with him and make him happy—*that* makes me selfish?"

She lifts her chin like a professor in a lecture hall. "You are common—and I don't say that as a criticism. Commoners look at the world through the lens of a single lifetime. In a hundred years, no one will remember your name. You are as indistinguishable as grains of sand on the beach.

"Monarchs see the world through the prism of legacy. Ask Nicholas; he'll tell you the same. What will we leave behind? How will we be remembered? Because whether we are reviled or revered—*we* will be remembered. Nicholas is a leader. Men are dedicated to him, they follow him naturally, you must see it."

I think of Logan and Tommy and James—the way they protected Nicholas. Not only because it was their job, but because they wanted to.

"When he is King he will better the lives of tens of millions of people. He will lead our country into a new age. He could literally change the world, Olivia. And you would deprive them of him—for what? A few decades of your own happiness? Yes, child—in my book, that makes you selfish."

I try to keep it together, but frustration makes me tear my hands through my hair. Because how the hell do you argue with that?

"So that's it?" I ask, crushed. "There's no way . . . at all?"

She's not angry when she says it, or mean. Just . . . final. "No, there isn't."

I close my eyes and take a deep breath. And then I lift my head—facing her, head-on. "Then I guess there's nothing left to say. Thank you for speaking with me."

I rise and turn to leave, but when my hand is on the door she calls my name.

"Yes?" I turn back.

"I have watched you these last months. I've seen how you are with the staff and the people, with Henry and Nicholas. I've seen you." From this angle, in this light, the Queen's eyes seem shiny. Almost glistening. "I was wrong the day we met when I said you wouldn't do. If things were different, you, my dear, would do . . . beautifully."

Tears rise in my eyes and emotion lodges in my throat. It's funny—when people are stingy with their praise, it always seems to mean the most when it's given.

I dip my head, and bend my knees and slowly lower into a full, perfect curtsy. I've been practicing. And for all she is—a queen, a mother, a grandmother—she deserves that honor and respect.

After the door closes behind me, I take a big breath. Because now I know what I have to do.

CHAPTER 22

Nicholas

The days leading up to the Summer Jubilee are always fraught with frantic activity and planning. There's a tension in the air, a weight that has to be waded through, because all the things that have to get done cling like leeches.

Dignitaries and heads of state come from all over the world and are hosted at the palace. There are photo sessions with the royal family—immediate and extended—and meetings and interviews with the press. The organized chaos grows as the day of reckoning approaches, like the burps and grumbles of a volcano, building up to its apocalyptic eruption.

I've gotten through it the way I do every year—with a smile spackled to my face and unspoken words locked safely in my head. But the last twenty-four hours have been particularly difficult. I say all the right things, do all that's expected, but it feels like a shroud lies across my shoulders, heavy and suffocating.

It feels like mourning . . . like the days surrounding my parents' death. When, in spite of the crushing grief pressing down on every cell in my body, I had to go on, keep walking, head high, one foot in front of the other.

I'm determined to enjoy tonight, though—really enjoy it. Olivia's never seen a real ball, with more pomp and circumstance and grandeur than I doubt she can imagine. And I want to soak up her reaction—every smile and sparkle of wonder that lights in her eyes. I'll hoard those moments, keep the memory of tonight close and safe, so I can pull it out and relive it after she's gone.

I wait in the morning room of Guthrie House for Olivia to come down after she's done getting primped and painted. Then I'll escort her over to the main palace, where we'll receive our final marching orders from the decorum police and the ball will begin.

I hear the swish of fabric at the top of the stairs, turn around—and get knocked on my arse.

Her gown is pale blue, satin and chiffon—low cut, with a taste of cleavage, framed by dips and swells that bare her shoulders but encircle her arms. It's an old-fashioned style without being costumey. There's a slash of rhinestone embellishment across the bodice, and the satin hugs her tiny waist, draping down to a skirt that's hooped but not overly large. On one side, the satin pulls up, held with the same gemstone decoration, revealing pale blue chiffon beneath, dotted with jewels. Olivia's hair is pinned up in ornate shiny black curls, with diamond combs winking out between them.

Fergus stands beside me, and the old dog practically sighs.

"The lass looks like an angel."

"No," I say as Olivia reaches the bottom step. "She looks like a queen."

She stands in front of me and for a moment we just stare at each other.

"I've never seen you in your military uniform," she says, eyes drifting over me hungrily from head to toe, before settling on my eyes. "It should be illegal."

"I'm the one who's supposed to be giving the compliments." I swallow hard, wanting her so much. In every way. "You look breathtaking, love. I can't decide if I want you to stay in that dress forever or if I want to rip it off you right now."

She laughs.

Simple, elegant diamonds dangle from her tasty little earlobes, but her throat is bare—just like I asked the stylist to keep it. I reach into my pocket and pull out a small, square box.

"I have something for you."

She blushes, before she even sees what's inside. And then, when I lift the lid, she gasps.

It's a snowflake—in an intricate, spin-wheel pattern—laden with a hundred small diamonds and sapphires. The diamonds are clear and flawless, like Olivia's skin, and the sapphires are brilliant and deep, like her eyes.

Her mouth goes slack. "It's . . . gorgeous." She fingers the velvet bed, but doesn't touch the necklace—almost as if she's afraid to. "I can't keep this, Nicholas."

"Of course you can." The words come out firm, almost harsh. "I designed it myself, had it made." I slip it from the box and step behind her, tying the silk choker ribbon around her throat. "There's only one in the whole world—just like you."

I press a kiss to the back of her neck, then her shoulder.

Olivia turns to face me, takes my hand, and lowers her voice. "Nicholas, I've been thinking—"

"Let's go, Googly Eyes One and Two—we're late," Henry—also decked out in full uniform—says as he walks into the room, tapping his wrist. "You'll have time to drool all over each other later."

I lean down and kiss Olivia's cheek. "You can finish that sentence tonight."

We assemble in an antechamber off the ballroom, while the sounds of the party, the chatter and music and the clinking of glasses, seep like smoke under the door. My cousins are here—

Marcus and his brood. After the briefest of greetings they stay far away from me, and I do the same. I also stay away from any refreshments they've been near . . . just in case.

My secretary, Bridget claps her hands, giggling and vibrating like the head of a social committee in school. "One more time, just in case—the Queen will be announced first, followed by Prince Nicholas, then Prince Henry, who will escort Miss Hammond into the room." She turns to my brother. "Everyone will be standing, so you will walk Miss Hammond to the marked spot near the wall, then return to your brother's side for the receiving line. Everyone's got it, yes?"

Trumpets blare from beyond the doors, and Bridget nearly bursts out of her skin.

"Oh, that's the signal. Places, my lords and ladies, places!" She pauses next to Olivia, squeezing her arm and squeaking, "It's just so exciting!"

After she steps away, Olivia laughs. "I really like her."

Then she lines up beside my brother. We talked about it—about Henry escorting her in, the expectations, the traditions . . . but standing here now, it all just seems so meaningless.

Stupid.

I turn around and tap my brother on the shoulder. "Hey."

"Yeah?"

"Trade with me."

"Trade what?" Henry asks.

I motion with my finger. "Our spots."

He leans over, looking at our grandmother's back. "You're supposed to follow Granny out. Be second in the receiving line."

I shrug. "She won't look behind her. She won't know until you're beside her—and then, she'll roll with it. You can handle greeting the guests second—I have faith in you."

"That goes against protocol," Henry taunts, because I already know he's going to say yes.

I shrug again. "Fuck it."

He chuckles and looks at me with pride in his eyes. "You've turned my brother into a rebel, Olive." He taps her hand. "Well done."

Then he switches spots with me.

Olivia's arm curls around mine, and her thigh brushes my leg through the fabric of her dress.

"That's better." I sigh. Because having her on my arm feels like it always has—like it's meant to be.

The ball is in full swing. Everyone's enjoying themselves—the music is less stuffy than in past years, the orchestra mixing renditions of popular music with classical. People are dancing, eating, laughing—and I stand across the room, by myself for a rare moment, watching.

Watching her.

It's the strangest sensation—the swell of joy in my chest that looking at Olivia always brings. The surging pride I feel as she moves with so much confidence, chatting with the wives of ambassadors, leaders, and assorted royalty like she's been doing it her whole life—like she was born to do it. And then the inevitable stab of agony lands—when I remember that she's leaving. That in just another few days, she'll be gone, lost to me, forever.

"Are you all right, Nicky?" Henry asks, with quiet concern. I didn't see him approach and I don't know how long he's been beside me.

"No, Henry," I say in a voice that doesn't sound at all like mine. "I don't think I am."

He nods, then squeezes my arm and pats my back—trying to prop me up, lend me strength. It's all he can do, because, like I told him months ago . . . we are who we are.

I push off from the wall and walk over to the orchestra leader. We speak for a few seconds, heads bent together. When he eagerly agrees, I head towards Olivia. I reach her just as the opening notes of the song float across the room.

And I hold out my hand. "May I have this dance, Miss Hammond?"

Understanding dawns on her face . . . and then adoration. It's the prom song she mentioned, that she loves but never got to dance to—"Everything I Do."

Her head tilts. "You remembered."

"I remember it all."

Olivia takes my hand and I lead her out to the dance floor. We've captivated the attention of the entire room. Even the couples already dancing pause and turn our way.

As I take her in my arms and lead her, Olivia whispers nervously, "Everyone's looking at us."

People have looked at me my entire life. It's something I've endured begrudgingly, accepted no matter how much it chafed.

Except for now.

"Good."

In the early morning hours, before dawn, I move inside Olivia—on top of her—with only breath between us, white-hot pleasure coursing and spiking through us both with every long, slow stroke of my hips. It's making love, in the truest, purest sense of the word.

Our thoughts, our bodies, our souls are not our own. They swirl and blend together, becoming something new and perfect. I hold her face while I kiss her, my tongue sliding against hers, our hearts beating in time. Sparks strike against my spine, tingles of electricity that hint at the shattering orgasm that's building. But not yet . . . I don't want it to end yet.

My hips slow and my pelvis rests against Olivia's, where I'm buried, touching the deepest part of her.

I feel her hand on my jaw and open my eyes. She's still wearing the necklace—it shines in the moonlight, but not as brightly as her eyes.

"Ask me again, Nicholas."

Hope whispers. Blessed, beautiful, thrilling hope.

"Stay."

Her soft lips smile. "For how long?"

My voice is hushed and rough with pleading.

"For always."

Olivia looks deep into my eyes and her smile grows, her head bobbing in the tiniest of nods.

"Yes."

CHAPTER 23

Olivia

Nicholas is practically giddy the next morning. We both are. Kissing and laughing—we can't keep our hands off each other. Because it's a new day. I never really understood that expression before. I mean, isn't every day a "new day"? But now I get it. Because our future—whatever that future may hold—starts today.

And Nicholas and I are walking into it together.

We have breakfast in his room. We take a long shower together—hot in more ways than one. We finally put our clothes on and venture out late in the afternoon. Nicholas wants to take me biking again. But when we make it downstairs, Winston—the "Head Dark Suit," as Nicholas calls him—is waiting for us.

"There's a matter we must speak of, Your Grace," he tells Nicholas, not looking at me at all.

Nicholas's thumb slowly caresses the back of my hand. "We're just on our way out, Winston. Can it wait?"

"I'm afraid not. It's rather urgent."

Nicholas sighs.

And I try to be helpful. "I'll hang out in the library until you're done."

He nods. "All right." He kisses my lips, softly, quickly, and then goes to do what he needs to do.

About forty-five minutes later, I'm still in the majestic palace library—it's two stories, with gleaming wood that smells like lemon polish, the shelves packed with one ancient-looking, leather-bound title after another. I flip through a copy of *Sense and Sensibility*, not really reading the words.

"We're ready for you now, Miss Hammond."

My head snaps up to find Winston looking down at me, his hands clasped behind his back.

"What do you mean, 'Ready for me'?"

This guy's poker face is epic. And more than a little freaky. His mouth is relaxed, his eyes impassive—it's the face of a mannequin. Or a very good, very cold, hit man.

"This way, please."

Nicholas

Olivia steps into the room, looking curious and so very tiny next to Winston's girth. Her eyes drift over Henry in the leather chair by the fireplace, then she smiles when she sees me across the room.

"What's going on?"

I search her face and my own memory—looking for some sign I missed. Something that would've made me suspect . . . but there's nothing.

Olivia worries her lip, staring at my blank expression.

Winston swivels the computer screen on the desk towards her. "These are the headlines that will run in the *Daily Star*. It's a tabloid."

HIS ROYAL HOTNESS'S UNWANTED SECRET HEIR

ROYAL TEEN PREGNANCY ENDS IN MISCARRIAGE – ALL THE DETAILS

Her face pinches in horror. "Oh no! How . . . how did they find out?"

"We were hoping you could explain that to us, Miss Hammond," Winston says. "Since you are the one who told them."

I hate that I agreed to this—agreed to let Winston take the lead, do the questioning.

"What are you talking about?" Olivia turns my way again. "Nicholas?"

Winston slides a sheet of paper in front of her. She stares at it hard, brow wrinkling with concentration. "What is this?"

It's a mortgage statement for Amelia's—for the building of the coffee shop and Olivia's apartment in New York—that was in foreclosure five months ago.

It was paid off in full last week.

Winston tells Olivia as much.

"I don't understand. I just spoke to Ellie yesterday—she didn't say anything." She takes a step closer to me. "Nicholas, you can't really believe I would do this."

My gut rebels at the idea—but the black-and-white evidence taunts me. "I'm not accusing you."

"Yeah, but you're not exactly defending me, either."

I take the paper off the table. "Explain this to me. Make it make sense." Even to my own ears, it sounds like begging. "Make me understand what happened."

She shakes her head. "I can't."

It's like a thousand weights are sitting on my shoulders, bending my spine, trying to snap me in half. "I would forgive you for anything, Olivia. Did you know that? Anything. But . . . I won't be lied to."

"I'm not lying."

"Maybe you told someone, accidentally. Maybe you mentioned it to your sister or Marty or your father?"

She takes a step backwards. "So, I'm not a scumbag but my family is?"

"I didn't say that."

"That's *exactly* what you said."

I throw the bank statement on the table. "For ten years there hasn't been a whisper of this in the press. Then weeks after I tell you, it's splashed across the papers and it just so happens your family's mortgage is paid off at the same time? What am I supposed to think?"

Olivia flinches, running her hand over her forehead.

"I don't know what to say."

My voice booms. "Tell me you didn't do this!"

She looks me right in the eye, chin raised, eyes simmering. "I didn't do this."

But then, when I don't say anything, her face falls like a collapsing castle of cards. "You don't believe me."

I look away. "Put yourself in my place."

"I'm trying to." Her lip trembles. "But I would believe you, so I can't." She shakes her head. "When have I ever given you a reason to think I want money out of this?"

"Maybe you weren't after money . . . in the beginning," Winston interjects, like a barrister setting up a question during a trial. "But then you came here and saw firsthand the wealth that was to be had. Perhaps with your departure so close, you made the choice to get what you could while you could."

"Shut your mouth!" Olivia lunges at him.

But I grab her arm, pulling her back. "That's enough."

Our eyes meet, hers so big and begging. Begging for me to believe her. And, Christ, I want to. But uncertainty twists my heart around in my chest, making it hard to breathe.

"I'll call my father," Olivia declares. "He'll tell you it's a mistake."

She slides her phone out of her pocket, dials and waits. After what seems like fucking forever, she looks up at me, nervously. "There's no answer. I'll keep trying."

While she redials, I ask Winston, "Where did the money come from?"

"We haven't been able to trace the transfer yet; we're working on it."

My voice is strong—commanding. "I need that information, Winston. It's the only way to know for sure."

Slowly, Olivia lowers the phone from her ear. And she looks at me, staring, like I'm a stranger. No—worse—like I'm a monster.

"After everything that's happened, everything I'm willing to give up for you, everything we've said and been to each other for the last five months . . . you need more information until you can decide if I'm the type of person who would take one of the most painful secrets of your life and sell it to a supermarket rag?"

There's a warning voice that tells me to stop. All of this. Right here, right now—go no farther. It says I have no reason not to trust her. That she could never do this to me. Not the Olivia I know.

But I turn deaf ears on that voice. Because it lies. I've listened to it before—over and over again when I was young and stupid and wrong.

I won't be wrong again. Not about this—not about her. It would . . . break me.

My face feels like a mask—stone cold and blank.

"Yes. I need more information."

And she shatters, like a windowpane that's been struck by a fist, right in front of me.

"Fuck you!" She steps back, yelling and crying and shaking her head. "Fuck you and this fucked-up place that raised you. You're so messed up. You're so warped inside—because of these games and these people. You can't even see it. And I can't stand to look at you right now."

"Then leave!" I shout back. "There's the door—get out! If I'm so hard to look at, go back to fucking New York!"

The second the words leave my mouth I want to snatch them back. I don't mean them. But words don't work that way. Once heard, they can't ever be taken back.

All they can do is echo.

The color drains from Olivia's cheeks and her eyes close. Her face turns towards the floor and her shoulders drop. Like she's . . . done. Like there's nothing left to her at all.

She takes a shuddering breath and without raising her head, without looking at me even one more time, she turns and walks out.

For a full minute, no one speaks. I stand there—like an idiot—staring at the space where she just stood.

Henry's words fill the silence. "You're making a mistake. And that was harsh, Nicholas, even for you."

I face Winston. "Find out where the money came from. Now."

Winston bows and leaves.

I feel Henry's eyes on the back of my head, but I don't turn around. I have nothing to say.

He doesn't feel the same.

"Hello?" He comes around and tries to knock on my head. "Is anyone alive in there? Who are you right now?"

He seems different to me somehow, taller or older. More . . . serious. I don't know why I didn't notice before, or why the hell I'm seeing it now.

"What are you going on about?"

"Well, you look like my brother and you sound like him, but you're not him. You're some alternate version of him—the one who gives all those scripted, meaningless answers in interviews. The Tin Man."

"I'm not in the mood to play games with you, Henry."

He goes on like I haven't spoken at all.

"My real brother would know that Olivia wouldn't—couldn't—do this. He'd know it in here." He pokes my chest. "So either you're too afraid to trust your own instincts or you're too afraid to trust her, but either way, you just let the best damn thing that's ever happened to you walk right out the door. And with the lives we have, that's really saying something."

I swallow hard, feeling cold and numb inside. Feeling . . . nothing.

My voice is as hollow as my chest. "If she didn't do it, it's one hell of a coincidence. I'll know what to do once Winston gets more information."

"It'll be too late then!"

I don't say another word. I'm done discussing this. But my brother isn't quite finished.

"There've been many times in my life when I thought Mum would be ashamed of me. This is the first time I've ever thought . . . she'd be ashamed of you."

And then he walks away too.

Olivia

I don't take a breath on the way back to my room. I'll lose it if I do. So I bite my lip and wrap my arms around my waist, passing security men in the halls, nodding to maids. But as soon as I'm through the door, I let go.

The sobs tear out of me, shaking my shoulders and scraping my lungs. It's rage and devastation mixed together, the worst kind of heartbreak. How could he do this? After everything I've done—everything I was willing to do for him.

I saw it in his eyes—those gorgeous, tortured eyes. He wanted to believe me—but he didn't. Couldn't. Whatever tiny wick of trust still lives inside him has been burned one too many times.

Did he ever really trust me? Did he ever believe that we could last . . . for always? Or was some part of him just waiting, watching, until I screwed him over?

Well, fuck him. Fuck him and his fucking palace. No more. I'm done.

"Can I bring you some tea, Miss Hammond?"

I gasp loudly and I think my heart stops. It's the maid for my room—Mellie, I think her name is. I didn't see her when I first walked in because I was crying into my hands.

Her fresh face is awash with sympathy. But I'm tired of being surrounded—sick of the maids and the security and, and . . . Twitter assholes . . . and the fucking secretaries and assistants. I just want to be alone. I want to crawl into a corner where no one can see me or hear me, so I can breathe . . . and cry my fucking eyes out.

A hiccup rattles through my chest. "Nn—no. No tha—ank you."

She nods, eyes down—like a good little servant. She slips past me discreetly, closing the door behind her. Trained oh so well.

I lock the door. Then I march to the bookcase that connects this room to Nicholas's and lock that too. I walk into the bathroom and turn the shower on to scalding. As the steam rises around me, I strip out of my clothes, choking on my tears. I step into the shower, slide down to the floor, and rest my forehead on my knees. And as the water pounds down over me, I let it all pour out.

Nicholas

I visited a children's hospital ward once, in a facility that specialized in treating the rarest, most confounding disorders. There was a young girl there—a tiny, bandaged, pretty thing—who was unable to feel pain. Something to do with how her nerves communicated with her brain. At first glance, you would think a life without pain would be a blessing—she'd never have a toothache, a stomach-ache, her parents would never have to dry her tears after a knee-scraping stumble.

But pain is actually a gift. A warning that something is amiss and action must be taken to correct the situation. Without pain, an otherwise minor injury could lead to deadly consequences.

Guilt works the same way.

It's a signal from the conscience that something is terribly wrong.

Mine eats at me—one slow, sharp bite at a time—in the minutes that I stay in the empty office. It claws at the lining of my gut when I make my way back to my room. It gathers in my throat when I pour myself a brandy, making it almost impossible to swallow it down.

I can't shake it, can't stop seeing it—the last look on Olivia's face. Defeated. Crushed.

It shouldn't feel like this. I'm the injured party. I'm the one who's been lied to. Betrayed. Then why do I feel so fucking guilty?

It stabs at me like the jagged edge of a broken rib.

The glass clinks when I set it on the table, then walk to the bookcase and through the corridor that leads to Olivia's room.

But when I push on the bookcase on the other side, it doesn't give—doesn't move an inch.

I'd forgotten about the latch.

My mother installed it herself. It was the only time I'd ever seen her with a screwdriver in her hand—and the only time I'd ever heard her refer to my father as a fucking wanker.

They'd patched up whatever they'd been arguing about—but the latch had stayed.

And was apparently now being put back to use.

I push at my hair and stalk out of the room into the hall, down to Olivia's door. I rap on it hard. But there's no answer.

A young maid nods to me as she passes and my chin jerks in response.

I try the handle, but that door is also locked, so I knock again—working hard to tamp down the pissed-offness growing with every second.

"Olivia? I'd like to speak with you."

I wait, but there's no response.

"Olivia." I knock again. "Things got . . . out of hand earlier and I want to talk to you about it. Could you please open the door?"

When a security guard strolls past, I feel like a fucking idiot. And that's just how I must look. Knocking and pleading outside a door in my own bloody house.

This time I pound on the door with the side of my fist.

"Olivia!"

Thirty seconds later, when there's still no answer, my guilt goes up in smoke.

"All right," I hiss at the closed door. "Have it your way."

I stalk down the stairs, spotting Fergus in the foyer. "Have the car brought around."

"Where are you going?"

"Out."

"When will you return?"

"Late."

His gaze rakes over me. "Seems like a damn stupid thing to do."

"Turns out, I've been doing damn stupid things for the last five months." I step out through the door. "Why stop now?"

Olivia

I put on my own clothes after my shower—my real clothes—worn gray sweatpants and a white V-neck T-shirt. I don't dry my hair, but twist it up into a bun, wet, on top of my head. My eyes feel puffy and swollen and probably look even worse. I drag my suitcases out from the closet and start packing—being sure to leave every single piece of clothing Sabine, the stylist, brought for me. They already think I'm a gold digger; I'll be damned if I give them any more ammunition.

When I'm done, I mean to walk down to the travel secretary's office, to get a car to the airport and a ticket home. But my legs have other ideas.

They bring me through the bookcase to Nicholas's room.

It's silent in that way you can feel there's no one in it. I see a glass of brandy on the table. I touch it with my fingertips—because he touched it. Then I walk over to his bed—that big, beautiful bed. I sink my face into Nicholas's pillow, deeply inhaling his scent—that amazing man-scent that's all him—a hint of ocean and spice.

It makes my skin tingle.

It makes my eyes burn. I thought I was all cried out, but I guess not.

With a shuddering breath, I put the pillow back.

"He's not here, Miss," Fergus says from the doorway. "He left earlier."

"Did he say where he was going?"

"No."

I walk up to the brittle, sweet man. "You were kind to me the whole time I was here. Thank you for that."

As I turn to go, his hand falls on my arm. "He's a good lad—he can be rash at times, but he has his reasons. Let him come to his senses. He loves ye, lass—as the day is long, he loves ye. Don't rush off just now. Give him a bit more time."

The Queen's words echo in my head.

"Time won't make this better, Fergus." I lean over and kiss his wrinkled cheek. "Good-bye."

Jane Stiltonhouse, the travel secretary, is at her desk when I fill her doorway. "I'm ready to go home now."

She's surprised at first—and then elated. "Marvelous."

Jane rises from her chair and slips a folder out from one of the drawers. "I have your first-class ticket to New York ready—courtesy of the Palace, of course. I'll send two girls to Guthrie House to pack your things."

"You don't have to do that. I already packed."

Her smile reminds me of poisonous fruit—dangerously sweet. "Anything provided by the Palace to you on loan—gowns, jewels, et cetra, et cetra—remains with the Palace."

"The only thing I planned on taking was the necklace Nicholas gave me."

She clasps her hands. "Precisely. The necklace must remain here."

Those words hit me like a subway turnstile jabbing into my stomach.

"But Nicholas designed it for me."

"Prince Nicholas had the necklace commissioned and he is a member of the royal family, therefore it is the property of the Crown. It stays."

"He gave it to me."

One of her pointy, penciled eyebrows rises nastily. "And soon he may give it to someone else. It *stays.* Are we going to have a problem, Miss Hammond?"

I'd like to show her how we solve problems like her where I come from. But I don't— because, really, what difference does it make?

"No, Miss Stiltonhouse. There's no problem."

And her mouth does a fabulous impression of Bruce the Shark from *Finding Nemo.*

"Very good. The driver will have your ticket; be sure to bring your passport. Do come visit again," her condemning gaze combs over my clothes, "if you ever have the means."

And I can't leave this place fast enough.

CHAPTER 24

Nicholas

That night, after a lonesome evening spent drinking myself into oblivion in a corner at The Goat, I don't dream about my mother, like I did the last time I was good and pissed. I dream I'm on a ship—a creaky, wooden pirate ship—with a stunning dark-haired figurehead with perfect, pale breasts. In the middle of a giant storm. Being tossed left and right, until one mighty, surging wave topples the whole thing over—sending me reeling into the sea.

When I crack my head on the hard, wooden floor, I realize I'm not on a ship. And the tossing wasn't a dream.

It was my little brother.

Tilting the couch I passed out on and spilling my sorry arse onto the bloody floor.

When I'm able to pry my eyes open, I see him standing over me like an angel of morning-after doom—with Simon standing next to him.

"What the fucking fuck, Henry?"

"I told you, you were wrong. I told you Olivia didn't do it."

Those words snap me into full, immediate consciousness.

Henry's eyes dart to Simon. "Tell him."

Simon looks pale—paler than usual. And not a little bit guilty.

"Tell me what?" I rasp.

He clears his throat. "Yes . . . well, you see—I've begun a new business venture for Barrister's . . ."

When he doesn't continue, I nudge, "And?"

"Pies."

Maybe I am still dreaming after all.

"Pies?"

"Yes—fresh and flash frozen—they'll be deliverable to anyplace in the world. We're going to knock Marie Callenders' and Sara Lee on their arses. And you know how much I enjoyed the pies at Amelia's when we were in the States, so . . . I purchased the recipes from Olivia's father. All of them."

My stomach is still stuck in the dream. It churns.

"How much?"

"Over six figures."

Slowly, I sit up, anger rising. "And you didn't think this was something you should have told me?"

He rubs the back of his neck. "Mr. Hammond wanted it kept quiet. He's been cleaning himself up—doing the twelve steps and all that. He wanted to surprise Olivia when she came home that the business was out of debt and she wouldn't have to run it all on her own anymore." Simon squirms. "And hell—I can never keep a secret from Franny, so I thought it best if you didn't . . ." His words trail off as he looks me over. "What did you do, Nick?"

What did I do?

The realization of what I have done lands like a moose kick to the balls.

I'm on my feet in an instant. And with the awful words I threw at her ringing in my ears, I run down the hall—shirt open, feet bare.

But the moment my hands touch the handles, before I even I open the doors, I know—I can feel it.

She's not here.

I stand in the middle of Olivia's room—that's how I think of it now—not the "white bedroom" or "my mother's old room." It's Olivia's.

Now, it's Olivia's *empty* room.

The bed is made but vacant. The white walls and furniture that looked so pristine and fair yesterday now seem gray and lifeless. I check the bathroom and the closet—I don't know why—but except for a few designer outfits encased in clear plastic, that I know aren't Olivia's, they're just as bare as all the rest. Any trace of her—her shampoos and trinkets and the little hair ties she's always leaving behind—have been wiped away.

Like she was never here at all.

I wander back into the bedroom and a shiny glinting on the dresser catches my eye. The snowflake necklace. It was hers—it was made for her; I gave it to *her* to keep.

To have and to hold.

Even that was selfish of me, I guess. I liked the idea of her having something tangible, something she could touch, a way for her to remember me . . . after.

And she left it behind.

A message doesn't get more loud and clear than that.

A maid walks past the open door in the hall and I bark at her. "Get Winston here. Now!"

I hold the necklace in the palm of my hand when Henry and Simon—and then Fergus—walk in.

"When?" I ask my butler.

"Miss Olivia left last night."

"Why wasn't I told?"

"You *told* her to go. I heard you tell her myself. The whole house heard you yell it."

I flinch.

"Just followin' orders." And his words drip with sarcasm.

Not today, old man.

Winston steps into the room, his lips etched in that constant, self-important smirk. And I want to punch it off his face. Why didn't I do that yesterday? When he suggested that Olivia would ever . . . *Fucking hell, I'm an idiot.*

"Bring her back."

"She's arrived in New York by now," Fergus says.

"Then bring her back from New York."

"She left, Nicholas," Simon points out.

And Henry begins, "You can't just—"

"Bring her back!" I shout, loud enough to make the frames on the walls tremble.

"Oh for fuck's sake." Henry grips my shoulders. "You tell the men to bring her back and they will *bring her back* by any means necessary. And then we'll add 'international kidnapper' to your résumé. She's not a bone, Nicholas—you can't order her to be fetched."

"I can do whatever I want," I hiss.

"Bloody hell," Henry curses. "Is this what I sound like?"

Panic. It rises like smoke up my throat—choking me—making my hands clench the pendant like a life preserver. Making me think wild thoughts and say idiotic things.

Because . . . what if Olivia won't come back? What will I do then?

Without her.

My voice turns to ash. "She'll come back with them. They'll explain it to her. Tell her . . . that I made a mistake. That I'm sorry."

My little brother looks at me like I've lost my mind, and maybe I have.

Simon steps forward, gripping my arm. "Tell her yourself, man."

The downside of responsibility and duty is that it gives you tunnel vision—you don't see the big picture, the options, because the options were never yours to have. You see only the track that you're locked onto, the one that takes you through the tunnel.

But every once in a while, even the most dependable trains jump their track.

"Prince Nicholas, you can't go in there." Christopher rushes out from behind his desk, trying to get between me and the Queen's closed office door. "Your Highness, please—"

I burst through the door.

The Japanese Emperor stands quickly and his security men go for their gunbelts. The Emperor holds out his hand to them. I see this all in the periphery. Because my eyes are fastened onto the Queen's—and if looks could kill, Henry would've just gotten a promotion.

"I'm canceling the press conference," I tell her.

Without blinking, she turns smoothly to her guest. "Please accept our sincere apologies for the interruption, Emperor Himura. There is no excuse for such rudeness."

The Emperor nods. "I have six children, Your Majesty. I understand all about interruptions." He glances my way on the last word, and reflexively I lower my chin and bow—a sign of respect.

My grandmother looks past my shoulder to the doorway. "Christopher, show Emperor Himura to the blue drawing room. I will join him momentarily."

"Yes, Your Majesty."

Once my grandmother and I are alone, her indifferent façade drops like a boulder catapulted over an enemy's wall.

"Have you lost your mind?"

"I'm canceling the press conference."

"Absolutely not."

"I'm going to New York to see Olivia. I've hurt her terribly."

"Out of the question,"she hisses, eyes glinting like the edge of a blade.

"I've done everything you've ever wanted! I've become everything you wanted me to be—and I've never asked you for anything! But I'm asking you for this." Something cracks inside me, making my voice splinter.

"I *love* her. It can't end this way."

She regards me, silently, for a several moments, and when she speaks her voice is gentler but still resolute.

"This is exactly how it needs to end. Do you think I'm a fool, Nicholas? That I didn't know what you were thinking?"

I open my mouth to reply, but she goes on.

"You thought you could postpone the wedding for a time—and perhaps you could have. But the fact remains, the day will come when you will be a husband and a father. You will be a *king*. And what will Olivia be then?"

"*Mine*," I growl. "She'll be mine."

I see her in my head—those smiling, rosy lips, the way her eyes dance when she looks at me. When she's happy—when I've *made* her happy. I think of the way her thick, dark lashes fan out against her perfect skin while she sleeps—peacefully, because she's sleeping in my arms. I remember the feel of her soft touch and the sheer, miraculous contentment I feel when I'm just lying beside her.

"The word 'mistress' doesn't carry the same weight it once did, but it is still not a pretty thing to be, Nicholas. And there are no secrets, not in this world, not anymore. You will have a purpose to fulfill, a destiny. You will have the admiration and devotion of a country. And Olivia . . . will have its scorn. Possibly the derision of the whole world. You've seen it play out—time and again. The nannies who take up with their married movie-star employers, the young interns ensnared by powerful men.

It's never the man who is shamed and ruined. It's always the woman—the *other woman*—who gets burned at the stake."

And I have no response. Because I didn't think that far. The future didn't matter—all that mattered was having Olivia, keeping her, being able to kiss her every morning and tell her, show her, how precious she was to me every night.

My grandmother's brows draw together, as if she's aggrieved.

"Are you really so selfish, my boy? Is that the life you want for her?"

The life I want for her?

I want the world for Olivia.

I want to show her every corner of it, explore it while holding her hand. I want the stars for her—and the moon and the heavens—and everything in between.

And for a moment, I truly thought I could give them to her. I believed there was a way.

Stupid.

Franny called me a fool. A double-damned idiot. For once, I agree with her.

When I answer, my voice is hollow—a ravaged, empty imitation of my own.

"No."

"Then let her go. If you truly love her, let her hate you. It will be easier for her that way." She puts her hand on my arm, squeezing with a strength that still surprises me. "And for you."

I rub my eyes, suddenly so . . . tired.

"Christopher has the list. I've narrowed it down to five. Look it over. They're wonderful women, Nicholas. Any one of them will make you happy, if you just allow it."

I move out of her office without another word, feeling dazed. I pause in front of Christopher's desk and he hands me The List. One page, five names, five pretty, smiling thumb-size faces. All the same. All meaningless.

Swallowing hard, I pass it back to the Queen's secretary. "Pick one."

His eyes jolt from me to the page and back again.

"Me?"

"Yes."

"Uh . . . which one should I pick, Your Grace?"

And I say the truest words I've ever spoken in my life.

"It doesn't matter."

CHAPTER 25

Olivia

The months I spent in Wessco flew by in a blink, in a snap of fingers—the way time always seems to move when you're happiest. But the last two days have limped, crawled by in endless, teeth-gnashingly painful seconds. I thought leaving Wessco was the hardest thing I'd ever do.

But I was wrong. Living without Nicholas is so much harder.

I called Ellie from the airport—told her I was coming home, asked her to meet me when I landed. But when I walked out of the gate it wasn't her that was there.

It was my dad.

His eyes were clear—sober and strong. And knowing.

I was already crying by the time he got to me. I didn't even try to hold back. He told me it would be okay; he promised that I would be all right. He said I was strong—like my mother—and that I would get through this. He rocked me in his arms and held me so tight.

My hero.

But it's been a struggle. I have to fight the urge to curl into a ball and cry because everything hurts. My chest is heavy with the weight of my heart, my head throbs with doubts—all the things I could've done differently. My arms and legs ache with the urge to run back to him, to fix it, to hug him and never, ever let him go. My stomach is twisted and nauseated. So sick that for a split second, yesterday, I considered the possibility that maybe I was pregnant—and that fleeting thought brought relief and joy. It's the worst reason to want a baby, but it would mean we'd still have a connection. And I'd have a reason to go back, to see him again.

I know I sound like a desperate, pathetic woman, but I just don't care. Having your heart ripped out of your chest will do that to you.

It's too early for morning sickness, but even if it weren't, I know I'm not pregnant. Those magical fixes happen only in romance novels and on soap operas. In real life, birth control is reliably, sometimes heartbreakingly effective.

"It's really you! Oh my God, can I get a picture?" the statuesque, twenty-something woman vibrating beside me asks.

"No. Sorry, no pictures," I mumble, staring at the dirty plates in my hands.

Business is booming. The line at Amelia's is out the door and down the block. They're not here for the pies—my father filled me in on his covert business deal with Simon Barrister the night I came home. The contract is exclusive, which means we're out of the pie business for good. And I'm happy about that, I am. Happy that my father is sober and healthy. Happy that Ellie will be able to go to college without the weight of money troubles on her back. Happy even for me—that I have choices now, that my life won't be spent doing something I hate for the family I love.

But Nicholas was right. Everyone has a price and everything is for sale.

The crowd that fills the coffee shop every day is looking for a piece of Nicholas. They all want to see the table he sat at—Ellie screwed a plaque into the back of one of the chairs: "His Royal Ass Was Here." Beside it, Marty scratched into the wood: "And it was fiiine."

I don't do autographs or pictures, but that doesn't stop people from asking. I've been working every day—trying to stay busy, but I mostly stay in the back. Away from all the greedy eyes and prying questions.

I dump the dishes into the sink in the kitchen, while the DISHWASHER WANTED sign still hangs, unclaimed, in the front window. The chatter of the crowd out front is so loud that I don't hear the person behind me come in. Not until I turn around and run smack into his chest.

Logan steadies me with a hand on my elbow.

"Pardon me, Miss Olivia."

That awful tight feeling pinches my chest, because looking at his face drums up memories that pound their way through my head.

"Why are you here, Logan?"

He gives me a confused look. "It's my shift. Tommy has the day off."

"No. No, I mean why are you *still* here?"

There hasn't been a word from Nicholas—not a call or a text. I expected Logan and Tommy to head back to Wessco as soon as it was clear I was back. For good.

His mouth tightens, and sympathy dims in his eyes. "Prince Nicholas asked me to protect your business, watch over your sister. Until I receive new orders, that's what I'll do."

"Maybe . . . he forgot you were here?"

Logan chuckles. "He doesn't forget about his men. If Tommy and I are here, it's because here is where he wants us to be."

I don't know what to do with this information—if it's some deeper clue about Nicholas's intentions or means nothing at all. But I don't have time to analyze it. Because a second later, my sister's voice echoes from out front.

"Everybody out! Let's go—it's siesta time, people—we're closed for the afternoon. Hey Marty, help a sister out, will you?"

Logan and I rush out of the kitchen. Ellie holds the door open, waving everyone out of it, despite the grumbles and protests, while Marty herds them in her direction like a modern-day shepherd.

"Your money's no good here." He waves at a guy offering him several bills. "Come back tomorrow."

"What are you doing?" I call above the line of heads.

Ellie holds up her finger until the last would-be customer has left. Then she locks the door and pulls down the dark green shade over the picture window.

"It's almost time for the press conference." She skips to the television on the counter, turning it on. "I figured you'd want privacy when we watch it."

My stomach has dropped to my feet a lot during the last few months, but this time, it drops to fucking China.

"I'm not watching the press conference."

"Oh yes you are, Negative Nelly." She drags me by the arm to a front-row seat. "Unlike you, I still have hope that His Hotness is going to pull his stupid head out of his fine ass."

"Even if he did, it doesn't matter. We were only supposed to last the summer. We were doomed from the start."

Marty comes up behind me, squeezing my shoulders. "Even if that turns out to be true, this will give you closure at least."

I hate that word. Closure. It's just confirmation that what you dread is actually true. Dead is dead. Over is *really* over. But there's no comfort in it.

"I don't want to watch."

I haven't searched Nicholas's name online, haven't looked at any of the paparazzi photos that are always so readily available. It would be like holding a still-raw, blistering burn against a hot stove—too much hurt to handle.

My sister folds her arms. "Liar."

Okay, she's right. The truth is, I don't want *to want* to watch. I don't want to miss him. I don't want to need him. I don't want to spend every moment of every day trying not to cry because I can't imagine a future without him in it anymore.

But . . . we don't always get what we want. Most of the time, we don't, actually. What did my mother say when we were little? *You get what you get and you don't get upset.* So I sit in the chair and dig my fingernails into my palm while Ellie switches the channel to the news station carrying the live press conference, and increases the volume.

To find out exactly what Nicholas and I both ended up getting.

I'm not the only one who's paid a price. Despite how it all went south in the end, I know Nicholas—every inch of his soul. I know what he felt for me was real—every touch, every smile.

I've imagined his regret when he found out the truth. I believe if he could've changed things, he would have. I believe he wanted to, more than he's wanted anything in his whole life.

But we can't change who we are—not a queen, a prince, or a girl from New York.

Like he told me once . . . royalty is forever.

The television focuses on an empty podium, the royal family crest etched into the shiny wood. I don't recognize the ornate background—two windows with heavy floral drapery, with a portrait of Nicholas's parents hanging on the wall between them. It's not Guthrie House—maybe it's another room in the palace, or one of the other properties he'd told me about, but never had the chance to show me.

There's building chatter from a group off camera, a burst of camera flashes, and then he's there, stepping up to the podium. The breath rushes from my lungs in one scraping, painful swoop, and the lump that suddenly lodges in my throat makes it hard to inhale.

God, he's beautiful.

And he looks fucking terrible.

His navy suit molds to his form perfectly—those wide shoulders, strong arms, warm, magnificent chest. But there's more hollowness to his cheeks and there are shadows beneath his eyes.

He seems . . . sad.

And that devastates me. Because despite how it all ended, he deserves to be happy—and I want that for him so much.

Henry sits down in a chair on Nicholas's right, resting his head on his hand, elbows on the table, looking tired. Simon's there too, one more chair over, and I think of Franny.

She's probably calling me Runaway Bitch right now.

"People of Wessco," Nicholas begins, taking a stack of white note cards from his pocket. "We've been through a lot together, you and I. You celebrated with my family the day of my birth," the corner of his mouth quirks up, "and I've been told some of the parties were quite rowdy. You watched as I took my first steps, attended my first day of school, rode my first horse—King, his name was."

Nicholas clears his throat and looks down, his dark hair falling over his forehead. "You grieved with Henry and I when we lost our parents—our pain was yours. You nurtured us, consoled us, held us in your arms as if we were your own—and in a very real way, we are. You saw me graduate university, undergo the same military training each of you have also undertaken—and I've strived in action and word to make you proud. To become the kind of man, leader and prince you all deserve."

He stares down at the cards in his hand for a moment, then swallows hard.

"My mother had many dreams for us, as all mothers do for their children. She wanted us to have lives filled with purpose, accomplishments . . . and love. The love my parents had for each other was a wonder to behold—you all saw it. They were meant for each other, made each other better versions of themselves. And you, like my grandmother, Her Majesty the Queen, have waited—not so patiently," Nicholas gives a small smirk and a chuckle echoes through the crowd, "for me to find a love like that of my own."

He looks nauseated. And his jaw clenches, like he's trying to keep the words in. Then he looks into the camera, brows drawn together. "Today, your waiting comes to an end. And I will speak to you about the future of the monarchy—of my future with the woman I will marry."

I bite the inside of my cheek. I don't think I can do this—God, why did I think I could watch this?

"She would have liked to be here with me today, but . . . circumstances . . . made that impossible." He pushes a hand through his dark hair, rubbing the back of his neck, looking down again at the cards in his hand.

"And so, I announce that I . . . that I . . ."

He stumbles on the words and I lose the ability to breathe.

He doesn't move, doesn't say a word for several seconds.

And then . . . he laughs.

A sharp, bitter sound, while pinching the bridge of his nose and shaking his head.

"I am a horse's arse."

Ellie jumps out of her chair. "I knew it! He's Jerry McGuiring you! He's Jerry McGuiring you, because you complete him!!"

"Shhh!"

"I had what my parents had," Nicholas says fiercely, gripping the sides of the podium. "I held it in my hands. The love of a woman who was not born into royalty but who is more noble of character than anyone I have ever known. Knowing her . . . changed everything. And loving her . . . brought me to life."

There's a wave of whispers in the crowd as Nicholas's brow furrows.

"And I betrayed her. I doubted her love and her honesty when I should've known better. And I'm sorry . . ." He stares into the camera—green eyes glowing—like he's looking right at me. "I'm so damn sorry."

After a moment, his eyes return to the crowd and his voice grows stronger, more definitive with every word.

"But I will not betray her again. I will not forsake the dreams my mother had for her sons, and I will not ignore what my own soul cries out for." His head shakes. "Not for country and not for crown."

He pauses, wetting his lips. "I'm supposed to stand up here today and give you the name of the woman who will one day be your queen. But I can't do that. Because I have screwed up." He snorts. "Royally."

Then he leans forward, his beautiful face sure and confident.

"What I can tell you, what I swear to you today, is this: I will marry Olivia Hammond or I will never marry at all."

And the crowd goes berserk.

Holy shit.

"Holy shit!" Ellie yells.

And Marty gasps. "You're gonna be a queen, Liv! Like Beyoncé!" He fans his eyes with his hand. "I might cry."

Only . . . I won't be. I can't be.

"He can't do that." I turn to Logan. "Can he do that?"

Logan's mouth is set in a worried line. His eyes flash to me—and he shakes his head.

One of the reporters stands up, and the back of his head comes into view in the corner of the screen, yelling his question above the din. "Prince Nicholas! The law is clear—the Crown Prince must marry a woman of noble lineage or, if he is to marry a commoner, she must be a natural-born citizen of Wessco. Olivia Hammond is neither of those."

I stare at the television, paralyzed by a hundred emotions swirling through me.

The crowd quiets, waiting for Nicholas's answer.

"No, she is not," he answers softly, looking down.

And then he straightens his shoulders and raises his head.

"And so, today, I, Nicholas Arthur Frederick Edward, abdicate my place in the line of succession and renounce all rights to the throne of Wessco. From this moment on, my brother, His Royal Highness Henry John Edgar Thomas, is the Prince of Pembrook."

The crowd roars like Brazilian soccer fans right after a goal.

And Henry wakes up, lifting his head. Blinking.

"Wait. What?"

Nicholas slaps his shoulder—smiling big and bright. "It's all yours, Henry. You'll do great—I know you will."

Then Nicholas holds up his hands. "No more questions—I have a lot to do. Thank you for your time." He turns to go, but then has second thoughts and comes back to the podium. "One last thing." He looks directly into the camera, and I feel his eyes like a touch to my skin. "You asked for a warning, Olivia, so here it is. I'm coming for you, love."

And the son of a bitch winks.

He heads off screen with a rush of reporters following him.

The coffee shop is silent—except for the stunned recap of the news anchor. As soon as Nicholas was off the screen, Marty walked outside, dialing on his phone, mumbling how the new guy he's dating better up his romantic-gesture game. Ellie's on the floor—I think she passed out somewhere between "Arthur" and "Edgar." Slowly, I turn to Logan.

"Did that just happen?"

Logan nods. "It did, lass."

"I can't believe . . . What did he just do?"

"He gave up a kingdom for you." There's a devilish shine in his dark eyes. "Always knew he was a smart one."

It takes a minute for it all to sink in. Repeating to myself seems to help.

"He's coming."

"That's what he said," Logan agrees.

"He's coming here . . . for me."

"Heard that part, too."

There's so much to do . . . but . . . priorities.

"He's coming here for me and I haven't shaved my legs in three days!"

I haul ass toward the stairs in the back, taking out one of the tables as I go.

Behind me I hear Logan mutter, "American women are nutty." Then he tells Ellie, "Get up, possum."

CHAPTER 26

Nicholas

Getting out of the State House is a shit show. Security has a hard time keeping the public and the press off of me. Literally—there's grabbing and handshaking, attempted hugs and blown kisses, everyone screaming congratulations or curses or questions or all three at the same time.

The world's gone completely mad.

And I can't remember ever feeling so happy.

So fucking free.

It feels like I could leap over the lot of them. Like I could fly if I had to. Because every step takes me closer to home. To Olivia. I can practically taste her on my tongue, and I swear every breath I take smells like roses and jasmine.

On the sidewalk, just near the car, my driver grasps my shoulder and yells in my ear, "The Queen's ordered us to bring you to the palace!"

I nod. Then I smack his hand upward, sending the keys in the air before I catch them.

"I'd best drive, then. That way, you're not disobeying orders."

He stutters. "Sir, please . . . The Queen—"

"Will get over it. We're going to the airport—call ahead if needed, but I want the plane ready for takeoff the moment we arrive."

I push my way into the car. The door's still open when a handful of security—and Simon—gather round.

"The airport will be mobbed, Your Grace," another security man argues.

"Then you lads should climb in—I may need your help getting to the runway."

A different man tries, "Sir, you can't just—"

"But I *can*." I laugh, feeling almost delirious. "Isn't it bloody fucking grand?"

Once I start the car, they stop arguing and jump the hell in. Simon's beside me in front.

"Where's Henry? Did we lose Henry?"

"He'll be fine," Simon assures. "He's getting pelted with questions, but the men have him covered."

I roll the car through the human sea and floor it once I'm on the open road. Mixed in with the joy is an urgency. A determined need pushing at my back like a gust of wind—because I can't wait to see Olivia. To hold her and kiss her until she can't stand. To make it all right again.

To begin this new, different life.

A life with her.

Nearer to the airport, I honk at the car in front of us who think they're out for a Sunday drive. And my mobile vibrates in my pocket for the twelfth time. I don't need to look to see who's calling. I give it to Simon.

"Keep this safe for me until I come back, will you?"

With a knowing smile, he asks, "When are you coming back?"

I laugh again. "I don't know."

And it's a beautiful thing.

"You should take my plane," Simon offers. "Her Majesty's already going to be furious. If you hijack Royal I, she may sic the air force on you."

It's good to have friends. Friends with their own planes is even better.

As we pull up to the airport, Franny calls on Simon's mobile. After a moment, he puts her on speaker.

"Nicholas."

"Yes, Franny?"

"I've never been so thrilled to be proven wrong. You're not an idiot after all."

"Uh . . . thanks?"

"Be sure to tell Olivia I said she's a Fleeing Bitch, but I forgive her. And you two must come for dinner when you return, yes?"

"You can count on it."

An hour later, I'm in the air—on my way to New York.

The streets are empty in front of Amelia's when I walk up to the door—the air eerily, strangely silent, almost like at a surprise birthday party, those moments just before the guests jump up and scream, scaring a year off the guest of honor's life. The shade is drawn in front of the picture window, and the lights inside are dark.

Maybe Olivia didn't see the press conference? My stomach roils—because maybe Olivia's not even here. Perhaps she went . . . *out.* A toxic mix shudders in my gut at the possibility that she went out *with someone.* A man who'd help her drown her sorrows and forget the heartache I've brought her.

The thought has me pushing the coffee shop door open with more force than I intended—and stumbling over the threshold. The interior is dim, but not dark—it's illuminated by a single candle. At a table . . . where Olivia sits.

And my entire being exhales with relief.

I take several moments to just look at her. Christ, I've missed looking at her. Soaking in the vision of her dark, swirling hair—shiny, even in the candlelight. The way the glow of the flame dances across her flawless pale skin, highlighting her heart-shaped face, her high cheekbones, the flush, pink lips that have possessed me from the start and the midnight-blue eyes that own my soul.

She watches me too, unmoving and wordless, her cheeks flushing as she stares—enough to make me wonder what gloriously filthy thoughts are fluttering through her mind. The door swings slowly closed behind me as I step farther into the room.

"It's a quiet night," I say. Because those words come easy—as opposed to the backlog of confessions and apologies that are fighting for prominence in my throat.

Olivia blinks. Almost like she's just grasping that I'm real—here—and not a vision she's imagined.

"Logan worked with the NYPD. He set up a three-block perimeter around the shop."

I nod, not taking my eyes off her. There's an excellent chance I'll never close them again. Sleep is overrated.

"Ah . . . that explains the barricade."

"Yes."

I rub the back of my neck, slowly drawing closer to her. "Did you . . . did you watch the press conference?"

Her face changes—softens at the corners of her mouth, heating her gaze.

"Yes."

I take another step, slowly, barely reining in the urge to take her into my arms and make love to her against the wall, the floor and on top of every table in the room.

Because before we get to that, there are things that must be said. Things she deserves to hear.

My voice is a raw whisper. "Olivia, about the things I said, the night you left. I'm—"

"Forgiven." Tears fill her eyes. I move the rest of the way to her just as she stands and jumps into my arms.

"You're completely forgiven. You had me at 'horse's ass.'"

I bury my face in the hollow of her neck, inhaling the sweet scent of her skin—honey and roses and her. My lips travel up across her jaw, finding her mouth, feeling the wetness of her tears against my cheek. And then our mouths are moving together, tasting and delving—wild and demanding. This is no sweet, storybook reunion. This is raw and desperate and unadulterated need. Being away from her, knowing how close I came to truly losing her, makes me rougher than I should be. My hands push through her hair, clench down her back, and grip her beautiful arse, holding her tight against me, feeling every breath that shudders through her.

And I'm not alone. She moans into me—I taste it on my tongue—her hands tugging on my hair, her legs wrapping around my waist, squeezing like she can't get close enough. Like she'll never let go.

And everything about it is perfect and right.

After a time, the desperation ebbs and our kisses slow—our lips turn to savoring and sucking. I feel Olivia's soft hands stroking the planes of my face gently and her forehead comes to rest against mine. We gaze into each other's eyes, breathing the same air.

"I love you," she whispers, her voice trembling. And more tears fall down her cheeks. "I love you so much. I can't . . . I can't believe you gave all of that up. How could you do that?"

She's crying harder now—and I realize she's grieving for me. Because somehow she thinks I've lost something.

I set her on her feet, brush back her hair and wipe the tears from her face.

"It was the easiest thing I've ever done. When I stood up there, in front of all those cameras, it was like when they say your life flashes before your eyes when you're dying. I saw all the years ahead—and not one of them mattered worth a damn. Because I didn't have you there with me. I love you, Olivia. I don't need a kingdom—if you're beside me, I already have the whole world."

"That's so beautiful." She cries. "And really cheesy, too."

And there . . . there it is—that stunning smile that hits me right in my heart.

And my cock.

She rests her head against my chest, her arms around my waist, and we stand just like that for several minutes.

Until Olivia asks, "What happens now?"

I kiss the top of her head and lean back.

"Well . . . I'm out of a job." I step backwards, grabbing the HELP WANTED sign from the window. "So, I was hoping the dishwashing position is still available."

Olivia's eyes sparkle—one of the most gorgeous fucking sights I've ever seen.

"Have you ever actually washed a dish?"

"Not one." I peck her lips. "But I'm a very eager learner."

"And what about us? What happens with us?"

"We can do anything we want. Every single day of the future is ours."

I sit down in the chair, pulling her onto my lap. She toys with the back of my hair, thinking it over.

"I want to go to the movies with you. And . . . to the park. Even if security has to tag along. And I want us to lie around in bed all day and order takeout."

"And walk around the apartment naked," I add helpfully.

Olivia nods. "All the normal things couples do when they're dating."

"It would be an interesting change of pace for us."

Olivia's fingers massage and rub at my neck. Feels amazing.

"So, we'll take things . . . slow?"

I bring her head down closer, whispering just before I kiss her, “Sounds perfect. I like slow. And you are going to thoroughly enjoy how I do . . . slow.”

EPILOGUE

Nicholas

Eight months later

S*low didn't exactly work out . . .*

"I now pronounce, henceforth, that they be man and wife. You may kiss your bride."

I don't have to be told twice.

I lift the gauzy veil trimmed with lace, cup her beautiful face in both hands, and press my mouth to Olivia's. Reverently—at first.

Then I kiss her deeper. Hungrier. Lost in the taste and feel of my sweet new wife.

Olivia giggles against my searching mouth. Henry whistles inappropriately beside me, and Simon coughs to try and cover it. Then the church bells ring, rattling our bones, the congregation stands, and I escort Lady Olivia down the aisle. Her dress is a strapless, lace confection, cinched at her tiny waist, long in the back—the train taking up almost the entire length of the aisle, carried by half a dozen little flower girls.

Outside, the crowds cheer, waving silk flags and white flowers and banners. The sun is shining, the sky is blue and doves are literally flying through the air. It doesn't get more perfect than this.

I lead Olivia down the gray stone steps to the open, gold-trimmed horse-drawn carriage—we only take them out for really special occasions these days. Once she and her gigantic train are nestled in, we wave our way through the streets, celebrating with the entire country.

And this time, I don't mind the cameras. Not even a little.

Eventually, we pull through the palace gates and I help Olivia down. Twenty footmen—in their full military dress—flank us. Their swords sing through the air when they're unsheathed and raised, forming a silver bridge that glints in the sunlight for us to walk beneath. Then it's upstairs, to the gold ballroom—where hopefully we'll be able to eat and drink something before we both die.

After that, we'll step out onto the main balcony of the palace, where the Queen will officially present us to the country with our new titles.

From then on it's pretty much a public make-out session, if all goes well.

My grandmother was spot-on about the magic of a royal wedding—which is why she didn't give us even a little resistance when Olivia and I told her we were getting married three months ago. All she asked was that she be allowed to take care of the arrangements. Considering we weren't sure if we'd even be able to pull off a city hall wedding in such a short time, we gave the Old Girl free rein. And she came through spectacularly.

The press has had their hands full with positive reports on the royal family—I mean, who doesn't enjoy a good "abdication of the throne for love" story? And the people are overjoyed. They adore Olivia—not quite as much as I do, because that would be impossible, but close.

Olivia, her father, and I have turned Amelia's into a nonprofit in the States. A string of "pay what you can" restaurants, where anyone can come in, sit at a table, and enjoy good food. They can choose to work off their bill or leave what money they're able to—or none at all. We've opened a second restaurant in the Bronx, with two more on the way this summer.

With the public firmly devoted to their royals and the media for once on our side, Parliament in Wessco fell into line and passed the legislation my grandmother and I had been working for. Employment and wages began recovering and have been climbing steadily ever since.

It's a happily ever after for everyone.

Well . . . almost everyone.

I spot my brother in the corner, scowling and sullen. It's the only look he wears these days. Not in the self-destructive way like when he first came home; more in a bratty way that doesn't concern me.

"Okay," Olivia announces, handing me her glass of Champagne, "before we head out to the balcony I'm going to attempt to use the bathroom."

We both look down at the miles of fabric that make up her dress.

"Do you want some help?" I ask.

"No—the bridesmaids will take care of that. Women have a natural instinct for how to get these things done. Although, besides Franny, this is the first time I've met any of those ladies. And now I'm going to pee in front of them." She reaches up and pecks my lips. "Being married to you is weird."

"It'll never be boring." I send her off with a swift pat to her arse.

On her way, Olivia passes Marty, giving him a smile and a thumbs-up. He winks at her—then goes back to flirting with Christopher, my grandmother's secretary, who's shamelessly reciprocating. I don't think I'll be the starring act in Marty's fantasies for much longer.

While Olivia takes care of business, I approach my brother, leaning against the wall beside him, arms crossed.

"Congratulations," he sulks. "Bastard."

"Thank you."

"Olive looks gorgeous. Prick."

"She does. I'll tell her you said so."

"I'm really happy for you. Wanker."

I laugh. "It's going to be all right, Henry."

He drinks from his flask, flinching as he swallows. "Easy for you to say. Prat."

I squeeze his shoulder. "Are you ever going to forgive me?"

He shrugs. "Probably. Eventually. Of course I will. When I'm sober."

"Any idea when that may be?"

"Henry, there you are!" our grandmother clucks from across the room. "We must speak about the memo I sent you . . ."

Henry lifts his flask and shakes his head. "Not today."

Ellie Hammond intercepts my grandmother before she reaches us, blocking her path. She tries to execute a full curtsy, but the hem of her dress gets caught in the heel of her shoe and she ends up almost falling on her face. The Queen attempts to step back, but Ellie grabs onto her—wrapping her arms around Her Majesty's waist and holding on like a baby sloth clinging to its mother.

Christopher jumps into action, trying to extract her. "Miss Hammond, please! We do not tackle the Queen—it's not proper protocol."

He manages to save her from the outrage. And Ellie steps back, fixing her hair, then bending her knees in a quicker, shorter curtsy and offering her apology.

With an accent.

"Begging your pardon, Mum."

Oh Christ.

"We haven't been formally introduced. I'm Ellie, Olivia's sister."

My grandmother looks down her nose at Ellie. "Yes, child, I'm aware of who you are."

My new sister-in-law bubbles with excitement over the recognition.

"And I just . . . well . . . I wanted to thank you for the gown." She smooths her hands down the champagne-colored silk. "Olivia said you paid for it and it must've cost a ton!"

"Indeed."

Ellie cups her breasts in her palms, squeezing. "And it makes my boobs look great!"

The Queen turns. "Christopher, get me a drink."

Ellie's hands twitter as she searches for more words.

"And I'm just . . . I mean I'm so . . ."

Then she's tackling my grandmother again. Flinging her arms around her neck in a miniature version of a bear hug. A cub hug.

"I just can't believe we're related!"

Over Ellie's shoulder my grandmother's face goes from shock to dry, begrudging acceptance.

"Neither can I."

The trumpets blare on the balcony over the sound of the crowd's cheers as each member of our wedding party, and then the Queen, are called out. Olivia and I are the only ones left. Bridget flutters around us, doing last-minute checks.

"No lipstick on the teeth, veil is straight, remember fingers together when you wave, yes, yes . . ." She brushes my hair off my forehead and tries to squirt an offending rain of hairspray.

I jerk my head back with a glare and she shuffles away.

Olivia giggles. And just a second later, I'm chuckling too.

"Ready, love?"

"As I'll ever be."

Her gloved hand slips into mine as our names are announced.

"Prince Nicholas and Princess Olivia, the Duke and Duchess of Fairstone!"

We step out onto the balcony as twenty thousand white rose petals fall from the sky. And the people applaud and shout, hold up their cameras and take pictures. The blissful energy blows through the air, dusting everything in a sheen of joy and sparkle. We wave and smile for a bit, and then with my hand on her waist, I dip my head and kiss Olivia softly.

With her hands on my shoulders, she leans back. "I don't think I'll ever get used to it."

"All the pomp and circumstance, you mean?"

She shakes her head, her eyes adoring. "No."

"Being a princess and a duchess?"

"Nope."

"Then what?"

She reaches up, leaning closer.

"That I get to be your wife."

Emotion hits me hard, making my heart feel too large for my chest. I stroke her cheek, because she's so lovely—and because she's mine.

Then I whisper, "Well, you'd better. We're royalty. That means . . . we're forever."

The End

DON'T MISS THE NEXT BOOKS IN THE ROYALLY SERIES!!

Royally Matched

Some men are born responsible, some men have responsibility thrust upon them. Henry John Edgar Thomas Pembrook, Prince of Wessco, just got the motherlode of all responsibility dumped in his regal lap.

He's not handling it well.

Hoping to force her grandson to rise to the occasion, Queen Lenora goes on a much-needed safari holiday—and when the Queen's away, the Prince will play. After a chance meeting with an American television producer, Henry finally makes a decision all on his own:

Welcome to *Matched: Royal Edition.*

A reality TV dating game show featuring twenty of the world's most beautiful blue-bloods gathered in the same castle. Only one will win the diamond tiara, only one will capture the handsome prince's heart.

While Henry revels in the sexy, raunchy antics of the contestants as they fight, literally, for his affection, it's the quiet, bespectacled girl in the corner—with the voice of an angel and a body that would tempt a saint—who catches his eye.

The more Henry gets to know Sarah Mirabelle Zinnia Von Titebottum, the more enamored he becomes of her simple beauty, her strength, her kind spirit . . . and her naughty sense of humor.

But Rome wasn't built in a day—and irresponsible royals aren't reformed overnight.

As he endeavors to right his wrongs, old words take on whole new meanings for the dashing Prince. Words like, Duty, Honor and most of all—Love.

Royally Endowed

A boy from the wrong side of the tracks…

But these days he covers his tattoos with a respectable suit. He's charismatic, good looking, smart and trustworthy—any girl would be proud to bring him home to her family.

But there's only one girl he wants.

She's an angel on earth, his living, breathing fantasy. For years he's known her, sometimes laughed with her, once shared a pint with her…he would lay down his life for her.

But she doesn't see him—not really.

A girl endowed with royal relations . . .

She dreams of princes and palaces, but in her quest for happily ever after, harsh truths are learned: castles are drafty, ball gowns are a nuisance, and nobility doesn't equal noble intentions.

In the end, she sees her true heart's love may just be the handsome, loyal boy who's been beside her all along.